AUTUMN
FINCH'S CROSSING BOOK 1

Amy Ruth Allen

FINCH'S CROSSING

Autumn

BOOK ONE

AMY RUTH ALLEN

Autumn, Book One, Finch's Crossing series
© 2015 by Amy Ruth Allen

www.amyruthallen.com

Cover Images by Chance Wheeler, Felicia Alfieri, and Maegan Tintari
Cover Design by Emma Grace, Inksplatter Design

ISBN: 978-0-9961269-4-6

For Leigh, always.

CHAPTER 1

*I*F STEAM REALLY could come out of a person's ears, Autumn Hamilton would have been a geyser. She was standing at the entrance of the Town and Country Nursery, a yellow chrysanthemum in each hand, scowling as she watched the exchange between her neighbor's granddaughter and the man who had come not only to take custody of her, but to extricate her from Finch's Crossing. Five-year-old Heather Christianson, who hadn't spoken a word since her parents died six weeks earlier, was pointing at a big pumpkin languishing in the field, still attached to the vine. The man, whom Autumn judged to be in his mid-thirties, and probably not too happy to be standing on the edge of a muddy pumpkin patch in his expensive Italian loafers, shook his head no.

"We'll get one later when we can come back with Nanna's truck," he said, loudly and slowly, the way people do when they are unaccustomed to speaking to children. "We have to buy Nanna's apples first, remember?"

Then he tugged Heather away from the pumpkins toward the pick-your-own orchard beyond. The little girl glanced longingly back over her shoulder at the pumpkins as she tripped along behind him.

Autumn was incredulous. How on earth could anyone deny a pumpkin, such a simple pleasure, to this tragic little girl? This was just another of many reasons why Ethan Rasmussen, the slick playboy lawyer from New York City, should *not* have custody of Autumn's favorite neighbor's granddaughter.

Shaking her head at the unfairness of it all, Autumn put the chrysanthemums she had purchased in her Jeep and was about to jump in and drive away when she suddenly changed her mind. Heather *would* have her pumpkin, she decided, and Autumn walked across the parking lot and into the pumpkin patch, not caring that her favorite red cowboy boots were sinking into the mud.

Jack Staub, who had owned the nursery, pumpkin patch, apple orchard, and Christmas tree farm for as long as she could remember, appeared by her side and offered to help her make her selection. Unable to gauge which pumpkin Heather had been enamored with, Autumn noticed a particularly unattractive specimen and spontaneously decided to purchase this mistake of Mother Nature for the man, as punishment for his callous disregard of Heather's simple wish.

"I'll take that one, please," she said to Jack, who was just a little surprised to see her make a decision so quickly. Jack had observed that whenever she bought something, she normally returned within a couple of hours. This was enough time for her to go home, arrange her purchases, change her mind, and drive back to the nursery.

"Which one?" Jack sought confirmation, because Autumn was pointing to the biggest, dirtiest, knobbiest pumpkin in the field.

She pulled a twenty-dollar bill out of her jeans pocket and had it at the ready.

"You sure?" Jack asked. "It's kinda lumpy." He spun it around on its stem and showed her where it was already indented and where the pulp had started to leak out. "Let me at least take it inside and wipe it off for ya."

"Oh, I'm positive," she assured him. "And give me that small, cute, smooth, almost-perfect one there, too."

Autumn grabbed the big ugly pumpkin first, not caring about the dirt that came off onto her jeans and T-shirt, and Jack balanced the smaller one on top, which she held in place with her chin. For reasons Jack didn't understand, but didn't question, she insisted on carrying the pumpkins herself. When she exited the pumpkin patch, victoriously stepping into the parking lot, she shook her long auburn hair out of her eyes as she surveyed the lot, looking for her target. There were only two cars in addition to her Jeep: an ancient silver Oldsmobile that belonged to Reverend Frye and a flashy, immaculate black Jaguar sedan. She grinned. She had found her target.

It was all she could do to carry her load the twenty yards over to the Jag, the small, perfect pumpkin balanced precariously on top of the ugly one. She set the pumpkins carefully on the ground and tugged on the door handle of the front driver's side door, but it was locked. Undeterred, she walked around the car and tried the front passenger door. It was open! She walked back around the car, retrieved her big ugly prize, and carried it gingerly over to the open door. She attempted to wedge the freak of nature in between the seats and the dashboard, but of course, it wouldn't fit. So she just plopped it onto the seat, mud and knots and all. Then she put the small, perfectly rounded pumpkin on top, intended of course, for Heather. Autumn grabbed the seat belt and belted in the bulbous orb good and tight, and when she was convinced it was secure, she shut the door. She spun around and race-walked as fast as she dared toward her Jeep, not wanting to attract attention to herself and trying not to look like someone who had just defiled a stranger's luxury car.

It was too late. The voice was deep and a lot closer than she expected.

"Hey you!" it boomed behind her.

She kept walking and pretended she didn't hear him.

"Hey! You. Lady with the big pumpkin," he said again. "I saw you break into my car with that dirty pumpkin."

Autumn turned around, laughing, hands on her hips. "Really? Did you just call me a big dirty pumpkin?"

This was more fun and excitement than she had had in a long time.

Then she felt two tiny arms wrap themselves around her knees and the weight of a little body sink itself against her legs.

The man was standing in front of her. "I saw you put that pumpkin in my car," he said angrily. "You can't deny it."

She was still laughing. "I won't," she said. "Guilty as charged." And she raised her hands in front of her, crossing her wrists, as if submitting to being handcuffed. "Call out the pumpkin brigade, throw me into the pumpkin patch, and let me serve my time, but first I have to say hello to this little munchkin."

Autumn went down on her knees so her face was level with

CHAPTER 1

Heather's, and she brushed the girl's blonde curls away from her forehead. The sadness in this little angel's face was heart wrenching. She had known Heather all her life, from the first time her parents brought the tiny bundle to visit her Nanna Martha, and from all the long weekends, birthdays and Christmases since.

Autumn kissed Heather's forehead and held her little face in her hands. "You okay, kiddo, considering?" she asked.

Heather nodded solemnly then turned to the man and stuck out her tongue at him with considerable enthusiasm, all the while still leaning against Autumn.

Autumn looked up at the man, not at all expecting to be taken in by his handsome features, and considered the flash of anger she had felt toward him for not buying Heather the pumpkin she wanted. His dark, wavy hair was controlled by a close cut, and his angry eyes were just as dark as his hair. He had the glow of health on his face, as if he had just returned from a Caribbean vacation where he played tennis and snorkeled all day. She got a closer look at his expensive, shiny loafers, now caked with dirt, getting secret satisfaction that he would very likely get the rest of his designer clothes dirty hauling the pumpkin out of the car.

She turned back to Heather. "Well, he can't be that bad. I think he bought you a pumpkin after all." Autumn grinned up at the handsome, perturbed man, then back at Heather. "It's in his car. Go look for yourself. Yours is the perfect one on top of the ugly one. The big ugly one's for him," she continued, glancing back toward the man.

The little girl began a triumphant sprint toward the Jaguar, stopping to give the man an unexpected, reluctant, and dutiful hug. He seemed surprised as he bent down to hug her back. Autumn refocused on the man who was now holding his hand out to her, ready, apparently, to get down to business.

"I'm Ethan Ras . . ." he began.

"I know who you are," she interrupted, rather rudely ignoring his outstretched hand.

He lowered his, but she couldn't tell how offended, if offended at all, he had been by her refusal to shake. "Then you know I'm an attorney with Morgan, Gladstein, Hi..."

She interrupted again. "Morgan, Gladstein, Hirsch. Yes, I'm well aware of who you are, and more importantly, what you're doing here."

She glanced over at Heather, who had gotten the door to the Jaguar open and was trying to wedge herself into the seat next to the pumpkins. However, she had only succeeded in getting herself and the car's interior muddy as she squirmed with joy, patting and caressing the pair of pumpkins.

"Well, if you know so much, then you must also know that you have no business interfering with me, or with Heather." He spoke uncharacteristically haltingly, with the tone of voice he usually reserved for the first-year associates at his law firm, who sometimes needed prodding. He immediately wished he had made his point more judiciously. Less bossy.

There was something about this woman that made him nervous and intrigued him at the same time. He had never in all his years been this unsure in a conversation. One of the strengths that had made him such a successful lawyer was his gift for being an unparalleled conversationalist. He could talk confidently with anyone—CEOs, the richest of the rich, famous people from every walk of life, anybody, really, from any walk of life. But this woman's boldness took him by surprise. It made her different for some reason, and he wondered if he would have the chance to find out why.

"Who said anything about interfering?" she asked mischievously. "I'm just trying to pay it forward, spreading the love, delivering gifts and goodwill to my fellow man. Just think of me as the Finch's Crossing welcome wagon."

"Uh, huh," he said. "I could use a little less of your goodwill. And it looks like you could, too." He pointed at the front of her *Charlie's Angels* T-shirt, which was now covered in dirt with a large smear of orange pumpkin guts clearly visible.

Oh crud, the first new, young, handsome, successful man Finch's Crossing had seen in about two decades and she'd already trashed her clothes in front of him. He must have thought she was such a country bumpkin. *Pumpkin bumpkin*, she thought to herself, almost laughing out loud. Oh well. He was the enemy, after all, swooping in to take Heather away from her grandmother.

"I don't see what's so funny," he demanded of her, crossing his arms over his chest.

She did the only thing she could think of, which was to repay his initial attempt to shake hands by now offering her hand to him. He hesitated, but reached out and surprisingly, warmly took her hand. He didn't shake her hand—he just held it for a second.

"Nice to meet you, Ethan Rasmussen," she said, smiling, and he let go of her hand. "I'm Autumn Hamilton, Martha's neighbor." She turned to walk back to her Jeep before he could offer a response. The conversation was clearly over.

He wished now he had said more, had engaged her. What did she do? Was she married? What was her story? Compared to every other stranger he had ever spoken to, this one had practically rendered him tongue-tied.

AUTUMN

After he watched her stroll across the gravel parking lot and slide into her Jeep, he whispered her name to himself. *Autumn Hamilton*. Something about the feel of her name on his lips gave Ethan a little shudder. He didn't know whether to feel good about meeting her, or to be afraid of her. Something told him it should be a little bit of both.

As she drove away, Autumn flashed on an image of Ethan Rasmussen, in his khaki pants with their razor-sharp creases, dragging the ugly pumpkin from his car onto Martha's front porch, orange pumpkin goop dripping onto his loafers and silk shirt. Maybe it would even get into his hair if he slipped on the gravel. Then she stuck out her tongue, as Heather had done just a few minutes earlier, and collapsed into schoolgirl giggles. It felt good to laugh. It had been a long time. But her happiness disappeared quickly, as it always did. She could only keep up the façade for so long.

CHAPTER 2

*E*THAN STARED AFTER the annoying, presumptuous, gorgeous, pumpkin-giving woman as she drove away. What had just happened? He had been pranked and disrespected and made to feel like a shy schoolboy by a woman in a dirty *Charlie's Angels* T-shirt, denim jacket, and muddy red cowboy boots. And somehow, contrary to his usual temperament, this really hadn't bothered him at all.

He stood beside the Jaguar and thought his head might explode as he became aware of Heather pounding the world's ugliest pumpkin with the keys on his key ring. She managed to penetrate the skin and send orangish liquid spewing across the kid leather interior of his car. She was a sly one, that Heather, and he was going to have to watch her closely. That hug she had given him a few minutes ago had been a ruse, totally staged to get his car keys out of his hand. In another life, he firmly believed she had been a pickpocket. He patted his pants pockets to make sure she hadn't lifted his phone or wallet.

This difficult process of integrating Heather into his life, and he into hers, was not getting any easier, he thought to himself. But things would be different soon. By dinnertime tomorrow he and Heather would be in his penthouse in New York City for a brief "get-to-know-you" visit before she moved in permanently. His turf, his rules. It was the psychologist's suggestion that they ease her into her new life slowly. Soon, he told himself, relieved, his life would return to some semblance of normal, or what he had come to think of as his "new normal." He was still the ultra-successful trial lawyer with a luxury lifestyle and a gorgeous, incredibly successful girl-friend, Ellen Bauer. Only now he would have a five-year-old girl in tow. How hard could it be?

As Heather went in for another chunk of pumpkin, Ethan sprang into action.

"C'mon, Heather," he said, holding out his hand, forcing a smile that came across mostly as a grimace. "Your grandmother will be wondering what happened to us. She wanted to make you an apple pie for tonight, remember?"

Heather ignored his outstretched hand and, leaving his car keys next to the wounded pumpkin, crawled into the back to buckle herself into the child safety seat Martha had insisted he use every time Heather was in the car. The seat left indentations on the leather seats, and that made him crazy. He couldn't help but notice that Heather had now transferred mud and pumpkin goop onto the backseat of the car as well. He watched, screaming inside, as she wiped her hands on the back of the passenger seat. He put the bag of apples next to her and tried to kiss her on the cheek, but she pulled away from him and crossed her arms over her chest. At least she'd stopped hitting him, he told himself, as he slipped behind the wheel and pointed the Jaguar back toward Martha's.

He glanced over at the pumpkin again and couldn't help but smile and think about Autumn Hamilton, who had, for whatever reason, taken it upon herself to trash the inside of his car with this horribly disfigured gourd. It was sinking in just how gorgeous she was. He had never seen such pure porcelain coloring, made all the more remarkable in contrast to her long dark hair and shining azure eyes. As his mind wandered to how she looked in her form-fitting jeans, he suddenly remembered Ellen. Long, cool Ellen, who was waiting for him, somewhat impatiently, back in New York.

As they drove home, Ethan tried to talk with Heather, knowing it would be a one-way conversation. It didn't matter. The psychologist had said Heather would start talking when she was ready. The worst thing he could do was ignore her. And he wasn't supposed to ask questions or try to trick her into speaking.

"So, Heather," he began, attempting to catch her eyes in the rearview mirror. "I think you like Autumn. It was nice of her to give us this butt-ugly pumpkin." He reviewed what he had just said, trying to make sure it was a statement and not a question.

He saw Heather slide her eyes up to meet his in the mirror, then abruptly look away.

"I guess that she must be nice if she gave us these pumpkins." He really didn't quite believe that statement, but was just trying to move the one-sided conversation along.

Again, the eyes slid into view, lingering on his a little longer this time, then disappeared. It was something, and he would take it. As recently as yesterday, when he spoke to her in the car she wouldn't even look at him in the rearview mirror.

His cell phone rang, and he took the call, despite Heather's disapproving sigh. It was the office. He had already been gone for a week. Some of his cases had to be reassigned, and clients were getting impatient. If he weren't a partner, he probably would have been fired by now.

"Barry," he answered more cheerfully than he felt. "How are you, buddy?" He had Barry on speaker, just in case. He couldn't remember if Pennsylvania was a hands-free state.

"Don't 'how are you, buddy' me, Ethan. Where the heck are you? I need your rear end back here right now."

Realizing immediately that Heather should not be exposed to Barry's anger and resentment, Ethan quickly grabbed his phone so he could take Barry Armstrong, one of the senior partners, off speaker. Lesson learned. Nobody on speaker when he was with Heather, just to be safe. Heather didn't need to hear all that. Then he fumbled the phone onto the floor and swerved slightly as he pulled it back within arm's reach with his foot.

"Sorry, Barry, ah, lost the signal for a minute. Can you hear me now?"

As Barry raged on Ethan saw the state trooper pass him, glancing at him as he drove by, then slowing and falling in behind him. Then the siren came on. So, Pennsylvania *was* a hands-free cell phone state.

Ethan pulled over to the shoulder and allowed himself one "dammit" and one restrained fist bang on the steering wheel. He glanced up at the rearview mirror to apologize to Heather for swearing and saw the flickering of a brief smile, actually more of a self-satisfied smirk, apparently at his expense.

CHAPTER 2

After the state trooper graciously released him with a stern, well-rehearsed warning, Ethan tried to talk himself down off the ledge that he seemed to have stepped out onto three weeks ago. Or rather, that he had been forced onto.

He had been devastated to hear of the death of his two dearest friends. He and Troy had been roommates at West Point and had served together in Afghanistan. After he left the Army, Ethan went to law school. Troy stayed in and climbed the military ranks, marrying Denise along the way. Despite their different career paths, they would always be soldier-brothers with a bond that only those who have served together, especially in combat, could understand.

Ethan and Ellen had attended Denise and Troy's funeral in Finch's Crossing and were getting ready to leave when an elderly gentleman had whispered something into Ethan's ear. Ethan had followed the gentlemen back to his office, after suggesting that Ellen go back to New York, when he was told the conversation might result in him staying in the area for a few days.

Ethan had been stunned to learn that Troy and Denise had designated him as their daughter's guardian in the event of their deaths. Though surprised, he understood because of what he and Troy had been through together. Ethan could, of course, have relinquished guardianship. That was not unusual and fairly easy to do. And Heather's grandmother was a natural choice to raise the little girl. Troy was an only child, so there were no aunts or uncles on his side to step in. Denise had a brother, but he was a Marine and spent much of his time deployed. In many ways, Ethan *was* an understandable choice, even though no one—not Martha, not Ellen, and not even the lawyer—would ever understand. He was the logical choice, except for just one thing. He knew nothing about how to raise a little girl.

Yes, his life would be forever changed from this point forward, but he could not in good conscience dishonor his friend's request to raise his child. He could see how some might think Heather's parents' choice was crazy and illogical. But Ethan had made his decision, and as was his way, he would stick with it, no matter what. But it was time to get on with it. It was time to go back to New York, with Heather, and resume his life.

By the time they pulled into Martha's driveway, Ethan had calmed down from his encounter with law enforcement. He was usually the guy making the officers sweat on the witness stand. He supposed it was just karma that this time he was in the hot seat, though he had been let off with a stern warning.

He unbuckled his seatbelt and turned in his seat to look back at Heather, ready to give her a warm smile and crack another joke about the pumpkins. Heather stuck her tongue out at him, again, unbuckled herself from the child safety seat, and was inside the house before he could even remind her to take the bag of apples in to her grandmother.

* * *

Martha ached with the loss of Denise, her only daughter, and her son-in-law, whom she had loved like a son. The telephone call in the middle of the night from the state police had been heart-wrenching, and then the hours and days and now weeks that followed had been equally as painful, although the dust was starting to settle some. The small family had been on its way to drop Heather off at Martha's house in Finch's Crossing. Denise and Troy had booked a room at a resort hotel outside of Pittsburgh for a romantic weekend. They had gotten caught in a downpour and had pulled over on the side of the highway to wait it out. It was dark, and according to the police report, a truck had hydroplaned and clipped their SUV parked on the shoulder. Denise and Troy had been killed instantly. By some miracle, Heather, asleep in her car seat, had not been seriously hurt. It was Heather who helped soften Martha's deep ache. Knowing she had to be strong for her granddaughter gave her something to focus on, other than her desperate grief.

Even before the funeral, Martha had begun to plan for Heather's permanent move into her house, getting Denise's old bedroom ready with a thorough cleaning, new curtains, and clean sheets on the bed. She would keep Heather out of kindergarten for a while, and she'd have to find out what types of food Heather liked. Things had changed a lot since she raised her own children. There were so many choices of cereals and snack foods and drinks these days. It was overwhelming.

Adam Frick, Finch's Crossing's only lawyer, had asked Martha to come to his office after the funeral, without Heather. She had protested at first, reminding him that Heather was still in shock and hadn't said a word since the accident. "I need to be there for her," she had said.

"It's important," he had replied emphatically, and so Martha had asked her neighbor, Autumn, to watch Heather for a few hours.

She and Ethan Rasmussen, one of Troy's friends she had only met briefly a few times, sat in front of Adam's desk. They both watched as the lawyer unfolded some papers and began to speak, telling her that she would not be Heather's guardian. She thought it must be a bad dream.

"That's impossible!" she cried, at the same time that Ethan said, "What! That can't be right."

"I'm afraid it's true," Adam said solemnly, knowing neither of the two sitting in front of him quite believed him. "After Heather was born Denise and Troy came to my office and asked me to draw up their wills, and they were very specific about their intentions. In the event that anything happened to both of them, Ethan was to act as Heather's guardian."

"But, why?" Martha pleaded, her voice shaking. "Did they leave a letter for us explaining their decision? I don't understand!"

Adam shook his head. "I'm sorry, Martha. And there's nothing I can do to change this. Their wills are airtight." He paused and then looked at Ethan. "Unless Mr. Rasmussen decides to give up guardianship and transfer it to you, which he has every right to do."

Ethan was shaking his head, and Martha couldn't tell if he was in shock or if he was indicating that he wouldn't give up custody. In fact, he was shaking his head in disbelief *and* to say he would not shirk his duty to Troy, and would honor his wishes and assume guardianship of Heather.

Martha and Adam looked at him expectantly, and he lifted his head to meet their eyes.

"If Troy and Denise asked me to look after Heather, which apparently they did, I have no choice but to honor that wish. I'm not sure why they did, but they must have had their reasons for choosing me."

Ethan continued, talking to Adam, but glancing sideways the whole time toward Martha. "This is a shock to me, too. But what am I supposed to do? I simply cannot *not* do this. Troy was my very best friend, and he has made this request of me."

CHAPTER 2

He turned back to Martha. "I can only imagine how much this hurts you, how you must feel that this makes no sense," he said gently.

"You have no idea how much this hurts me," Martha snapped. "First I lose my daughter, and now you are going to take my only grandchild away from me. You'll be too busy in New York to look after her properly, and she'll be away from the people she knows and loves. This is just wrong."

"Martha," he said gently. "I'm not *taking* Heather—she was entrusted into my care by your daughter and son-in-law. For whatever reason, they wanted her to be my responsibility. And I'm not going to vanish with her. New York is only a few hours away. I will make sure you see her a lot. I promise. I know how much Heather loves you. I know how much you love Heather." Ethan had no idea if what he was saying were in fact the right things to say. How could anyone know how to react in a situation like this?

Now, looking out the front window at Ethan hefting a gigantic, misshapen pumpkin out of his Jaguar, getting dirt and pumpkin juice all over his car and his clothes, Martha's rage at him for refusing to relinquish guardianship of Heather had dissolved into general sadness and disappointment. And fear for Heather. Genuine fear. Heather obviously didn't like Ethan in the least. She shot him dagger looks at every possible opportunity. But Ethan had engaged a child psychologist near Finch's Crossing, whom he, Heather, and Martha had seen four times now, and he had another counselor lined up for when they returned together to New York City. He had hired a nanny and enrolled Heather in a private school near his apartment. She sensed that his meticulous planning and his logical approach to problems and decisions had helped make him one of New York's most successful trial lawyers. But none of that would help him raise a devastated little girl. She grudgingly admitted to herself that he was doing all the right things and taking the situation very seriously. Martha just wished she could understand *why* he was doing this to them, why he hadn't relinquished custody. That would have been the most logical thing and kindest thing to do. Family belonged with family. Heather belonged with her.

Martha was grateful that Ethan had let Heather stay with her as he tried to figure out how to arrange, or more accurately, rearrange, his life to accommodate the little girl. But now he was back to take Heather away from her for the first time, for a long-weekend to acclimate her, and him, before she made the permanent move. Martha desperately hoped that in time he would come to his senses and change his mind.

CHAPTER 3

AUTUMN HAMILTON UNDERSTOOD that she was one of those rare and lucky people who know exactly where they belong in the world, who are not driven by wanderlust, and who are certain the grass is rarely greener. She had lived in the small town of Finch's Crossing, in Pennsylvania's Laurel Highlands, all her life, and she still lived in the house where she had grown up. It was the same house where her mother and grandmother had lived before her. It wasn't just tradition that kept Autumn from ever wanting to leave her hometown, but the undeniable sense of belonging she carried deep inside her. She was indelibly connected to the essence of Finch's Crossing, to the slate sidewalks and cobblestone side streets and graveled alleyways, and to the familiar smiling faces she would always see along them. She counted on the old-fashioned lampposts to illuminate the streets at precisely six every evening.

Her heart was linked to the annual events like the July 4th celebration and the Fall Festival, with the arts and crafts bazaar and food vendors who had at one point come from all over the region. She *needed* the Christmas parade, with its Santa Claus float, fire trucks with screaming sirens and flashing lights, and Shriners weaving their tiny cars along the parade route. And she was forever drawn to the rich variety of architectural styles exhibited in the rows of houses, many built before the turn of the century. Finch's Crossing exuded an absolutely predictable ebb and flow of small-town life, and it was as familiar to her as her own face.

At 7:58 a.m. every weekday, Miss Eva, the postmistress, raised the flag in front of the Finch's Crossing Post Office and collected the letters dropped overnight in the familiar blue mailbox. At eleven, Ducky, the letter carrier, would either be outside the library taking a break before resuming her route or warming a stool at the lunch counter if it was raining or snowing. The elementary school kids would head to Hoffman's Drugstore for candy and sodas at two-thirty after school let out. Autumn knew Finch's Crossing's every heartbeat and never grew tired of the steady, persistent familiarity of it all.

Every fall it was Autumn's ritual to decorate her family home as if preparing for a major holiday. She arranged sprigs of bittersweet on the mantle in the living room and collected acorns and chestnuts deposited by the old and stately trees that guarded the streets. Piling these harbingers of the season into stylish bowls, she placed them lovingly and carefully in every room of her large room, celebrating that her favorite time of the year had finally arrived. Her front porch practically exploded with pumpkins, other gourds of every color, size, and shape, and the biggest and most exuberant chrysan-

CHAPTER 3

themums she could find. Dried corn stalks were bundled and placed upright on either side of the front door. She typically couldn't get enough of fall decorating. But this year, even this usually joyful ritual wasn't enough to fell her growing and inescapable sadness.

When Autumn arrived home after her encounter with Ethan Rasmussen at the nursery, she calmed herself by walking from room to room, admiring her handiwork. She now remembered that they had met before, briefly, at Heather's christening. That must have been four and a half years ago now. He and his Barbie doll girlfriend hadn't even stayed for the reception. She was surprised that they had even deigned to honor the commoners with their presence in the first place. Obviously, Autumn hadn't made any impression on him, as he hadn't remembered her.

She exchanged a bowl of acorns in the morning room, a cozy nook off the kitchen, with dried husks of corn that had been resting on the tall bookshelves that flanked the marble-mantled fireplace in the living room. The house was a large Victorian built in a time when families were large and furniture was dark and substantial. Autumn took her time walking through her home, trailing her fingertips across the occasional table or chair back and along the spines of books she imagined her grandmother reading as a young woman in the window seat in what was now the guest room. She paused outside her studio, her anxiety level skyrocketing, and then she hurried past, purposefully not looking.

Autumn couldn't decide whether it was ironic or just coincidental that she had developed such an affinity for the season she had been named after. Her three sisters had also been named after the seasons of the year by their bohemian parents. Summer, the baby of the family, and Spring, a model in Los Angeles, also went by their given names. Only Winter, an architect in Pittsburgh who was as hard and cold as her name implied, went by a nickname, Win.

After their father passed away (they had lost their mother ten years earlier) each of the Hamilton girls had chosen what she wanted to keep from their parents' significant estate. There had been no fighting or bickering or hard feelings that so often occur when families attempt to divide money, property and keepsakes. Autumn had wanted their childhood home and furniture. Spring had taken the lion's share of their mother's significant silver and crystal collection and all the heirloom jewelry, which included many one-of-a-kind Tiffany pieces worth tens of thousands of dollars. Summer and Win had split their parents' considerable remaining cash assets. Their grandparents' farm in the Catskills belonged to all of them jointly, an arrangement that had carried over from their grandparents' will.

Only Autumn had chosen to stay in Finch's Crossing. She supposed she couldn't blame her sisters for leaving. They all had experienced taunts in school, especially in high school, and had had very few friends. It was probably just jealousy on the part of the bullies. The Hamilton sisters were gorgeous, smart, and appeared confident and polished.

"It's the seasoning sisters," their classmates would jeer. "Hey, what's the weather today? Did you bring the weatherman to school with you today?"

At least the other kids didn't know their middle names—Rainbow, Sky, Earth, and River—which would have made their school days a true misery. The day Winter graduated from high school she declared that from then on, she would be known as Win, and she had since refused to answer to Winter.

Lost in a book or sketchbook, Autumn somehow had managed

CHAPTER 3

to shake off the schoolyard taunts, but it was not that easy for her sisters. It was the worst for Win. In elementary school the kids had called her "Frosty the Snowwoman," but by the time she graduated from high school, she had been labeled "The Ice Queen." Winter knew she was considered aloof, but every attempt she made at connecting with her classmates seemed to go nowhere. And before long, she gave up and closed herself off completely.

After each of them graduated, Autumn's three sisters scattered to the winds, choosing colleges as far away as possible and returning infrequently to Finch's Crossing for the occasional holiday. Autumn missed her sisters. Especially now. Summer would understand what she was going through. And Spring, with all her efficiency, organization, logical thinking, and ability to put things in their proper perspective, would have her feeling right in no time. Winter probably wouldn't understand, but she would provide such a distraction that Autumn would likely forget, at least for a time, that she was struggling mightily.

Autumn was grateful for her best friend, Meg Overly, whom she met her freshman year in high school. They had become fast friends and remained close, although Meg's idiosyncrasies and gruff manner sometimes kept Autumn from confiding in her.

Coming down the stairs, Autumn straightened a grouping of mirrors, then four Audubon prints hanging over a chest of drawers on the landing. She ran her finger over the top of one of the frames and was pleased that there was very little dust. She arrived on the first floor. She was procrastinating. And she knew it. She also knew it had to stop.

Taking a deep breath for courage, she dragged her feet across her grandmother's Oriental rug in the entryway, continuing through the living room toward the back of the house. She finally stepped into her light-filled studio and immediately felt the warmth of the sun on her face, though this time the warming rays felt more like accusatory daggers.

She ignored the stacks of large canvases leaning against the wall as she walked by them, the gentle breeze of her passing causing dust particles to flutter and swirl around her knees. The drop cloths beneath her were so hard that she could almost hear the paint spatters crackling as she walked over them.

After she sold her first significant painting, Autumn had expanded the first floor of her family home with this 1,000-square-foot, mostly glass-walled studio overlooking the flower-cutting garden. It was here that she worked, happily and productively, producing beautiful and haunting abstract paintings that had been acquired by some of the world's finest contemporary art museums and many private collectors. Her work was in the corporate collections of several Fortune 500 companies and a few prestigious university art museums. Her business was her art. And it was lucrative. And if her business was her art, her art was her life. She could not imagine a life without creating. She had occasionally wondered what she would do if she could not make a living as an artist, never dreaming she would ever stand on the precipice of that possibility. Without the art that nourished her, she had imagined her soul would wither away, and she would wilt into nothing. How true the musings during a happier time had been.

Autumn was known for working in shadowy, silvery, almost reflective tones of white, ivory, and cream, and her abstract paintings had been universally praised and desired. She was lucky enough to have had her first solo show while still in graduate school, and two

CHAPTER 3

agents snatched her up, each representing her on a separate coast. Later, her white florals had been popular for a while and had sold quickly, significantly enhancing her name recognition. But interest dropped off and then disappeared, and the remaining canvases were now stacked, unceremoniously, against the walls of her studio, like proverbial albatrosses. They had been banished from the galleries because they were taking up space needed for "fresh" and "up and coming" artists.

Sighing, she sat on her stool at the island in the middle of her studio and surveyed the pristine tubes of paint in hues of pale green in neat rows before her. She had bought those two months ago, thinking a new color might jolt a creative spark within her and reveal even the smallest inspiration that might spur her on. The paintbrushes were waiting for her, just as she'd left them in jars of thinner, only the thinner had evaporated, and the brushes were as stiff and brittle as old cornstalks. The last time she had been in this room, maybe two weeks ago, she had stacked rags in neat piles and rearranged pencils, charcoals, pastels, and erasers next to the tubes of acrylic paint.

In some ways, she was almost glad her florals were no longer selling. Painting them had become automatic, almost formulaic. She had ceased to feel them, to feel anything at all when she painted them. Her heart no longer raced, no longer beat with fury and purpose or kept pace with her brushstrokes. Her original paintings had been sometimes delicate and deliberate, but more often they were instinctive and unexpected, and more than occasionally, brilliant. But now when she tried to access that creative fount that once flowed through her so strongly—to feel her work, to feel her heart race and her breath catch in her lungs—she only found an emptiness that until very recently she hadn't realized was there. Somehow, it had crept inside her, boring a deep, empty well.

Her initial thought had been to try to capture that emotion, that emptiness, that inability to feel, in her work, and she returned to the abstract form that had served her so well at the very beginning of her career. Dark, jagged, and haunting images appeared before her. She was not pleased. She couldn't believe that shades of white could create such dark, disturbing images. That work made her shudder, and she quickly destroyed the five paintings in the new series she had created.

She had refused to show them to her agent in Pittsburgh. It seemed clear and obvious that if she could figure out where the emptiness had come from, she could work on getting rid of it, which she believed would restore her creativity. She knew the most important thing was to get rid of the emptiness. She wondered what had changed in her life that could have sapped her creativity and blocked her so completely. But quite simply, there had been no changes in her life. She had the same routine and the same friends. She lived in the same house and did the same things. She had recently considered that the problem wasn't that something had changed. Perhaps the problem was that *nothing* had changed.

She had kept up the façade of being the happy, carefree artist, and no one ever knew that she was blocked artistically, and felt empty as a human being. She knew it was such a cliché, but she really felt like she had a hole in her soul. What was that expression she had heard? "Fake it till you make it." Well, she had been faking it, but there had been no making it, figuratively or literally. But she soldiered on. Maybe this strategy *had* helped some. She hadn't isolated herself completely. She wasn't avoiding her studio altogether.

Autumn glanced around the room at the stacks of unsold paintings. Each work was like a favorite childhood doll that had been squished, torn, and put upon until it was dirty and broken. You couldn't get rid of the doll, even though it had become pathetic to look at. She needed these outdated, unwanted, and unsellable paintings. Perhaps they would sell eventually. For so many years she had made an excellent living selling her work. But not anymore. She finally had to face the truth. And the truth was harsh. Autumn hadn't really painted in more than a year, and she hadn't sold a painting in more than two.

CHAPTER 4

MAYOR PEGGY BRIGHTWELL sat in her spacious office in Finch's Crossing City Hall. She was a cheerful woman in her fifties, with the same traditional ash-colored bob haircut she had coifed for the past thirty years. The only thing that had changed were the lengths to which she went to cover the grey. Her wise and understanding dark brown eyes and winning smile, she believed, had helped her win every election, often unopposed, for the past twenty years. She had nerves of steel. This was required if a mayor was to survive cantankerous council members, irate citizens, and each new crop of high school freshmen who thought they had just invented social justice and public protests.

Peggy felt she had to be particularly strong and always show her game face. Her husband had fallen from a roof during a contracting job ten years ago. He had broken his back and was permanently disabled and unable to work. He could walk, slowly, but he couldn't work. Fortunately for Peggy, Bob Fletcher was positive and progressive and seamlessly took over the role of house husband. He couldn't do a whole lot physically, but he was a natural organizer and manager. But he was not much of a disciplinarian. Their teenage sons were nothing short of juvenile delinquents, engaging in everything from lifting candy, soda, and chips from the IGA grocery store to hacking into the school system's mainframe computer to change their grades and the grades of those fellow underachieving students who could afford to pay them. And they were only in middle school. Despite the struggles and frustrations at home, Peggy had bigger problems at City Hall. And she was running out of time. If she wanted to leave a legacy she'd have to move fast.

She surveyed the wood-paneled office she had occupied for two decades. The Brightwells had been prominent citizens in Finch's Crossing since its founding in 1874. She imagined this was the reason she had chosen to keep her last name when she and Bob Fletcher married thirty years ago as seniors at Carnegie Mellon University in Pittsburgh. She was by no means a feminist, at least not back then, and her decision to remain a Brightwell caused quite a stir. But she knew deep down that she wanted to run for public office, and she also knew that retaining her prominent maiden name was a strategic move.

She toyed with the office supplies on her desk, tapping a pen against a legal pad on her blotter, straightening the pile of sticky notes, and positioning the stapler and tape dispenser next to each other. Pictures of her family and the many civic awards she had received over the years dominated the bookshelves that stood floor to ceiling against the windowless west wall of her office. When it became apparent that she would probably be staying in office for a while, she had done some redecorating at her own expense, bringing in a pretty needlepoint rug in bright blues, reds, greens, and golds. She hung green velvet drapes and replaced the masculine leather couch and club chairs with a tan chintz sofa and matching armchairs.

She moved from her desk to this comfortable seating area, taking her legal pad with her. It was time to get down to business. She had to face some hard facts. The town's annual Fall Festival, a tradition for forty years, had experienced dwindling attendance for the past few years, culminating in last year's pathetic showing of less than a hundred people. She had watched as the merchants, horrified, tried to hide their panic. It was so bad that they had cancelled the festival this year. Besides the Christmas shopping season, which also had dropped off thanks to online shopping and big-box stores in neighboring towns, the merchants relied on the festival for a significant chunk of their annual income.

Finch's Crossing had once been one of the most prosperous townships in Westmoreland County at the center of the coke-making industry. Its early citizens built large Italianate and Victorian mansions on sleepy, tree-lined streets and opened successful businesses. Even though the coal money had gradually dried up, Finch's Crossing's five thousand residents and its merchants had held their own for decades, luring tourists who came for the nearby outdoor adventure sports and to see attractions like Frank Lloyd Wright's Fallingwater. But empty storefronts on Pittsburgh Street and the exodus of young people seeking greener, and most likely more exciting, pastures all combined to usher in the least prosperous time in the town's history.

Peggy looked at the list she had been making on the legal pad. Only half of the merchants had websites, and if she was being honest, they weren't very good, and some were downright awful, with black backgrounds, tiny yellow text, and no contact information. Some of them hadn't been updated in months, even years. Knopf Jewelry was still advertising a twenty percent off Easter sale, and Teppy Eicher's Et Cetera Boutique and Christmas Shop, hadn't been updated since she added the Christmas expansion two years ago. And Lila Geyer's Morris Ladies Wear now carried men's and children's clothes, which you would never know from visiting the website. Melissa Overholt's Burnt Orange Antiques Emporium, Stan Brilhart's hardware store, and Miss Elsie's Tea Room all had similar online disasters. And social media? That was another deficit. Only Melissa had a Facebook account where she uploaded photos of new inventory. Peggy imagined this was why she enjoyed a larger clientele than her commercial neighbors. Still, though, twenty customers a week wasn't much better than fifteen. Peggy imagined tiny Miss Elsie Hixon, well into her seventies, trying to use Twitter, and cringed.

And to make matters worse, the slump in business had had a disastrous impact on the town coffers. The downward trend in sales meant lower sales tax revenue. Businesses closing or relocating meant less business taxes and impact fees, all of which meant less money for schools and vital services like fire and rescue. The result was an ever-dwindling revenue stream. Now was the time to be prudent with the town's budget, Peggy chastised herself, not go out on a limb. But she knew if she didn't do something differently, nothing would change. Well, the time for self-doubt had come and gone. She had already made her decision and signed a contract with a young man from Cleveland who had promised to bring the merchants into the social media revolution, albeit about ten years after it had begun. Oddly, it was her delinquent sons who had pointed out the town's social media deficit. Peggy sighed, marveling at the ups and downs of parenthood.

The knock at her office door startled her, though she was expecting Kyle Oswald at ten and he was on time.

"Come in," she called, not knowing what to expect, as she had hired him over the phone. She could have gone to Cleveland to interview Kyle after she chose him from the stack of responses she got from her ad, but she did not want to spend town funds for travel. He had suggested a Skype call, but as she had no idea what that was, she politely declined and conducted the interview over the phone.

She watched as a young man, probably twenty-nine or thirty, strode confidently into her office. He was good-looking in a nontraditional way. He had an oblong face and a rather large nose, but his cheekbones were chiseled, and he wore his blond hair military-style, all of which suited him and combined to make him very handsome. His eyes were a startling green, almost like a piece of jade.

"Welcome, Kyle," she said cheerfully, trying to live up to her Brightwell name, and motioned for him to sit on one of the chairs opposite her. "I just can't tell you how glad I am that you've agreed to take us on as your next project."

And she was glad, and relieved, as he was the only candidate willing to work for the pitiful salary she could offer.

"How ya doing, Mayor Peggy?" he said, and she instantly remembered his very youthful and casual way of speaking, but assumed that this came along with being an eccentric Internet guru and entrepreneur. "Couldn't pass it up. Like I told you, I used to spend my summers in Pittsburgh with my grandparents before they retired to

Georgia. Besides, from what I can see, you really need my help."

"Well, that's very true," she agreed. "Is there any hope for us?" she asked wistfully.

"That depends on the desired outcome," Kyle replied. "You always need to start with the objective and work backward. In this case, you're looking to bring tourists and shoppers back to Finch's Crossing, revitalize what you have now, and energize the people who are trying to hold everything together. Am I close?"

Peggy nodded. They had spoken over the phone of course, but this morning he had articulated what they needed in a no-nonsense manner. She liked him instantly. From what she could tell, he seemed like an itinerant entrepreneur of sorts, and while he wasn't the typical county employee, she knew that in this time of crisis she had to be brave.

"We will see results immediately, right?" she asked expectantly.

"That's not really how this works, Mayor," Kyle responded, suddenly aware of the desperation in Peggy's voice. "This isn't a magic wand. All the web design and online marketing work I do is a series of small, strategic steps. It takes time for everything to fall into place."

"But certainly by Black Friday," she pressed. "There's enough time between now and then surely?"

Kyle hated to disappoint her. He could see how important this was to her.

"Yes, by Black Friday. I never make promises to my clients in this line of work, but I will make an exception for you. And I promise you I will work as fast as I can for you. Right now, you are my only client."

"It sounds like you've been, ah," she struggled for the word, "freelancing since you left school?" she hoped she wasn't sounding accusatory.

"Yes, ma'am," he answered politely, wanting so badly to make a good impression. "Trying to find the best place for my skills, you know. That sort of thing."

"Well, your references were stellar. They couldn't say enough good things about you. In fact, all three wished you had stayed with them longer. They were all so disappointed that you had chosen to move on."

"Yes, ma'am."

"Well, in any event, I'm glad you're here," Peggy said, rising and extending her hand. "When would you like to get started, and what can I do to facilitate your work?"

"Just need to dump my stuff at the hotel, and then I'm all yours," he responded.

As part of his pay she had arranged to cover his room and board at the Greystone Manor Inn.

"By the way, how long do you think you'll need me for?" he asked as he was getting ready to leave. "We never did agree on a contract time."

Peggy stared out the window to Pittsburgh Street below. It was virtually empty.

"As long as it takes," she said. "Just as long as it takes."

They agreed that he would settle in, have some lunch, and explore the town on his own for the rest of the day, getting the lay of the land and observing the merchants. In the evening, he would proceed to the computer lab at the high school, where she would introduce him and say a few words about her plan, and where he would begin introducing the local merchants to the basics of com-

CHAPTER 4

puters with the intention of eventually teaching them how to market their businesses with computers and the Internet. Peggy had no idea how they would respond. And now, looking at this confident young man with his dark jeans, black and white Pumas, and starched white dress shirt flapping open at the cuffs, she was just a little worried.

Kyle drove down Pittsburgh Street, unable to be as observant as he knew he should be due to his unfamiliarity with the town. He surprised himself at his ability to follow Mayor Peggy's directions from memory, and he felt a sense of accomplishment when he turned onto Hickory Street and into the parking lot of the Greystone Manor. He sat for a moment to catch his breath and push back his racing thoughts.

I must be crazy, he thought. *There is no way I can pull this off. What if they find out what a fraud I am?*

Kyle didn't know much about the Manor, as it was known by locals, only what the mayor had told him as she explained his housing stipend. Apparently, the grand stone building was built by a descendant of the town's founder, Jacob Finch, for whom the town was named. Jacob brought his family to the area from Maine to escape New England's harsh winter climate. When he came upon the proverbial fork in the road—a muddy cart path to the south or a stream that could be followed west—he chose neither and instead settled where he had stopped, buying land outside a small, unincorporated village with only a scattering of buildings. When the railroad opened in Finch's Crossing in 1873, the fortunes of Jacob—and his friends and neighbors—were forever changed. The railroad would cross Jacob's land, and he sold it for a handsome profit and moved his family to a grand Greek Revival-style house on fashionable Mulberry Street. When the town was incorporated in 1874, Jacob, who was simultaneously elected its first mayor, named it Finch's Crossing as a reminder of the fateful afternoon at the crossroads that had changed his fortunes.

As he sat in his van, Kyle couldn't help but wonder if the crossroads in his own life would lead to similar prosperity and good fortune. He could only hope. With a final deep breath for courage, he stepped out of the van and walked to the front path that took him past large trees and up to a large and imposing stone mansion with white columns on either side of door and a glass solarium on one end. It was beautifully landscaped with neatly trimmed ground cover, boxwoods, and colorful chrysanthemums artfully placed everywhere.

Maybe they won't care what I've done when they see what a good job I can do, he told himself as he walked through the front door.

The lobby was sumptuously decorated in the Victorian style of dark woods and jewel-toned upholstered furniture and drapes. Before he had a chance to check in at the registration desk, a loud voice boomed at him, and he turned his head to the left to see a middle-aged man, dressed in starched khakis and a blue dress shirt, descending the stairs toward him, hand outstretched in greeting.

"Hello, hello! You must be Kyle," he said and introduced himself as Duncan Olack. "I'm so pleased to welcome you to the Manor."

They walked through the lobby, and Duncan continued his friendly banter.

"Peggy told us to be on the lookout for you and make sure you didn't get lost on your way up here, which we know is almost impossible in a town this size, but Peggy wanted to make sure."

He paused for a quick breath and guided Kyle toward the reception desk then stepped behind the counter and began to type on the computer keyboard. "Let's see, here you are. Kyle Oswald. I see you are with us for a few weeks, possibly longer. That's fine, just fine. The mayor has paid for two weeks in advance and has given you a sixty dollar per diem, which is more than enough to cover all your meals here at the restaurant. Is that all your luggage?" he asked, pointing at the duffle bag now resting at Kyle's feet.

"I travel light," he said cheerfully, but thinking to himself *yeah, this is my only luggage, and all I have in this world is in it.*

He wondered to himself how tacky it would be to ask for his per diem in cash, rather than be trapped to dine at the Manor's restaurant. He knew the menu would be pricey. He'd rather eat cheap and have the cash for other necessities.

"Well, we are so glad to have you with us here, and I just know you'll have us all shipshape in no time." Duncan gestured grandly, joined him on the other side of the reception desk and continued. "We are incredibly proud of Greystone Manor and know that you will be quite comfortable here."

Kyle took a moment to look around and noticed the beautiful crown molding and stone fireplace. Built-in bookshelves and various nooks were packed with knickknacks, though Kyle knew they were not like the cheap salt and pepper shakers and tiny ceramic cats that his grandmother collected. He looked up to the ornate ceiling with the carved reliefs.

"Greystone Manor is Finch's Crossing's best kept secret," Duncan continued, and Kyle followed him up a grand staircase, admiring the gleaming mahogany banisters and listening to his chatter.

"It was built in 1909 by an industrialist who, as you can see, spared no expense in construction and detail work. That's my apartment," he said pointing to a door as they walked past. They went up another staircase and stopped at a doorway at the end of the hallway.

"We have two floors of rooms and of course the restaurant, library, and solarium you saw when you walked in. The third floor is a grand ballroom that we never use." He sighed. "It's a relic from another era, I'm afraid. All that's up there now are banquet tables and chairs we need to get rid of."

He presented Kyle with an actual key to the room, not a key card.

"We've put you in the Laurel Suite," he said. "It's our largest room and our only suite, and Peggy thought you'd be more comfortable here since you'll be with us for a while. She had a microwave and small refrigerator brought in. There's free Wi-Fi, and anything else you need you just come find me. I think the Manor is the only place in Finch's Crossing that is fully wired and computerized, so we can certainly accommodate your work."

After Duncan's footsteps were out of earshot, Kyle turned the key in the brass lock, pushed open the heavy wooden door, and walked into the room. As his host had promised, it was a suite with a large bed and a small sitting area with a love seat, coffee table, and lamp. A two-person dinette set sat to the left of the bay window. He could use that as a desk, he thought. The microwave and fridge were tucked into a corner. On top of the fridge was a fruit basket, with an envelope tucked between two apples. "Welcome to Finch's Crossing," it read, and it was signed by Duncan.

Kyle opened the fridge and to his surprise found that it was well stocked with sodas, bottled water, and breakfast and lunch items. He closed the door slowly and sank onto the bed. Never before had anyone been so nice to him. He vowed to be extra vigilant to safeguard his secrets. He couldn't let Mayor Peggy down. He sensed her

CHAPTER 4

uncertainty during their meeting, no matter how hard she had tried
to hide it from him.

CHAPTER 5

*A*UTUMN HAD HEARD about a computer class focusing on Internet marketing that Peggy had organized for local merchants, and not wanting to go alone, she insisted on dragging her best friend, Meg Overly, along with her. They decided to grab a quick dinner at the Greystone Manor.

Meg was tall and willowy with a pretty face and striking grey eyes framed by lush lashes that belied her tomboyish persona. Her blonde hair was kept sensibly short, and her typical wardrobe was, according to Autumn, disastrous. Meg wore jeans, work boots, and flannel shirts in winter and jeans, work boots, and short-sleeved T-shirts the rest of the year. Autumn could understand these outfits for work, but it was a constant irritant to her that her pretty friend never lifted a finger to fix herself up, and Autumn often accused her of hiding behind a unisex façade.

CHAPTER 5

Like Autumn, Meg had been a serious introvert in school. Maybe that's why they had become fast friends and remained that way in the two decades since. Autumn had her art, and Meg had ridden horses all through school and even college, taking her mare, Belle, to Briar Rose College in rural Virginia, where she was able to continue competitive riding while studying biology and zoology. She knew her college education was to prepare her to return home, and, as an only child, take over her parents' successful business breeding and training German shepherds for law enforcement. Like Autumn, she would never leave Finch's Crossing. And, also like Autumn, she never really wanted to, though she would complain about the backward town from time to time.

As they studied their menus, Meg asked casually, "So have you heard anything from Ethan Rasmussen?"

"Why on earth would I hear from him?" Autumn asked incredulously, putting her menu down.

Meg shrugged. "From the way you talked about it earlier I sensed some kind of spark between the two of you during the pumpkin patch incident. Seemed like you were flirting with him."

Autumn was silent. When the waitress appeared, she ordered a sensible grilled chicken salad. Meg, who could eat anything she wanted and remain as slim as a schoolgirl, opted for a cheeseburger and fries.

"It's not fair," Autumn observed as the waitress left them. "You never gain any weight."

"Well, I'm always moving, on the go, hauling dogs, exercising them, heaving gigantic bags of dog food into the truck. You sit around for a living. No offense."

"I wouldn't flirt with Ethan for love or money," Autumn said distractedly, returning to the subject to set the record straight.

"Word around town is that he's handsome. Wait, no, I think the word I heard was *hot*," Meg cooed, artificially breathless.

"Handsome is as handsome does," Autumn responded haughtily with a toss of her hair. "He might be good-looking, but he's a pompous know-it-all who actually doesn't know anything." She took a breath. "And he's selfish, too, taking Heather away from Martha."

The food had arrived, and Meg was shoving multiple fries into her mouth at once. "Yeah, real selfish, upending his bachelor life to take care of a traumatized little girl to honor the wish of his best friend," she said with her mouth full. "Sounds pretty selfish to me."

"You know what I mean," Autumn insisted.

"Well, the way you talk about him, my dear, I think thou dost protest too much."

"That's absurd. I haven't given him a second thought since that day in the pumpkin patch," she lied. In fact, from time to time since their encounter, her mind had wandered to his handsome face. She remembered how he looked in his exquisitely tailored shirt that hinted at broad shoulders and muscled arms and chest beneath.

"So," Meg continued, obviously happy to be teasing her friend. "Do you want to see him again?"

Autumn was surprised at the flip-flop her stomach made at the mere mention of perhaps seeing him again. "Of course not," she said.

"Do you remember Trevor Geyer from freshman year?" Meg asked, putting her elbows on the table and resting her chin in her hands.

"Sure I do. He was my first crush," Autumn remembered. "But I don't see what that has to do with anything. Wait…you've heard that he's having trouble with his wife, and you think I should get together with him? That's crazy!"

"Don't be silly," Meg retorted. "I wouldn't touch that man if you paid me, and neither should you. He's bald, and has a beer belly. Anyway, I knew you were interested in him before you told me, remember?"

Autumn nodded and Meg continued.

"And do you know how I knew?" she asked.

Autumn shook her head.

"You got this funny little smile that wasn't really a smile but kind of a dreamy curve to your lips whenever you talked about him!" Meg said triumphantly. "And whenever you talk about Ethan Rasmussen you have that exact same look!"

"That's quite a poetic observation for a math and science gal," Autumn observed.

Meg shrugged and raised her eyebrows. "I try," she said simply. "Don't try to change the subject."

But Autumn had closed her lips into a hard, straight line, making Meg laugh. "See, you're trying *not* to have that look! You like him, you love him," Meg said in a singsongy voice. "You want some more of him!"

"I consider Ethan Rasmussen off limits," Autumn said emphatically. "When I saw him six weeks ago at the funeral he was with his girlfriend, or maybe it was his wife, though I didn't see a ring on either of them."

"I knew it!" Meg exclaimed, slightly banging her hands on the table for emphasis.

Autumn recalled the sleek, elegant woman who had stood stoically beside Ethan at the funeral. Her slim black linen suit, somehow unwrinkled despite the drive from New York City, hugged her slim curves. Her hair had been tied back in a loose bun at the nape of her neck. She even wore a little hat that on anyone else would have seemed absurdly out of place in Finch's Crossing.

"Aha!" Meg continued her teasing. "The fact that you were considering him at all and checking ring fingers is an indication that you are interested, *and at a funeral...*" Meg threw her head back triumphantly. "I bet having Heather in his life will break them up. From what you've told me about Ellen she doesn't seem like the kind of woman who would raise another man's child, much less a child that wasn't even his."

"Meg, that's an awful thing to say. We don't even know what kind of person Ellen is."

"I know, but I call 'em like I see them. You know that."

"But you *didn't* see her."

"You did. And I can go by what you told me."

Autumn *did* know that Meg "called 'em like she saw them," and it sometimes irked her—like right at that moment. But she couldn't deny that Meg's blunt honesty and strong opinions sometimes revealed a different, and often more accurate, perspective on people and events, which Autumn had come to appreciate.

After they had paid their checks and gathered their coats to go, Autumn suggested they walk to the high school for the computer class and pick up Meg's truck afterward.

"I don't want to go a stupid class," Meg whined. "I'm already a computer whiz. In fact, Steve Jobs has me on speed dial!"

"Meg, you are awful," Autumn scolded her friend. "Steve Jobs was an American genius who died a few years ago, much too young, I might add."

"Oh, yeah, sorry. You know I forget those things. Well, it'll just be a time suck. Besides, I'm not a merchant," Meg whined.

"Are too."

"Am not."

"Oh, for the love of Pete. I know for a fact that you pay annual dues to the Chamber of Commerce *and* that you are a thousand-dollar sponsor of the Merchants Association, so don't pretend like you don't give a flip about downtown because I know that you do."

"Just so you know, before you start thinking I'm some secret millionaire, my parents pay that sponsorship," Meg said. "Besides, I've got a pregnant shepherd, and I expect her to give birth any second now so I need to get back to the kennel."

With that, she got into her truck and headed home, leaving Autumn to enjoy a ten-minute walk to the high school alone.

Mid-September still held a lingering feel of summer in the Laurel Highlands, but soon temperatures would drop. Autumn walked down the Greystone Manor's driveway and headed down Chestnut Street and up toward the high school on Arthur Avenue. She knew Meg was lying about the pregnant dog. If it were really true, she wouldn't have gone out to dinner, especially if a dog was that close to having her puppies. But she forgave Meg. For whatever reason Meg had for not wanting to go, Autumn had her own. She didn't really need to go to this class herself. In fact, she didn't even want to go, but it was certainly better than going home to the empty canvases and unused paint tubes that ridiculed her from their perches.

* * *

Kyle was thrilled to see a packed room when he entered the computer lab. He surveyed the gaggle of merchants, and it struck him immediately that they appeared to be in their late fifties and older. Mayor Peggy hadn't been exaggerating during his interview when she lamented the greying of the town's population, and warned him that only a few of the merchants used computers in their shops. He knew he had his work cut out for him when Teppy Eicher, the Christmas Shop woman, searched the back of the computer for the power button, even though it was obvious the machine was already on.

As everyone settled in, Stan Brilhart held up a mouse and asked, "What's this thing for?" Kyle really hoped he was joking. Meanwhile, he noticed the tiny, blue-haired Miss Elsie slip a mouse pad onto her lap like a napkin. She exclaimed, "I bet I could sell these as potholders in my shop!"

Kyle knew she was not joking, and instantly regretted the promise he had made to the mayor earlier that day.

As everyone settled in, Kyle was relieved to see Mayor Peggy come through the door. She shook his hand, then turned to face the group and gave her best mayoral smile. She wanted them to think that she had everything under control and was doing all she could to revere the downward spiraling economic condition of Finch's Crossing.

"Welcome everyone! So glad you could make it tonight. I know how busy you all are." *Not busy enough,* she was thinking. "I gather you have all met my friend Kyle Oswald, who will teach a series of classes during the next few weeks in preparation for Black Friday." She flashed Kyle a quick smile. "Kyle is here to help all of us in downtown Finch's Crossing." She paused for a couple of seconds for effect. "Kyle is going to bring us into the twenty-first century, which apparently started a few years back." This brought chuckles.

CHAPTER 5

"He is not going to make us computer experts. That's not his job. He's going to show us how to market our businesses using the most up-to-date methods, which happen to involve computers as well as smart phones, tablets, and all the other gadgets just about everyone has these days. So remember, we need what he has to offer. The old-school way is not working. It never will work again. So I encourage you, listen to what Kyle has to say. Be open-minded. Give his ideas a try."

With that, she walked right down the middle aisle and took a desk in the back row. She hoped everybody interpreted her staying as showing her commitment to the downtown merchants.

"Okay, everyone," Kyle began, hoping his voice did not betray the trepidation he felt. "This is a mouse," he said, pointing to Stan's outstretched hand as he attempted the "What's this thing for?" joke again, apparently for the benefit of the latecomers who missed his early show. Stan held up the mouse on display as if he were Vanna White. Kyle simply continued. "You use it to navigate around the computer."

He began his slow wade through the parts of a computer and how to use them, explaining social media marketing, and touching on websites and search engine optimization. Of course, with the limited time he had, he could only hit the high spots. Before he realized it, it was after nine, and he could tell everyone had had enough for one night, and was ready to leave.

"Same time tomorrow night, everyone?" he called after them as they crowded out the door, talking about him as if they thought he couldn't hear them.

"Nice young man," Stan was saying to no one in particular. "But I still don't understand how all this socializing is going to help business."

"Do you think he's single?" Melissa Overholt asked Lila Geyer. "My niece's husband just left her, and I think she would like him even if he does have a big nose."

He heard Miss Elsie's high, shrill voice down the hall.

"That SEO he keeps talking about. I didn't understand a word he said about that. Sounds like a pyramid scheme to me, all that searching and optimizing for other people."

A beautiful woman with auburn hair and striking blue eyes came up to him and gave him an encouraging smile before she followed the group out the door. She could tell he was a little shell shocked. "It'll get better—you'll see. I'll see you tomorrow night."

As he circuited the room switching off all the computers, Kyle said a silent, grateful prayer. It all felt so unreal, and he could hardly bring himself to believe that he was actually here, with a steady job and roof over his head and a steady paycheck. Well, steady at least for a little while. All his hard work, sacrifice, and planning had paid off. He had landed on his feet despite the odds. He locked the room with the key that the mayor had given him, and it was heavy in his hand as he cringed at the memory of the fake references on his resume. When Mayor Peggy had called them, she had actually spoken to a high school buddy who was an amateur actor. Kyle had used a disposable cell phone and a call-forwarding function that allowed him to use three different phone numbers and asked his friend to play the part of three fictional employers. It had worked like a charm.

I wonder what Mayor Peggy would do if she knew the truth about me, he thought to himself, hoping that it would never come to that.

CHAPTER 6

*A*UTUMN SAT, as she sometimes did, at the easel in her studio, staring at a blank canvas.

"Oh, I'm so glad you're here," she yelled, as she heard Meg slam the side door. "I'm in the studio. Come on in."

She heard Meg take long strides across the house. Like the dogs in her care, she was fast and purposeful, and was there in an instant.

"What's the matter?" she asked, looking around the room. "Where's the fire?"

Autumn had resumed her staring match with the canvas. "What do you mean?"

"What do you mean, what do I mean?" Meg plopped down on the toile-covered chaise in the corner. "Why are you so glad to see me?"

"Oh, that." Autumn swung her stool around to face her friend. "I need a distraction. Please observe," she motioned at the blank canvas. "It's winning," she said breezily, and smiled. "And it's been winning for a while. I really need to sell a painting." She hadn't meant to say anything to Meg, but it felt good to say just a little, like inhaling just a little bit of air to relieve yourself after you've been holding your breath for, well, a year.

"Don't be ridiculous," Meg said. "You'll bounce back. Besides, don't you still have two agents selling your work? An East Coast and a West Coast agent?"

"Well," Autumn started, but Meg wasn't finished. "From what I understand you are one of those rare contemporary artists who have the luxury of working full time as artists. As in, no day-job required. When you sell a painting, you hit pay dirt. Am I right?"

"Well," Autumn said again as Meg plunged on. "So, just get on the phone and get those agents to sell a painting. Problem solved."

Autumn smiled lovingly at her friend. In Meg's world, when you wanted something to happen or someone to see things your way, you picked up the phone, yelled and screamed, and threatened physical harm, public embarrassment, or both, and the desired outcome was usually achieved within minutes. This tough-talking, no-nonsense business style was a result, Autumn assumed, from working with law enforcement clients who didn't mince words and used phrases that weren't meant for public ears.

"I'll pose for you," Meg said suddenly. "You can draw my pretty face, and they'll put it in the Art League art show next year alongside the hummingbirds and close-up photographs of spiderwebs."

Autumn hesitated, and before she knew it, an automatic response had kicked in and she was holding a sketchbook and charcoal pencil. Meg's suggestion had been so innocent and offered out of love that Autumn felt no pressure to perform. No need to find an emotion to express. She simply had to do what she had done a thousand times before: look at her best friend. Autumn folded herself into the easy chair across from Meg and began to sketch.

"Stop moving," she commanded. "You have the worst habit of flipping your bangs out of your eyes."

"Well, can I at least talk?"

"As long as you don't move your lips."

"Funny. You know the rumors are still flying about the pumpkin stunt you pulled on Ethan Rasmussen at Jack's nursery."

Autumn ignored the statement. "Has anyone ever told you your eyebrows are crooked?"

Meg's hands went flying to her forehead.

"Don't move," Autumn groaned.

"Well, you can't tell someone their eyebrows are crooked and expect them not to react. Now stop stalling," Meg pressed. "Jack was talking to the Sunset Boys seniors' gang about it yesterday at Hoffman's Drugstore, and by the time I paid my check the story was that you were throwing those miniature pumpkins at the guy's Jaguar and took out one of his headlights."

"So?" Autumn asked. "What's the big deal? If I don't care, why should you?"

Autumn changed positions so she could study Meg in profile, and was struck again by just how pretty she was, her fine features and cheekbones a contrast to the physical strength required by her work.

"So when is he taking Heather back to New York?" Meg asked, all of a sudden very serious.

Autumn shrugged. "Not sure exactly, though Martha did mention that he would be gone for a few days getting everything ready."

"Does anyone know anything about him?" Meg asked. "I mean, here's this guy, out of the blue, who's given custody of a little girl who obviously belongs with her grandmother. He could be a perv for Pete's sake."

"Meg!" Autumn yelled. "You can't say things like that about people. That's how rumors get started and lives get ruined."

"Whoa, don't go all Oprah on me."

Autumn ignored the remark. "Besides, do you think Adam Frick would let her go with anyone he hadn't checked out thoroughly? And from what I understand, before he read the wills to Ethan and Martha he consulted some colleagues in Pittsburgh and at Harvard University about contesting it." Autumn paused. "It will be strange not to see her with her parents. Without Troy and Denise. They visited a lot, you know."

Denise Everson had attended school with Meg and Autumn. The three hadn't been friends exactly, but as next-door neighbors, Denise and Autumn were friendly enough. They ran in different circles. Truthfully, Denise actually *had* a circle, as opposed to Autumn and Meg, who just had a pair. She married Troy right out of high school and moved away.

"Do you want to be the subject of idle gossip the rest of your adult life?" Meg asked, steering Autumn back to the original subject of the Sunset Boys' highly embellished version of the Great Pumpkin Patch Encounter.

"Oh, Meg, they're just harmless old men who have been retired so long they don't know what to do with themselves. It doesn't matter. Now put your head back the way it was."

"I think we're the only two people under the age of fifty in this town, excluding the kids, of course," Autumn said, changing the subject. "Have you ever thought of moving away?" She kept her eye on the sketch pad. "Somewhere where they don't roll up the sidewalks after six in the evening and the local bar stays open past nine?" She couldn't believe she was thinking these thoughts, much less saying them aloud.

"What do we need to stay out that late for?" Meg asked defensively. "I'm always up early because I have to feed and exercise the dogs, and you are always telling me how much you like to be up with the sun because that's when the light is best for painting. Are you telling me that you would leave your family home and move to a city just so you can be at a bar at midnight?"

Meg had moved her entire body now and was leaning toward Autumn, concern on her face.

"No, of course not. I guess it's not the nightlife I miss. Do you get lonely, Meg?"

Meg didn't speak for a long moment. "Well, when the work's finished and I'm done for the night, it sure would be nice to have someone rub my feet and help me pick the ticks off," she joked.

"That's not very romantic," Autumn chided.

"That's the farming life for you," Meg laughed.

"You aren't a farmer," Autumn corrected.

"Am, sort of."

"You are *not* a farmer. I give up! I have some interlibrary loan books that just came in. Walk to town with me?" Autumn was glad to change the subject. She wasn't sure if she was ready to slip out her façade just yet. Not even with her best friend.

"Not the library!" Meg complained, unfolding herself from the chaise and stuffing her arms into her discarded jean jacket. "The last time you made me go in there old Mrs. Ward forced me into getting a library card."

"Good grief, Meg. It was library card registration month," Autumn said, putting on her own jacket and following Meg through the house. "You were doing a public service, not enduring an act of torture."

The two walked through the quiet neighborhood. Meg's family had bred and trained German shepherds to be police dogs in Finch's Crossing for more than fifty years, working with police departments from all over the country. Meg would rather be hauled out of her home on a gurney, to be transferred straight into a hearse, before leaving Finch's Crossing. She wasn't going anywhere. She wondered where Autumn's new hint of wanderlust was coming from. And it made her consider, for a change, her own loneliness.

Arriving on Pittsburgh Street, they stopped short in front of the old music store. Boarded up and empty for several years, the door was now open, and there was some kind of chanting music coming from inside. Peeking in the windows they saw a woman arranging music stands in a circle on a small stage in a far corner of the store. Bookshelves lined one wall, and against another wall, a long wooden counter buttressed by bar stools gleamed with a fresh shine. There were painting easels in the middle of the room, put here and there between zebra-striped chairs and what looked like bongo drums.

"What do you think it is?" Meg asked, as if she were observing an alien creature. "It looks to me like a thrift shop threw up in there."

Autumn shook her head. "Looks like a concert hall-bookstore-art gallery something or other."

They hadn't heard the woman come out of the shop and turned at the sound of her voice. She was wearing a black pencil skirt, a black-and-white-striped knit top, and a beret. Her ink-black hair was styled in a severe blunt bob with bangs cut straight across her forehead. Her lips were painted fire-engine red.

"This," she said icily, "is Finch's Crossing's first ever atelier."

"Atele-what?" Meg asked.

"It means studio or workshop," Autumn explained.

"You're partially right, Autumn," the woman said condescendingly, with an emphasis on Autumn's name. "But I prefer the more general definition. What I've created here is an organic space where people can gather for poetry readings and impromptu concerts, walk through fine art, and enjoy a cup of real coffee as it was intended to be prepared, ground from dark-roast beans harvested from the hillside fields of South American countries."

"Hello, Natalie," Autumn responded, recognition gradually emerging from her memory banks. "I didn't know you had moved back."

She felt Meg stiffen next to her.

"Just a few weeks ago. I moved back from Pittsburgh and decided I would share my gift with my fellow citizens of Finch's Crossing."

"Well," Autumn said doubtfully, but wanting to find something positive to say, she offered, "It certainly is a unique idea."

"Unique?" screeched Natalie. "It's absolutely brilliant. What better place to open an establishment of such refinement than in this cultural desert, this wasteland absolutely devoid of the finer things? There is no place to go but up."

"The arts and culture are thriving right here in Finch's Crossing," Autumn replied, defensively, for she was thinking of her own creative downturn.

"You can't count old Mrs. Story's display of crocheted doilies in the library," Natalie snapped. "And Miss Elsie's Tea Room doesn't count as culture. She doesn't serve anything but Lipton's. *Lipton's!* I went in there the other day looking for Earl Grey, and Elsie thought I was meeting someone *named* Earl Grey."

Autumn and Meg looked at each other.

"Well, Lipton *is* a tea," Autumn shot back.

"We have a Chinese restaurant now," Meg contributed, gesturing to the Number One Wok restaurant across the street.

Technically it was Chinese American. Laverne and Dallas Pritchard were Texans who had retired to Finch's Crossing a few years ago and opened an all-you-can-eat buffet because they loved Chinese food and the closest restaurant was thirty minutes away.

"I'm going to push out the Art League's and library's exhibit spaces and put Miss Elsie's Tea Room out of business in one swoop," Natalie boasted, gesturing grandly.

"That's kind of ambitious, not to mention harsh, don't you think?" Autumn asked.

"Wow," Meg said, wiping her clammy hands on her jeans.

Natalie continued, ignoring their comments. "What this town needs is some culture. Do you realize that our children are growing up without the influences of the classical composers in their lives, not to mention the great masters or Greek philosophers? I'm going to take us back to the classical age where we used our minds, not our thumbs, as enrichment to the tableaux of our lives."

Natalie barely paused for breath before continuing. "Can I expect *you* at my grand opening next month?" Natalie asked, turning her gaze to Autumn, making it clear that Meg was not included in the invitation. Without waiting for a reply, she bustled into the recesses of her new atelier. "Ciao," she shot over her shoulder.

CHAPTER 6

"I can't believe she's back. I thought she'd be gone for good," Meg groaned. "And she looks like a cross between Betty Boop and Pepé Le Pew in that getup. I didn't recognize her at first."

"Me neither, until she started speaking," Autumn observed, and they laughed.

Natalie had been one of those mean girls who made merciless fun of Autumn and Meg because they were late bloomers in high school, and neither one of them had had dates to either the junior or senior prom. But she hadn't been one of the kids who teased Autumn about the "seasoning sisters." No, her taunts were much more targeted and mean-spirited. She once told the girls' gym class that Meg was really a boy and they shouldn't change or shower in front of her.

"She was a piece of work. Always thought she was better than everyone else, spreading rumors about us," Meg said. "If I don't see her again for a thousand years that would be fine with me. What did we use to call her?" Meg was trying to remember. "Oh yeah, Miss Priss. Well it looks like Miss Priss has turned into Miss B..."

"Don't say it, Meg," Autumn commanded.

"Okay," Meg grumbled. "But you can't stop me from thinking it!"

Autumn had suggested they stop into Miss Elsie's for an afternoon snack after their unpleasant encounter with Natalie, but Meg had begged off, making an excuse about checking on the imaginary new puppies. And that's exactly what it had been—an excuse. Their discussion about being lonely, however brief, had unnerved Meg. And now, this run-in with Natalie Prescott was almost more than she could take. After what Natalie had done to her in high school, Meg couldn't stand the sight of her.

After retrieving her truck from Autumn's, she drove home, distracted and troubled by the thought that from now on she might have to see Natalie every time she went to town. Meg was impulsive, sometimes to the point of rudeness, saying what she thought without bothering to think how it might impact the person she was talking to. But seeing Natalie again had rendered her tongue-tied. Usually her comebacks were clever and interesting, instant and biting. But in mere minutes, Natalie had managed to take her back twenty years to the girls' locker room where she felt like an ugly duckling. But it hadn't just been high school. She and Natalie had gone to the same college, and Natalie had brought all her mean-spirited cruelty with her.

When Meg arrived at the kennel, she checked on her dogs, gave instructions to Sammy Dawson, her only employee, then went into her small office and sank into her chair. Although she hadn't admitted it to Autumn, she *was* lonely. Her parents had retired to Florida six months ago, much to her surprise and dismay. It had never occurred to her that her parents, now in their seventies, would want to slow down.

Yeah, she was lonely, with an ache that almost hurt when she thought about it, so she tried her best not to think about it. She looked out the window of her small office to her childhood home, beyond the oaks, dark in the shadows of twilight, not a single light burning. She hadn't set foot in that foreboding, quiet house in five months.

"You're ready," her parents had told her as they were packing up their new SUV, when she knew, in fact, that she was not ready. Oh, she could run the business. That wasn't the issue. She was just not ready for the quiet that would settle in once her parents retired to Florida. She was used to her father's tapping on the keyboard of his computer as he wrote articles for trade publications. News junkies, her parents had the television on almost constantly, and CNN was pretty much always buzzing in the background. She would miss her mother's comforting presence as she bustled and puttered in the kitchen.

The first few nights after they left, Meg had been unable to sleep and simply walked from room to room, turning on the lights then turning them off again. Sometimes she would visit the dogs, finding comfort in the rustling and snoring she heard as she let herself noiselessly into the kennels. When they sensed her presence, they woke up, stretched, and yawned, tails wagging, eager to play and please.

So, she had packed some necessities and clothes and moved into the efficiency apartment attached to Ten Oaks administrative office and once used by the part-time groomer. Her parents had kept it cozy, tidy, and fully stocked over the years, taking turns staying over when one of the dogs was having a particularly difficult pregnancy. Meg loved the secure, cabin feel of the whitewashed walls and the tiny living room with the braided rugs, blue-and-white-checked easy chair and ottoman, and a small dinette table for two. The apartment had everything she needed, including miniature appliances just large enough for one person. The shower stall was barely large enough to turn around in, but she didn't care. It did the trick. After a month, she had even gone so far as to buy a television and hook up the cable.

Sighing, she closed the computer and turned to her phone messages. It was after seven. No use answering any of them now. Startling her, Sammy came around the corner, a bag of dog food hoisted on his shoulder.

"You still here?" he asked.

"Yep," Meg answered, pretending to study the phone messages. "Had to fumigate the house again. Those cockroaches just moved right back in."

"I see."

"Yep."

"Okay, then, see you tomorrow," Sammy called as he stacked the dog food with the other bags outside the office and headed out for the night.

She knew he knew. But he wouldn't say anything. He needed this job. Newly married with two small children, Sammy was working two jobs to get through college.

She waited until she saw Sammy's Explorer disappear around the driveway bend. Then she entered the runs, turning on all the lights as she went. Stopping at the first kennel, she lifted the latch and scooped up one of the pups into her arms. Now ten weeks old, the little fellow had been excluded from the pile of yawning and sleeping litter mates, and Meg couldn't bear to watch him lying alone in a corner any longer. She never named the dogs. Like her parents, she used a numbering system. It helped her avoid growing attached to them. But tonight, the ache of loneliness was particularly strong so she scooped up the puppy.

"C'mon, buddy," she said, kissing the black and tan fuzz ball on the head. "You're with me now. You and me against the world. I think I'll call you Spike," she told the puppy as she settled him on the bed in the apartment and rubbed his belly.

CHAPTER 7

AUTUMN HADN'T EXPECTED to see Ethan again so quickly. She knew he had taken Heather to New York, so she was surprised to see his shiny Jaguar in Martha's driveway. She had baked cookies and was using them as an excuse to check up on her neighbor and friend, who she knew was hurting terribly.

She could hear the excited voices and laughter as she walked up the steps to Martha's open front door. One voice in particular: Heather's. Autumn chastised herself for feeling a little twinge of irritation along with immense relief. Why did it have to be Ethan who had coaxed Heather back to her once happy self? Why couldn't it have been Martha? It should have been Martha.

"Hello," she called as she let herself in and saw the trio sitting around the coffee table, with Heather chattering away like a little magpie.

Heather ran to Autumn when she saw her.

"Autumn!" she screamed, and hugged her knees. "I went to New York City where they have big apples, only I didn't see any of those."

Autumn squeezed her tight. "Yes, I know. It looks like you had a good time with Ethan."

She drew back and looked over at Ethan shyly and said, "Yes. He is not a bad man. He is an okay man."

Autumn let her eyes find his, smiling slyly. "Perhaps you're right, Heather. *Maybe* he's not a bad man after all," emphasizing the "maybe" just enough for Ethan to notice, but not Heather.

It had been Ethan's greatest breakthrough since all this began. They were standing in front of a rack of children's winter coats at Bloomingdale's. Heather seemed genuinely engaged and was going down the rack, touching the sleeves of various styles and colors. Ethan was surprised at himself. He was actually enjoying this.

He had been following her down the rack, and he stopped when she did. She held the sleeve of a $200 fuzzy swing coat.

"If that's the one you want I'll buy it for you," he said, probably too enthusiastically.

She turned toward Ethan and to his amazement whispered, almost apologetically, "I really don't like purple that much."

She had spoken! Ethan's mind raced. What was it he was supposed to do when she started talking again? The psychologist had been very clear. And very adamant. He should act as if she had been speaking all along. He was not to show any surprise, or in any way reveal how remarkable her words were.

"That's okay, sweetheart." He hoped she could not hear the trembling and excitement in his voice. "I am sure they have that coat in

CHAPTER 7

other colors. If they don't, I'll ask if they can order it for you."

Now Heather sat on the couch happily munching the cookies Autumn had brought and describing her new room in Ethan's penthouse (Ellen had painted it pink like cotton candy), the school she was going to attend (it had "big kids"), and the food she had eaten (Ellen had brought over "Soochee" one night).

"And Ellen took me to a big toy store, and then we bought new clothes. See?" She stood up and pointed to her sweater. "It's pink like my room. And then we went to the park and rode the horses that go round and round and then…"

Ethan finally cut her off. "How about you get ready for bed, and Nanna will come tuck you in after a little while, okay?"

She didn't look very happy with the suggestion, but didn't complain as she trudged up the stairs.

"You've made a lot of progress in a short period of time, Ethan," Martha said. "I have to admit that I doubted you, but I'm not afraid to admit when I'm wrong. I owe you an apology. But I still feel Heather would be better off here. With me."

Whoa, thought Autumn. He had his girlfriend bribe a five-year-old with toys, new clothes, and a spin on the merry-go-round for two days, and suddenly he's father of the year? What was Martha thinking? Sure, a change of scenery obviously had been good for Heather. But how long would that last?

Ethan brushed it off. "I know you're not comfortable with me taking Heather, Martha, but I promise you that she will have the kind of life that you will be proud of. And you are welcome to visit us anytime in New York, and of course I will bring her here to visit as my schedule permits. And I'm not totally alone, you know. I hired a nanny, and Ellen has been a real godsend. I don't know what I would have done without her. She's really stepped up to the plate, and as you can see, Heather adores her. She's in good hands. I promise you."

"I appreciate that, Ethan. I really do. It's going to take getting used to. It was hard enough to lose Denise and Troy, and now to lose Heather…" She broke into a sob and excused herself.

Ethan shook his head in frustration, hating the pain he was causing. He gripped his hands together and rested his chin on them, his elbows on his knees.

Autumn knew it wasn't her place to interfere, but felt she had to intervene at least once on behalf of her friend.

"Won't you reconsider?" she asked gently while Martha was still composing herself in another room.

Ethan was dressed more causally in khakis and a cashmere sweater. She could see the confusion and hesitation in his dark eyes. She almost got lost in them as she listened to his answer.

"I don't expect you to understand, Autumn, but I am duty-bound to carry out my friend's wishes. Do you think Troy and Denise would have chosen me for Heather's guardian if I were anything less than an honorable man?"

"But can't you see what this is doing to Martha?"

"She'll be okay," he said without looking at her. "You heard what she said—she just has to get used to the idea. It's an adjustment for all of us."

"But are you sure you are doing what's right for Heather?" she asked. "Sure, she had a great time in New York for the weekend, but that was all candy and rainbows. What are you going to do when she cries in the middle of the night because she misses her mommy and daddy, or grandma, or worse, when she gets sick?"

"Ellen will help me when she can, though she has her own interior design business to run. And Inga will be there. She came highly recommended from one of the top agencies in the city," he said quietly, and winced at the unspoken judgment he felt emanating from her. He didn't know why, but suddenly, what Autumn Hamilton thought of him mattered.

"I appreciate you bringing her back for a quick visit so soon," Martha told him as she came back into the room. "I'll have her ready first thing in the morning," she promised.

Ethan put on his jacket, ready to head out to the Greystone Manor for the night. Autumn followed him, feeling the chill since she hadn't bothered to get her coat. They stood facing each other on the front steps.

"I don't need another lecture," he said firmly.

"Is that why you think I came out here?" she asked, and he nodded yes.

"Well, it's not." She rubbed her hands along her arms. "I wanted to tell you that you can feel free to call me anytime if you need any help or just want to bounce some ideas off of me. Martha has my number and email address."

"Okay, thanks," he said, turning to leave.

"And one more thing," she said, her heart pounding a bit. "I wanted to say, too, that even though I don't agree with what you're doing, I admire you. This isn't going to be easy for you. Heather's going to turn your life upside down, but you're going ahead with custody. I know you think that I'm angry at you," and he interrupted her.

"Don't tell me what I think or feel," he snapped, and then immediately apologized. Why had he done that?

"Please, just let me finish," Autumn said. "I do believe that you are an honorable man, Ethan. I just don't know if you're up to the challenge."

A surge of adrenaline shot through his chest at the sound of his name coming from her lips.

"That feels like a backhanded compliment, or maybe a dare," he responded. "I'll see you soon, Autumn," he said warmly, and boldly touched her arm. "It's all going to be all right. You'll see. I got this."

After Ethan had gone back to the hotel, Martha poured them each a glass of wine, and they settled in Martha's comfortable living room with its oversize sectional couch arranged in a U-shaped configuration overlooking the fireplace, giving the room a snug, cozy feeling.

"Autumn, you know I had my doubts about all of this. Still do. But what am I supposed to do? I have no legal recourse. If I put up too much of a stink, he can just take her away forever. I think I need to give him a chance. Look at the progress Heather made in just one weekend. Kids are resilient. You've seen that just now. Yes, emotionally it hurts like the devil. But it will get easier. I pray every night that it will. It's not like I'm never going to see her again."

* * *

"You need a website," Autumn told Meg as they sat in the small booth in Hoffman's Drugstore as September was itching to crawl into October.

"No, I don't."

"Yes, you do."

"No, I DON'T. Just let me eat in peace already."

"Just trust me on this one." Autumn jerked her head to the right to indicate Kyle Oswald sitting at the lunch counter. His white shirt stretched across his back, and Meg could see that he was trim and fit. She wondered what his biceps looked like. He turned his head, and she almost swooned when she saw his profile.

"Wow, who's he?" Meg asked, craning her neck hoping to get a better look, not caring that he was watching her watching him.

"The new consultant Peggy Brightwell hired to help the merchants. You would have met him if you had come to the class with me. But... oh yeah, you had puppies ready to birth."

Meg stared into her coffee cup, and despite her mightiest effort, she couldn't completely stifle the smile that insisted on presenting itself.

"Ha, told you! You think he's hot!" Autumn threw her napkin at her, simultaneously calling over to Kyle and inviting him to join them. He turned, and smiling gratefully, made his way toward them.

"Send him back," Meg suddenly hissed, as soon as she saw Kyle's baby face.

"No," Autumn hissed back. "Why?"

"Look at him. He's twelve. Fourteen tops."

Autumn just stared at her blankly.

"Hrumph," Meg huffed. "If you're not going to call him off, then I'm leaving." She started to gather her things and reached for her check, and that's when Autumn grabbed her wrist.

"You're not going anywhere. That would be incredibly rude. Besides, he's not twelve, he's twenty-nine."

"Yeah, and I'm Miss America. Let go."

"Miss Elsie gave me the scoop, so you know it's true. He's..." Autumn cut herself off as Kyle approached the table.

"Hi, there," she said, switching her tone. "Won't you join us?" She gestured to the seat next to Meg. "This is my friend, Meg Overly."

"Well," he grinned, "seeing as how you are the only people under the age of fifty I've met since I've been here, don't mind if I do."

He slid in next to Meg, who managed to give him a half smile.

"Hello and good-bye," she announced. "I have that meeting."

"Oh," Autumn shot back, "I forgot to tell you. That meeting was cancelled. You're free for the rest of afternoon." She turned to Kyle. "So, how are things going?"

Kyle looked at Autumn. "Forgive me. I remember you from class the other night, but I don't think I caught your name."

"It's Autumn." She braced herself for the obligatory comments about such an unusual name, but none came.

Instead, all she got was, "Very nice to meet you, Autumn." It was almost weird to meet a young person this polite.

The bell at the front door jingled as a group of young women entered.

"Look!" said Meg gleefully. "More young people! Maybe you can talk to them." She readied to leave again, but Kyle did not budge to let her out.

"You seem awfully anxious to leave for someone who has no-where to go," he said with a lazy, confident smile. "It occurs to me that perhaps this is something I should take personally." Then turning to Autumn, he said, "To answer your question, progress is slow, and resistance is high. But we're getting there. Last night I signed everyone up for Facebook pages, and they all friended each other. Miss Elsie found her grandkids and sent them friend requests. Tonight we're going to handle photos and posts."

Meg snorted, and Kyle turned toward her. "Do you have a Facebook page?" he asked her.

"Don't need one," she responded.

CHAPTER 7

"She doesn't even have a website," Autumn offered. "I've been trying to persuade her for years to get one, but she won't budge."

Meg took a bite of sandwich and said, with her mouth full, "Don't need one."

"What makes you think that?" Kyle asked.

Meg swallowed and took a gulp of soda. "Three words," she said, holding up a fist and counting off the numbers in time with her consecutively protruding fingers. "Word of mouth."

"I don't get it," Kyle said.

"My family has been breeding German shepherds for law enforcement for decades. We don't need to advertise. The business just appears."

"A website's not just advertising," Kyle explained. "Think of it as a resource for your customers or potential customers. You could post photos of your dogs, videos of the training, pertinent articles. It's not just about getting more business. It can be just about your *web presence.*" He emphasized the phrase "web presence," as if it held the secrets of the ages.

Meg studied Kyle's face. He his oddly arranged features were striking, and his intense expression somehow made him seem incredibly virile. Half listening to him as he sang the virtues of websites, she contemplated what he might look like if he were five years older. She tried not to notice his brilliant green eyes that had the power to swallow women whole.

She took a sip of her soda just as she heard a tinkly voice behind her.

"Are you ready, Kyle?" she heard Natalie ask, appearing at their booth and putting a hand on his shoulder. "I pulled out a lot of great photos for you to use on my website." Natalie's voice was like a fingernail on a chalkboard and gave Meg the accompanying shiver.

"I was just getting ready to head over," Kyle said, looking at his watch, then standing and readying himself to leave as Natalie walked away. "It was nice meeting you both," he said, and then looked directly at Meg.

"If you want I could start your website, and you could look it over, no charge. If you like what you see, we'll go on from there."

"Don't need to," Meg grumbled, stuffing the last bite of sandwich into her mouth and avoiding those startling eyes.

"And why's that?"

"I already know I don't like it."

"I see," Kyle said, amused. "Well, maybe I'll try anyway. You might like what you see. Tell you what, I'll draft a few mock-ups and bring them by for you to take a look at." He grinned and left them.

"Now look what you've done," Meg accused Autumn. "Bring them by where? I hope he doesn't think he's coming out to the kennel."

"What? What did I do? Help you make a new friend? Yep, you're right, that's just terrible of me."

"Ha, ha. I don't need any new friends."

Meg watched as Kyle opened the front door for Natalie, ushering her out with his hand on the small of her back. Once on the sidewalk Natalie tilted her head in her annoying coquettish way and said something, making Kyle burst into laughter.

"Well you certainly won't get any, acting like you do. I don't see why you had to be so rude to him."

"I wasn't rude."

"Well, you certainly weren't friendly," Autumn shot back.

"I was neutral," Meg suggested.

"If that's neutral then you're worse off than I thought. Besides, I don't think it's going to matter with Kyle."

"And why's that?" Meg asked.

"Because apparently, your crusty personality doesn't faze him. I think he likes you."

"Does not."

"Does too. As he was leaving with Natalie he looked back over his shoulder. Men only look back if they're interested."

Meg snorted loudly and slid out of the booth, rolling her eyes at Autumn's unwavering and cheery optimism.

"Nice," said Autumn. "Very ladylike. I know you like him—I could tell by how long you stared at his biceps. You don't look at anything for more than a few seconds if it doesn't interest you."

"Well, what if I did?" Meg shot back. "He's too young for me so it doesn't matter. End of story."

CHAPTER 8

*T*HE EVENING OF Natalie's Atelier opening, Autumn picked up Martha, and they rode together out to Ten Oaks to get Meg. The house was dark, and Meg wasn't waiting outside the kennel so Autumn went into the office, where she found her in her usual jeans, work shirt, and dirty work boots. Her hair was sticking up, and it appeared as if there was hay in it.

"C'mon, you'd better get dressed. We're late."

"What do you mean, 'get dressed'?" Meg demanded. "I AM dressed." She gave a wicked smile and gestured at her jeans. "I will have you know these are my GOOD jeans, and I pulled them out just for Miss Priss."

"And the shirt?" Autumn prompted.

"It's just a regular shirt I pulled out of the dirty clothes hamper."

"Oh geez," Autumn said. "This ought to be good."

CHAPTER 8

Natalie gave Meg a long, hard, and very dirty stare as they entered the surprisingly packed studio ten minutes later.

"So glad you could fit my *petit* opening into your schedule, Meg," Natalie said nastily. "You see that my other guests have enough respect for me to dress accordingly. I know how busy you are with those *grands chiens* of yours. It is a shame that you did not have time to change clothes after work to attend my *grande affaire*."

"Oh, but I did," Meg replied. "Oodles of time." And she sauntered off. She was surprised by the crowd of people in attendance, but then again, Natalie's atelier was a novelty so of course people would attend out of curiosity. And for the free food.

Weaving in and out of the sea of people, she walked around the periphery of the room pretending to be absorbed in the artwork Natalie had hung on the walls. It was a natural thing to do, and no one would suspect that she was actually looking for something in particular. Natalie had plenty of kooky art, but Meg was relieved that she had no photography. Not for the time being, at least. She eyed the curtain at the back of the room, contemplating for a split second whether or not to slip past and rummage around whatever weirdness Natalie was storing in the back. And she might have done just so, but Martha appeared next to her, flustered and fanning herself with her hand.

"Can you believe how many people are here?" Martha asked, as she looked around the room.

Martha had gone her own way as soon as she had arrived with Autumn and Meg. She made the rounds of the room, stopping to exchange a few words now and then with a friend or acquaintance, all the while looking for Jack Staub, on the one-in-a-million chance he had decided to accept Autumn's invitation for him to meet them there. She doubted he would. Jack was more comfortable in the garden than anywhere else. She just wished he could be comfortable in *her* garden. How many loads of mulch, gravel, and fertilizer did she have to order before he got the hint?

She found an empty place against the far wall where she could lean and scan the crowd. She was getting tired of finding places to put all the stuff she had bought from Jack. The last time he delivered the mulch she had ordered, but didn't need, she had called Reverend Frye and told him if he could find someone to haul the mulch away, the church could have it for the flowerbeds in the churchyard. Gracious, she had never had so much mulch in her life. When would Jack realize that she was ordering truckloads of stuff she didn't need, just to see him? Wasn't it obvious when he delivered the latest load of mulch and gravel that the most recent load had suspiciously disappeared without being used in her yard? How could he not wonder what she had done with it?

Then she saw Meg and, grateful to see a friendly face, made her way across the room in time to crane her neck and follow Meg's frowning gaze to where she saw Natalie deep in conversation with an oddly handsome young man in dark jeans and a white shirt with the cuffs unbuttoned.

"Who's that with Natalie?" she asked.

Meg brought her glance back to Martha's face.

"No one," she said, a little too dismissively.

When Autumn had stepped into the crowded room following Meg and Martha, she immediately accepted a glass of champagne from a barefoot, roving waiter dressed in all black and wearing a long ranger-style mask with a purple-sequined porkpie style head apparatus of some sort perched precariously on his head. It matched

Natalie's purple, sequined beret and black lipstick.

Scanning the gathering, Autumn spotted Duncan Olack and edged through the crowd to join him. He was standing awkwardly by the music stands, where several tall musical instruments were resting on their stands. She gave him a peck on the cheek in greeting and then clinked her champagne glass to his and took a sip.

"This is quite an event," she mused. "I doubt Finch's Crossing has seen anything like this in, well…ever." She turned around to the music stands and pointed to a collection of what looked like wooden horns or pipes. "What are those things?"

Duncan followed her eyes. "Those, my dear girl, are the strangest looking musical instruments I have ever seen, and I believe they are called didgeridoos."

Autumn was genuinely impressed. Duncan continued, "I saw a gentleman playing one in the subway the last time I went to New York. They are considered by many to be the world's oldest instrument and are thought to have originated from the Aborigines of northern Australia."

Now Autumn was really impressed, and even Duncan was surprised he remembered all this. He thought to himself that an event like this was probably the only place in the whole world he would ever have a conversation about a didgeridoo.

He wrapped up his impromptu music lesson saying, "I predict that within the hour we are going to be subjected to a torturous concert that everyone will pretend that they just *loved*."

* * *

Now that they were back in New York, Ethan was on his own.

AUTUMN

Yes, Inga the nanny was there to tend to Heather while he was at work, but when she was not there, it was all up to him. And he was terrified. Ellen had helped out with Heather for that first get-to-know-you weekend, and she had been terrific, like she always was with a new project. But Ethan could tell her heart wasn't in it, and by the time Heather had moved in permanently, she always had an excuse as to why she couldn't help with any Heather-related task.

Heather's enthusiasm for the city hadn't exactly grown the way he had hoped it would. She was still afraid of the traffic and the crowds on the sidewalk, and she gripped his hand for dear life whenever they were out together.

As for him, he was having trouble learning to share his space with a veritable mess machine. During his four years at West Point he had learned to be immaculate. "A place for everything and everything in its place" became his motto. After Heather moved in, and her boxes of belongings arrived from her parents' home, he realized that the "organized" time in his life was over. How one little girl could make such a mess he could not fathom. She left her toys everywhere and typically lost one of everything—one sock, one shoe, one arm to a Barbie, one barrette in a pair. And he spent much of his mornings chasing down these items that simply *had* to be found before she could leave for school.

And he was certain that she manufactured crumbs in her pockets and then sprinkled them around the house. It was exhausting trying to keep up with her, her little girl stuff and her little girl chatter about ponies and fairies and hair accessories. As much as he was growing to love her, he found himself watching the clock every morning as he waited for Inga's arrival.

His attempts at cooking were just as excruciating. In fact, they were pretty disastrous. Spatula in hand, dish towel over his shoulder, he attempted various hot, nutritious breakfasts. He felt like a fry cook in a greasy spoon. And by the time he left for work, grease spots dotted his tie, until he finally learned to cook in his T-shirt. Dinner was invariably takeout, though sometimes Inga would cook a meal or two for them.

"It's okay, Ethan," Heather said one morning as he was burning toast and crucifying two poached eggs. "Daddy couldn't cook either."

He froze over the stove top, spatula hanging above the pan. This was the first reference she had made to her parents, in his company, since coming with him to New York.

He tried to remember what the psychologist had said about that as he scraped the bits of eggs off of the pan. Was he supposed to encourage her conversation, or change the subject? Ask her if she missed them? That was stupid. Of course she missed them.

Darn it, the toast was burning. The spatula dropped toward the floor as he grabbed the dish towel to wave it under the smoke alarm, and he watched in dismay as gooey bits of egg yolk splattered over his loafers when the spatula finally hit the floor.

"What did Daddy try to cook, sweetheart?" he asked, turning to place the burnt breakfast in front of her.

"Cereal," she replied, deadpan, and she slipped off the stool, went to the pantry, and grabbed a miniature box of Honey Rings.

"I'll get the milk," he said, defeated.

He'd have to ask Inga to come in earlier and help him with breakfast. At the rate he was going, they would both starve, or learn to live on cereal and takeout.

His work had taken a beating, and it became immediately apparent that he could not, in fact, "do it all." He had taken a temporary cut in pay, reduced his hours and opted to work at home rather than stay late at the office.

His assistant, Myra Tate, had been terrific during the transition, helping him to stay on top of his schedule, appeasing his clients, and liaising with the other partners, who quite frankly were getting tired of accommodating Ethan's new circumstances. She was a vigorous, efficient, no-nonsense woman in her sixties. Ellen had approved of her immediately because of her age and her plain Jane appearance. Ethan approved because she kept his life orderly and him sane. But as the pressures of raising Heather closed in on him, he found himself snapping at her for mistakes *he* had made. And he hated himself for it. He had quickly come to the point where he felt so out of control—uncharacteristically out of control. Ever faithful, Myra ignored his angry outbursts as if they were nothing.

During one particularly tense trial he had forgotten to ask Myra to scan and email some important documents to an important client.

"Myra, that's just unacceptable," he barked over the phone one evening when he was working on a case at home. "I want that done first thing in the morning, and I don't care if that means you have to go into the office at 5 a.m. Just do it."

When he finished, he glanced over at Heather, who briefly locked eyes with him before cutting her gaze away abruptly, as she used to do with him in the rearview mirror that first week they were together in Finch's Crossing.

She slid a pink crayon out of the box and colored in a flower on her drawing. "You shouldn't yell at Myra," she said, telling him what he knew as soon as he had hung up the phone. "It's not nice to yell. You have to call her back and tell her you're sorry, and then have a time-out."

And he did. After he apologized to Myra, he put Heather to bed and gave himself a time-out with a large whiskey and soda and, exhausted, fell asleep on the couch.

CHAPTER 9

KYLE RETURNED TO the Greystone Manor after the atelier opening, his mind preoccupied by two women— one whose advances he'd have to put a stop to and the other who wasn't about to respond to his advances. Natalie had hired him to do her website, but he wasn't giving her anything else, despite her repeated attempts and unsubtle hints about her intentions. He would need to make that perfectly clear very soon. But it was Meg who dominated his thoughts. He didn't get it. Why was Meg so dead set against him? He had tried to catch her eye that evening, but she had refused to look at him. And Natalie had trapped him in a corner telling him about some poetry slam she was planning, and by the time he untangled himself from her talons, Meg was no longer there. He laughed to himself ruefully. Never in his life had he thought he was the kind of person to find himself locked in a love triangle.

CHAPTER 9

For the next three weeks, Kyle threw himself into his work, spending long hours with each of the merchants, giving them one-on-one lessons about maximizing their social media presence and optimizing their websites. He showed them how to purchase online ads and respond to Twitter alerts, fully intending to make his time at Finch's Crossing worthwhile. His first test would be the pet parade on Halloween afternoon. He knew the merchants had been reluctant to put any effort into a one-day, minor holiday event, but he had convinced them. He was pleased that they were warming to him and his ideas.

On the day of the parade, Mayor Brightwell surveyed the crowd on Pittsburgh Street. It wasn't exactly the stampede of shoppers she had been hoping for, but it was a start. A strong start. It was Halloween afternoon, and the trick-or-treaters were out in their bright, and often strange, costumes, many tugging on leashes, anxious to line up and start marching.

The pet parade had been Meg's parents' idea, so she was forced to present the proposal at the Merchants Association meeting, where the reception was lukewarm. But when she pointed out that the canines and their children would be accompanied by parents who had money to spend along Pittsburg Street, they had agreed.

Peggy had asked Kyle to do the publicity, and he obviously knew what he was doing. As each day passed, Peggy was more and more convinced that she had made the right choice in hiring him.

Kyle scanned the shoppers on the streets, noticing a lot of people he didn't recognize. There was a steady stream of traffic in and out of the shops, and he was delighted to see people exiting with bags holding their purchases. He peeked through the windows at Miss Elsie's Tea Room and smiled at the full tables and waitresses scurrying about. His work was showing a return on investment, and he hoped that would please the mayor. He needed to win her over completely if his plan was going to work. After the holiday season, he would show the merchants the increased traffic on their websites and ask them to compare last year's sales to this year's. He still had a long way to go, though. He couldn't build ten websites overnight. Eleven, actually, he reminded himself as he spotted Meg trying to corral a group of children and dogs.

"You look like you need some help," he said, as he went over to offer a hand.

She looked up then away. "No, thanks, I got it under control. Hey there, you, kid in the purple wizard cape, park it and make that dog sit."

He watched, dumfounded, as the young wizard child did exactly what she said. Even the dog obeyed.

"You don't have such a good bedside manner," he suggested.

"Don't need one. This isn't a hospital." She looked away so she could roll her eyes without him noticing. "Kids respond to authority. You, Little Red Riding Hood or whatever you are, stop petting Little Mermaid's dog. It bites." The poor child snapped her hands back and buried them into her costume's pockets. "Cinderella! No prince will ever marry you if you don't get that beagle under control!"

Kyle chuckled, raising his camera and clicking off a few shots before Meg realized what he was doing.

"If you want to help, put the camera down and help me get these little hoodlums into a straight line. Dogs on the left. Leashes short and tight."

He obeyed, happy that she was at least acknowledging him.

"Parents!" she barked. "Stand to the side but close enough to step

CHAPTER 9

in if your dog goes wacko or decides to share his business with the rest of the world."

As the children and dogs merged into what was probably going to be the straightest line they could hope for, Meg paused where a German shepherd puppy sitting at attention on the sidewalk, seemingly in the care of Autumn. Meg looked at Autumn, gave her a half smile and a full wink, and then fixed her gaze on the pup. She gave a barely audible command, and the little cutie came over and sat next to her. Kyle raised his camera and began to shoot as Meg crouched down to pet and cuddle Mr. Impossibly Adorable, allowing him to lick her face and nuzzle her neck. She then scooped him up, and with the pup comfortably in her arms followed the kids down Pittsburgh Street, barking orders and pointing her fingers as she went. Kyle scrolled back through the pictures he had just taken, all of which had captured a Meg so different than the one she pretended to be that he felt a surge of emotion rise in him. Not self-conscious, but completely enraptured in the moment with her dog, with everyone else's dogs, and all the excited kids, Meg was radiant. The expression on her face was pure joy. She had no inkling of how beautiful she was.

Kyle followed the children and dogs as they marched—more in a clump than a line—down Pittsburgh Street. There was a lot of barking and tail wagging, but Kyle kept his eyes on Meg's cowboy hat, trying to catch up to her, not wanting to miss another opportunity to talk with her.

The parade ended at the post office, where the Mayor announced the winners for best costume and cutest dog and then handed out dog treats for everyone. Kyle caught up with Meg across the street in the IGA parking lot, where she was sitting on a low wall, her puppy by her side, watching the awards ceremony. Kyle sat down beside her.

"Hey," he said.

She looked at him with a disinterested glance. "Hey."

"I've been working on your website," he told her. "I think you're really going to like it."

"I told you I don't need one," she said ungratefully, but her ungraciousness did not deter Kyle. She was thinking about all the time she had wasted organizing the pet parade. Her parents may have turned the management over to her, but they were still full owners, and if they wanted Ten Oaks to sponsor, and organize, a pet parade then that is what she would do.

"I'm thinking you probably need about five pages to start with. Nothing fancy, just a basic site that we can expand later."

"I'm not paying you," she shot back without looking at him.

"I didn't ask you to. Anyway, back to the site. You could have a page about the pet parade, you know, to show your pro bono work. I've got some great pictures."

He had purposefully left a shot of her smiling with the puppy, her cowboy hat pulled low on her brow, on the viewfinder so it would be the first one she saw. He wanted her to see herself the way he saw her. He held out the camera, and she took it, rolling her eyes, and began to look. She scrolled slowly through the pictures of herself without saying a word. After the last one, she handed the camera back to Kyle, stood up, whistled for the dog, and spoke to him coldly.

"I didn't give you permission to take my picture. Don't you ever do it again." And she walked away.

Kyle ran to catch up with her.

"Meg," he said, surprised and confused. "Those are beautiful photos of you. You look so happy and natural. Don't you see?" He held out the camera to her again, but she kept walking, ignoring him. After a few blocks of silence, he stopped, but she kept going.

"All right then," he called to her disappearing back. "It was great to see you. I'll let you know when I get your website finished. Maybe we could get together and look at it over dinner?"

He had hoped for a wave. Heck, he'd even be happy with a nasty look, thrown over her shoulder. But there was nothing. Which only doubled his determination to get to know this beautiful, cranky, and stubborn woman.

Kyle walked slowly back to the Greystone Manor, despite the late October chill, and admired the rows of neat houses along the tree-lined streets. Lying in bed at night as a child and listening to his parents screaming at each other in their cruddy Cleveland apartment, he would imagine that he lived in a small town like Finch's Crossing, with neat and tidy neighborhoods, where people smiled and said hello on the street, and no one was yelling. He would squeeze his eyes tight, hunker down under the covers and imagine living in a place where he felt safe and loved. He realized that Finch's Crossing *was* the town of his childhood yearnings, and that despite his past, he felt safe in the community's kind embrace. Just six months earlier he had been closed off, flatly refusing to let anyone penetrate his exterior and get to know him. He couldn't risk anyone finding out the truth about him. But now he *wanted* to get to know people and have them know him.

Meg's behavior was not unlike his own just a few months ago, Kyle realized. He knew that he had unintentionally crossed some line with her by unearthing something that went way beyond her gruff personality. She was scared of something, or someone. And he knew it couldn't be him.

When he reached the Manor, he went to his room more determined than ever to find the real Meg—the one he captured in the photographs—and help her any way he could. A little bit of help and prodding from the right person, he knew from experience, could go a long way. And sometimes that help had to come from people who didn't know you very well.

* * *

In early November, Stan Brilhart was bustling around the storeroom of his hardware store, sorting loose hardware that had spilled out over the years, when the blaring bleat from his computer interrupted him. He looked over at the machine, as if it had just talked to him. Then it bleated again. He put down the box of picture hangers he had been sorting and, sitting down at his desk, he wiggled his mouse to wake up his computer.

The keyword alert that Kyle had set up was blinking on his screen, and a tweet had pulled up beside it. Someone called "Rover10."

"Locked out of my Rover, Finch's Crossing area Walmart. Need a locksmith. Can u help?"

Stan sprang into action, leaping from his chair and rushing into the shop.

"I have a tweet," he yelled to no one in particular. "I have a tweet!"

As he made his way to the front register, he knocked down a display of key rings and mini flashlights.

"Where's my kit? Someone's locked out of their car at Walmart. I've got to go."

He had all the nervous energy and excitement of a first-time father who had just been told that his wife had gone into labor.

Johnny Newill, who kept inventory and stocked the showroom a few days a week, came rushing after him with his locksmith case containing all the tools he would need.

"Did you tweet back?" he asked, out of breath.

"What?" Stan asked.

"You know, did you answer and tell the guy you were on your way?"

"No, I didn't think of that. Do you think I should?"

He was already on his way back to his computer. Just like Kyle had shown him, he prepared a message to send back to Rover10.

"Finch's Crossing locksmith to the rescue. Be there in 10. Stan Brilhart."

Johnny was looking over his shoulder. "How many characters is that?"

"Geez, I have no idea."

"I think you should add your cell phone number, too," he mused. "Looks more professional."

"Oh, for crying out loud, son," he said, as he typed in the numbers and hit enter, then dashed out of the shop, almost running over Miss Elsie in the process.

"What's with him?" she asked Maureen at the front register.

"He got a tweet."

"Really? He got a tweet?"

Miss Elsie walked out the door, trying to catch up with Stan without paying for her light bulbs.

"Wait," she called after him. "I want to come, too."

Stan was halfway down the street. "Well, hurry up, woman," he commanded and waited until she caught up to him and helped her into his van.

AUTUMN

As he pulled away from the curb Miss Elsie rolled down the window and hollered out, "Someone tell Kyle Stan got a tweet!"

* * *

"Autumn, I'm desperate," Natalie was saying on the other end of the line. "I need your help. Please. Can you come over?"

Within the hour, Autumn was sitting in Natalie's atelier, perched uncomfortably on one of Natalie's prized zebra-print, straight-back chairs. She knew what was coming. Since the opening Natalie's only customers were a few tourists from out of town, and word on the street was they weren't buying the strange mix of art Natalie had elected to exhibit. Despite the nice write-up in the *News-Observer*, attendance at her poetry readings and classical music concerts had been dismal, attracting only the senior citizens on fixed incomes who came for the free food. If it weren't for the music lessons she gave to schoolchildren, Natalie would be in financial ruin.

Natalie was practically wringing her hands as she paced up and down the room.

"I've sunk every penny I have into this place," she wailed. "I'm even living upstairs in the tiny apartment to save expenses."

"But I thought you inherited your parents' house?" Autumn asked.

Natalie nodded and wiped her nose with a tissue. "I did, but I've rented it out to cover the rent on this place." She gestured frantically around her. "My life's dream has become the albatross around my neck. I don't think I can stand it a minute longer!"

"Don't you think you're being a little dramatic?" Autumn asked.

"Not at all. I'm about to lose this place. I have enough for two months' rent and utilities, and then I'm out. Flat on my back. Ruined. A disgrace. I'll have to slink back to Pittsburgh and ask for my old job back at the Tell Gallery. I hated that place. It stifled me to no end…it suffocated my creative spirit, it …."

"Natalie! Stop it!" Autumn found herself yelling.

Natalie looked at Autumn as if she had just shot her.

"Just drop the act, this phony, overdone, woe-is-me act," Autumn continued. "And while you're at it, bring yourself down a notch or two." Autumn couldn't believe she was talking to anyone like this, but it seemed to be working. Natalie had sunk onto one of the couches and had stopped crying, so Autumn continued. "You have to stop lording yourself and your refinement over everyone in this town. You're pushing people away. Don't you see that? No one wants to eat food they can't pronounce and listen to poetry they don't understand and hear operas in a language they don't know. Why don't you figure out a way to involve the community in what you're trying to do? Hold poetry workshops and art classes. Show the work of local artists. Make this a real working studio, someplace where people can learn how to express their own creative side instead of trying to figure out someone else's. You need to explore all your options and do whatever you can to save your business. And whatever you do, stop calling this place an atelier. No one knows what it means."

Natalie glared at Autumn. "I invited you here to help me, not to be berate and insult me," she huffed. "Of all the people in this town, I thought you would be the one who would understand what I'm trying to do here."

"Look," Autumn said softly, wanting to say that she hadn't been invited as much as begged to come. "I didn't mean to insult you. I just was trying to show you that if you don't make some changes your business isn't going to survive."

"Well, isn't that rich coming from you, Autumn Hamilton," Natalie hissed. "Little Miss Perfect, Little Miss Everything Comes So Easily to You, with your big art career and your paintings that sell for tens of thousands of dollars each. Well for the rest of us, it's not that easy. Some of us actually have to work for a living."

The two women sat across from each other, and Autumn, stunned, waited for Natalie's apology. When it was obvious it wasn't coming, she stood up to leave.

"I'll help you any way I can, Natalie. When you're ready, just let me know."

After she had gone, Natalie fixed her makeup and railed in her mind against Autumn Hamilton. She was glad she had made her so miserable in high school. It was time to get that momentum back.

The next morning, she came across a piece in the *News of the Weird* online news magazine that struck her as a possible solution to her problem. What a genius the woman in Texas had been. Natalie could get a badly needed influx of cash to prevent her business from hemorrhaging into nothingness. And who would have to know? And she would be more successful than the Texas woman. She just knew it.

CHAPTER 10

*N*OVEMBER IN FINCH'S CROSSING blew in cold and damp, and the leaves that were left on the trees suddenly lost their once-brilliant luster. The weather outside reflected Kyle's dark inner churnings. The way Meg had turned on him at the Halloween pet parade had left him confused and more than a little hurt.

It was a few days after the parade, and he was holed up in his room at the Greystone Manor, working twelve-hour days in preparation for Black Friday, which just about everyone in retail considered the most important shopping day of the year. He was determined to prove his worth to the merchants, and especially to Mayor Peggy. If he made himself indispensable, perhaps there might be a future for him here. And maybe if he stayed around long enough he might figure out a way into Meg's heart. He was certainly going to give it his best effort.

Sitting at his desk, he wiggled the mouse to wake up the computer. The screen revealed a collection of large German shepherd stock photos he had purchased online, arranged under large text reading "Ten Oaks Kennel." Meg's website was going to be beautiful. He had chosen the site's colors to complement the dogs' black and brown coloring, and he had created a page with information about the history of law enforcement and military use of dogs in the field and in combat. With a little help from Meg's part-time employee, Sammy, whom he had run into at Hoffman's Drugstore, he had learned which police departments used Meg's dogs, and tracked down videos of those dogs in action. He had even spent hours in the *News-Observer* archives and at the Westmoreland County Historical Society researching Ten Oaks and writing a history of the company. The historic photos he had paid to have reproduced made for an incredibly rich portrait of the Overly family business. He couldn't wait to show it to Meg. After the disaster at the pet parade, Kyle was more determined than ever to win Meg over. He saw the website as a kind of peace offering. There were no pictures of her on it. At least not yet.

As he clicked along, placing the final photos, he thought about how Meg avoided getting close to people and showing how she really felt about things. His behavior really did mirror his own recent behavior. Not so long ago, he had *had* to avoid social situations. That was nearly impossible given that he was in school, attending classes, working full time, and studying in the library. Everywhere he went, not only were there people, but people he *knew*. When his circumstances first changed, he found himself immediately withdrawing from his friends and acquaintances. He could no longer afford to go out for dinner after class or to the movies on the weekends. But it wasn't just that. He was ashamed. He knew he would have been devastated if people had learned the truth about him. He believed that he didn't have a choice, and so to safeguard his secret and keep his pride, he avoided his friends and social situations as much as possible. He couldn't help but wonder what Meg was hiding.

As thoughts of his recent past spiraled one on top of another, he felt a panic rising in him. What would happen if people learned the truth about him? And what if Duncan asked him to leave the Greystone Manor? Where would he go? Back to his van? He might find himself homeless. Again. He felt sweat bead up on his forehead. His quickening pulse told him that if he didn't talk to someone about this soon, he was going to burst.

He grabbed his cell phone off the bed and dialed, grateful to hear his friend pick up on the second ring.

"Hey, Eric," he said, trying to keep the panic from his voice. "It's me, Kyle."

"Hey, buddy, long time no talk," Eric replied with genuine enthusiasm. "Glad I could help you get that job, man. Is it working out okay?"

"Yeah, it's great," Kyle replied flatly.

"It doesn't sound so great," his friend observed. "What's going on?"

Eric was the only person in the world who knew the whole awful story, every detail that he wished he could wipe from his mind forever—details that instead haunted him and shook his confidence.

"I really like it here. It's just I don't know how long I can keep lying like this. I feel like I'm going to explode. Or even worse, someone's going to find out, and it'll all be ruined."

"Look, Kyle," Eric reassured him. "You're not really lying. Okay,

I'll admit, those reference checks, those were lies. But everything else isn't. Not telling them certain things does not equal lying. Have they asked any direct questions?"

"No."

"Everyone deserves a chance. In the end, you didn't do anything wrong. The charges were dropped, remember? I respect you so much for what you went through. All that you endured, man. I wish you would have told me sooner. I could have helped, you know."

"I was too embarrassed," Kyle said quietly. "But you ended up saving me anyway, and I will always be grateful."

"No sweat, man. We've been friends since kindergarten. There's just about nothing I wouldn't do for you."

"Ditto," Kyle replied, feeling calmer and lighter, as if the knot in his gut had untied itself.

"Hey, when are you coming back to see your parents? I need a new website. Things are kinda taking off for me. I'm thinking about moving to New York."

"Eric, that's fantastic!" Kyle was genuinely pleased for his friend, and the two talked about the catalog modeling Eric was doing and the bit parts on a new sitcom.

By the time they hung up, Kyle's panic was gone. He walked to the bureau on the other side of the room and looked at his reflection. He had no idea how he would ever repay Eric. His friend had rescued him when he was at his lowest point and too proud to ask anyone for help. If it hadn't been for Eric, he wouldn't be in Finch's Crossing. Developing a new website for Eric would be a start, but a mere drop in the bucket compared to what he owed him.

He would think of Eric's website later. First things first. He was almost finished with Meg's site, but he wanted it to be perfect before she saw it. He looked at his watch. He knew the kennel would be open for another few hours. He'd put the finishing touches on it and head over before she closed for the night. As he worked, he thought of the pictures he had taken of her and the way her faced had glowed when she cuddled her puppy. There was no doubt about it. He was falling for Meg Overly, whether she was ready or not.

* * *

Across-the-street neighbors for years, Peggy and Martha often shared a cup of coffee in the mornings before Peggy headed for City Hall. Martha looked forward to these mornings with happy anticipation because all that stretched ahead of her was a long, lonely day, just like the one before, and the one before that. It was funny—Heather had only lived with her for a few weeks, but she felt her absence as she were her own child.

Peggy had been so busy with her campaign to turn the town around that the visits had been fewer and farther between than she would have liked. But one morning in early November, Martha heard the familiar knock on the kitchen door and was delighted to see Peggy, coffee cup in hand, smiling back at her.

"Have time for a cup?" she asked.

"Well of course I do," Martha responded with feeling, and she ushered Peggy into the warm kitchen. The two friends sat at the table with steaming mugs of rich, dark coffee.

"Congratulations on the success of the Halloween parade!" Martha said warmly. "You had a great turnout, Autumn tells me, and a lot of people in and out of the shops."

"I'm so relieved," Peggy shared. "This is so important to me . . ."

she trailed off as she began to cry.

Martha reached across the table and took her friend's hand. "Peggy, it's all going to be okay," she said, comforting her friend. "Halloween was a great start, and Black Friday will be even better. I just know it."

Peggy composed herself and played with her coffee cup. "But it's not going to be okay," she sighed. "I have breast cancer."

"Oh, Peggy," said a stunned Martha. "Oh, I'm so sorry."

"It's stage two, so not as bad as it could be. The doctors are hopeful, but I'm so tired. This is going to be my last term, and before I leave office, I want to turn this town around and leave a legacy. Right now my legacy is empty storefronts, scared merchants, and a Fall Festival that has dwindled into nothingness. I can't bear the thought of leaving on that note."

"Peggy, you have served this town faithfully for twenty years," Martha reminded her kindly. "You have done so much—you must believe that. I can't even count how many things you've accomplished. You secured private funding for the mobile library, and you got that addition that was so badly needed to the elementary school with state funds. And you found a way to lower taxes without impacting fire and rescue services. In fact, if I recall, because you worked with the 911 center, they were able to streamline their system and improve service. And you found a way to update their aging technology."

Peggy sniffed. "Well, yes, you're right. But you know how it is. Everyone wants to know 'what have you done for me lately?' It's the most recent thing they remember."

"I know this legacy idea is bothering you, Peggy," Martha said, squeezing her friend's hand. "But you can't worry about this now.

You have to concentrate on getting well. Have you started any treatments?"

"No. I just found out. I'm going to have a double mastectomy after Christmas, and then they'll decide about chemo. And you're right, of course. If I'm going to beat this, I have to concentrate on my health."

"Peggy, please know I will help you any way I can—preparing meals, taking you to and from the hospital, picking up your children from school."

Peggy laughed. "You don't know what you're in for with those boys. They'll try your patience just like a toddler would." Then, turning serious, she said in a whisper, "Please don't tell anyone about this. I'm not ready for that. Not yet."

* * *

Sammy had the afternoon off, and so Meg decided, what the heck, and gave herself permission to close the kennel early and take a few hours off. She deserved a break, she told herself, after doing her good deed and annual civic duty at the pet parade. Thinking of the kids in their goofy costumes, she rolled her eyes and checked the latches on the runs and made sure all the dogs had fresh water. The things she did for this town, she told herself, shaking her head. When she was certain everything was secure she sat down at the computer and checked her email. She thought fleetingly of the photos Kyle had taken of her. They *had* been good, and she sort of regretted the way she had treated him. Sort of. He had just taken her by surprise, and she hated being caught off guard. And she hated having her picture taken when she wasn't looking. She realized that she wasn't angry with Kyle for taking her picture. He had just brought back memories that she would rather stay buried.

Maybe she would apologize to him the next time she saw him. Maybe. It would depend on how cozy he and Natalie were getting. She powered down the computer, locked the office, and with Spike at her heels retired to her cozy apartment for some serious Netflix and junk food time. The apartment's only flaw was its tendency to be hot and stuffy, so she usually left the door between it and the office open. She changed into a pair of shorts and a Briar Rose College T-shirt, grabbed a quart of Häagen-Dazs from her tiny freezer, and settled on the bed with Spike curled up beside her. An hour later, she was dancing around the tiny apartment to the strains of ABBA's "Dancing Queen," and she didn't see Kyle until he was yelling her name.

"What are you doing here?" she screamed at Kyle as he filled the doorway. Her heart was beating so fast she could hear a whooshing in her ears. "You scared me to death."

"I'm sorry," he stammered, taking in her long, muscular legs and lean body. "I didn't mean to. I knocked," he added lamely.

Meg was always so covered up in baggy clothing he was surprised to see her shapely figure.

Meg snapped her fingers in front of his face. "I'm up here, buddy," she yelled, and he jerked his eyes up to meet hers. "You haven't answered my question. What are you doing here? I don't remember inviting you."

"I came to show you your website." He held up his laptop as if to offer proof. "And I didn't think I needed an invitation to come to your place of business since it's open to the public. I didn't realize that I'd be coming into your home, too."

CHAPTER 10

"You weren't. You didn't. You won't be," Meg snapped.

"Do you always wear short shorts and play *Dancing with the Stars* while you're working?" he teased her. "And eat ice cream with your dog?" he added.

She turned and glared at Spike, who was still curled up on the bed with the empty ice cream container stuck on his front paw.

"Some watchdog you are," she scolded him, and Kyle took that moment to slip past her.

"Nice office," he said, teasing her. He sat down at the table with his laptop, pushing aside the salt and pepper shakers and a box of cereal.

He nodded his head out the window to the big, dark house beyond them. "What's going on there?"

"It's being fumigated," Meg lied.

"Look, there's no reason to be embarrassed about living in a barn. Are you having money trouble?"

"You have no idea what you're talking about," Meg replied icily.

"Don't worry, I won't tell anyone."

"There's nothing to tell," she responded, still furious.

"Okay, if that's how you want to play it. It's fine with me. Now, moving on." He opened his laptop. "I think you're really going to like what I've done."

Meg made no move toward him, but instead crossed her arms across her chest. He had never met such a stubborn human being in all his life. Nor had she.

"Tell you what. How about if I just email you the link, and you can look at it when you aren't so busy," he gestured around the room.

Meg didn't reply, so he emailed her the link via the general email address he had gotten from Sammy's business card. They both heard the "ding" announcing the incoming email message on Meg's cell phone.

Rising to leave, smiling brightly and staring into her eyes to hold her gaze, Kyle simply said, "It was a pleasure doing business with you, ma'am."

After Kyle had left she remembered her resolution, just a few hours before, to be nicer to him. So much for that. But he had taken her by surprise, and she hadn't counted on him materializing like an apparition. She sat on the bed and buried her face in her hands. He had seen her dancing like an idiot. He must think she *was* an idiot. She rose from the bed and shut and locked the door to the apartment. It wouldn't matter how stuffy it got, she would never be surprised like that again. Ever.

Even if she *did* like him, there was Natalie to consider. She still had those pictures and was just spiteful enough to use them if she became jealous of Kyle's advances toward her.

* * *

Ellen was obviously displeased. She had instructed Ethan to meet her in the lobby of the Agnew Building, from where they would take the elevator up to the 65th floor, and where they had a dinner reservation at the world-renowned St. Vincent's Restaurant. A reservation for two.

She gave Ethan a quick peck on the cheek and then glanced down at Heather, flashing a forced smile and slightly touching her on the top of her head, unsuccessfully feigning affection. When the elevator doors opened, the three of them entered, and they were the only passengers on the ride to the 65th floor.

CHAPTER 10

Ellen stepped close to Ethan, and with her lips pressed against his ear, she whispered, but loud enough for Heather to hear, "What? Babysitter cancelled at the last minute?"

Ethan was confused. "Babysitter?" he asked.

"Darling, we made this reservation over three months ago."

This time Ethan got the fake smile, although now it was tinged with annoyance. "Our reservation was only for two."

"I didn't think about that," Ethan stammered. "But certainly, they will make accommodations for us. I mean, we come here all the time." Heather, whose hand was in Ethan's, tightened her grip and stepped closer to him. "If they don't, we'll just go somewhere else."

"We can't just go somewhere else," Ellen almost hissed. "I heard one of my biggest clients is going to be here tonight. It is important for me to be seen here. To be seen here *tonight*."

Ethan was grateful when the elevator doors swooshed open, and they were greeted by the smiling face of Pierre, the maître d'. "Mr. Rasmussen! Ms. Bauer!" he exclaimed, as if their appearance at the restaurant was a complete surprise. "And who, might I ask, is this lovely angel accompanying you tonight?" Pierre sunk down on one knee, and before Heather could protest, he took up her hand and kissed it gingerly. She nudged in even closer to Ethan, but, glancing sideways at Pierre, she gave him the cutest smile he had seen in a long time.

"This is…"

"She's my…"

Ellen and Ethan had begun to speak at the same time, talking over each other's words. They paused, each politely giving the other the opportunity to speak, when to their astonishment, Heather stepped up and said to Pierre, pointing to Ethan, "He's my guard."

Ethan smiled proudly. "It's a long story. I'll fill you in some other time. We're famished. I think our reservation was for two. We made it so long ago."

"Not a problem at all, my friend. Follow me." Pierre cocked his elbow, and Ellen took his arm, and Ethan and Heather followed them to a table set for four right by the huge glass window looking out over the gleaming city.

Within seconds of being seated, Henry, their usual waiter, appeared, and as he deposited a beverage in front of each of his guests, he began, "Ms. Bauer, I took the liberty of choosing for you a glass of 2009 Pristine Springs Riesling from Washington State."

Henry and Ellen had an unspoken agreement where he would surprise her on each visit with a glass of wine of his choice.

"And for Mr. Rasmussen, the usual Royal Coast Single Malt and soda, and for this little darling, a Shirley Temple, made with the finest grenadine available: Chateau Mont Loudon Grenadine." He smiled down at Heather.

Ellen spent most of the meal preoccupied, glancing this way and that, searching for her big client, hoping desperately to be seen. She managed polite small talk with Ethan, and even took a friendlier tone with Heather.

Wine must be kicking in, Ethan thought.

As they finished up their dinners, Heather leaned over to Ethan and shyly asked, "Where is that music coming from?"

"You mean that piano playing?"

She nodded her head yes.

Ethan looked back over his shoulder toward the bar area. "They have a guy playing over at the bar." And then he had a thought. "Would you like to go watch him play for a minute?"

He glanced over at Ellen. "Okay?"

She approved, probably not wanting to have to explain Heather's presence should her big client happen by.

"You two go ahead. I have to make a quick call anyway. I'll catch up."

Ethan and Heather arose from their seats, and taking her hand, Ethan led Heather over to see the piano player. When they reached the bar, they stood and watched the pianist for a second, and then, trying not to just stand there and stare at the guy, they sat down in a small, leather, L-shaped booth in the corner of the bar, with Ethan's back against one wall and Heather's against the other so they were almost facing each other. Ethan couldn't recall a time when she had expressed any interest in music, especially piano music, but he was pleased. He leaned his head forward a little bit and peered into the dining room where he could see that Ellen was still seated at their table. She caught his eye and smiled and waved then turned her attention back to the conversation she was having on her cell phone.

Heather seemed mesmerized as the pianist played on. Ethan loved seeing the look of wonder on her face, and he leaned his head back against the wall in satisfaction. But his head bumped up against something, and he turned to see that it was a painting. The colors caught his eye, so much so that he stood and faced the wall. Wow. It was a haunting floral piece rendered with off-whites and reflective greys, and it was simply exquisite.

His first thought was that Ellen would certainly appreciate this piece, being an interior decorator and all, so he must discover the painting's creator to impress her, to show her that his artistic side was alive and well. He closely examined the work for a signature, and in the lower right-hand corner he found that this masterpiece was in fact signed. He could barely make out an "A" and maybe an "H." Apparently, this artist didn't really care if anyone knew who he was. Ethan narrowed his focus on the signature, and, to his surprise, unmistakably deciphered "Autumn Hamilton." Could this be the Autumn Hamilton he knew? Who else could it be?

Ethan's heart did a back flip and then raced for several seconds until a few deep breaths brought it under control. How could it be that she had a painting hanging in the bar of one of the most famous restaurants in New York? And then Autumn's beautiful face formed in his mind. She was so gorgeous. But not just gorgeous. He saw her kindness. Her humanity. Her strength. He saw her *standing* beside him, with Heather between them, clinging to each of their hands, smiling from ear to ear.

"We can go now, darling." Ellen had in fact caught up with them. "Looks like my client is going to be a no-show. Anyway, thanks for dinner." She gave Ethan his second peck on the cheek of the night. "My town car is out front. Hope you don't mind if I head home alone since we are going in opposite directions."

Ethan didn't mind. Not at all. He had Heather. And he had the exquisite image of Autumn Hamilton, and her painting, to keep him company on the ride home.

CHAPTER 11

"Where are we going?" Martha asked, as she climbed into Autumn's Jeep.

"You'll see."

The older woman shot a sideways glance as Autumn started the engine and headed out.

"I'm not sure I like the sound of that."

It didn't take her long before she realized where they were going.

"I don't need anything from the nursery," Martha said coolly. It was obvious from Jack's absence at the gallery opening that he wanted nothing to do with her.

"Oh, that's okay," Autumn responded matter-of-factly. "I just want to pick up a few things."

"Liar," Martha said. "You just think if you parade me in front of Jack Staub enough times that he'll break down and ask me out for an egg cream at the soda fountain at Hoffman's Drugstore."

"What's an egg cream?" Autumn asked.

"Oh, never mind," Martha fussed, extracting a lipstick and compact from her purse to freshen her makeup. "How do I look?"

"Like a woman on a mission. And Martha, you have to be on a mission. Jack is far too shy to make the first move."

"I don't have the faintest idea what you're talking about," Martha said, turning her face to the window so Autumn couldn't see her smile.

"Don't be discouraged that he didn't meet us at Natalie's opening. It wasn't his thing. Can you imagine him standing next to that barefoot waiter in the purple hat and face mask, and listening to that horn music that sounded like cows mooing?"

Laughing at the image, they pulled into the nursery driveway and parked next to the fresh-cut Christmas trees Jack was beginning to arrange.

"So, what do you need today?" Martha asked.

"Nothing," Autumn answered. "I lied to get you to come with me."

"Told you. Liar, liar, liar."

Autumn nudged Martha. "Go inside and pretend you need to buy something."

"Like what?"

"It doesn't matter. Just walk in and pick up the first thing that catches your eye and go to the register to pay for it."

"Oh, for goodness sake," Martha whispered. "I suppose this is the only way to get you to stop badgering me. But you have to stay here. I can't have an audience. I'm nervous enough as it is."

She squared her shoulders and made her way to the shop door, which was propped open with a brick. Oh, gracious, she thought, hoping Jack hadn't heard her exchange with Autumn.

Martha had known Jack all her life. They had gone to school together from kindergarten through senior year in high school, but they ran in different crowds. She really didn't get to know him until she realized years later he owned the nursery.

She walked past bags of bird feed and fertilizer on her right and a bin of small hand-tools on her left on sale for fifty percent off. She paused and scooped up as many as she could carry, not even looking at them, and took them to the register where Jack stood, eyes on his ledger. He looked up when she cleared her throat.

"Hello, Martha," he said quietly. "You sure you meant to pick up all flat heads?" He picked up one of the screwdrivers she had put on the counter.

She looked down, horrified to see that she had picked up six identical screwdrivers.

"Well, you know, they are so easy to lose or misplace," she laughed nervously. "You can never have enough screwdrivers. That's what I say."

He rang up her purchases and put them in a paper bag, which he slid across the counter to her.

"Thank you, Jack." She paused. "How have you been?"

"Awright," he responded, pretending to wipe something off the counter.

"Well, that's good, that's good. And business? How's business?"

"Awright," he said again, this time glancing up for a brief moment before he ducked his head again.

His handsome face was leathered from years of being in the sun. His snow-white hair was impressively thick for a man his age. She couldn't help but notice how nicely he trimmed his eyebrows. So many men his age just let them grow wild.

"Okay, then," Martha said, deciding to end her humiliation, and his torture, but then he glanced up again.

"You been getting along awright, Martha?"

"Oh, ah, yes," she sputtered, surprised by his question. "Thank you. Thank you very much."

They stared at each other for a few seconds, and then Jack returned to his ledger.

"Well then," Martha said. "Good-bye." She turned and practically ran out of the store to where Autumn was waiting by the Jeep.

"Let's go," Martha ordered. "Now."

"Did you speak to him?" Autumn asked as they climbed into the Jeep.

"I guess you could call it that," Martha replied, burying her head in her hands. "I made a total fool of myself. I did what you said and picked up the first thing I saw, but I wasn't really looking, and I ended up buying six identical screwdrivers. Who does that?"

"Well, you could have been getting them for gifts," Autumn offered.

She glanced at Martha, who hadn't responded. "What's the matter?"

Martha turned to look at Autumn. "Oh, my goodness. This *can't* be happening. I left them there. I paid for them, and he put them in a bag, and I walked out without them. What must he think of an old fool like me?"

"I'm sure he doesn't think anything of the sort about you," Autumn tried to reassure her friend. "People do that sort of thing all the time. I sometimes go in with my dirty dry cleaning and pay for the clean clothes but forget to take them and have to come back for them."

"Well I'm not going back inside now. In fact, I'm never going back to Town and Country Nursery as long as I live. You'll have to get my wreaths and poinsettias this year, Autumn. And I'll start getting my mulch from Story's in Mt. Pleasant." She sighed heavily and worried, her hands in her lap. "And now you have me all flustered, and I have so much to do before Ethan and Heather come this evening for the weekend."

Surprised by the news, Autumn tried to sound nonchalant, saying, "Oh, Martha, that's wonderful. I know how much you miss Heather."

"I want to spend as much time as I can with Heather, but I'm not sure what I'm going to do with Ethan. As far as I'm concerned, she's mine all weekend."

"Oh, he's staying, then? Not going back to New York?" Autumn inquired, suppressing a smile.

"Well, that's what he said," Martha answered.

Autumn decided to do a little fishing. "Well I'm sure he and Ellen will find something to keep them occupied while they're in town."

"Oh, but she's not coming," Martha responded. "Something about having to work. A big client who needed her this weekend."

"A big client who needed her this weekend," Autumn echoed. "Huh."

"I have an idea. Come for dinner tomorrow night, Autumn. Heather would love to see you, and you would help break the ice. I feel so uncomfortable around Ethan, and I don't want Heather to sense anything's wrong between us."

Autumn turned the invitation over in her mind. On the one

hand, she still hadn't forgiven Ethan for what he'd done to Martha. On the other hand, if Martha needed her, she ought to go, and it would be great to see Heather. And, if she was being honest with herself, Ethan intrigued her.

"Are you all right, dear?" Martha asked, staring at Autumn quizzically. "You look a little flushed. I hope you aren't coming down with a fever." She crossed her arms over her chest. "See, I told you we shouldn't have come out. I've made an idiot of myself, and you've gotten a cold. Hmpf."

"I'm not sick," Autumn said. "It's just hot in the Jeep." And she turned the heat way down as if to prove her point. "And I'd love to come to dinner."

* * *

On Friday nights, Meg and Autumn usually enjoyed dinner at the Greystone Manor and then drove to Mt. Pleasant for a movie. Autumn knew she'd catch some flack for cancelling their long-standing "girls' night" and braced herself as she dialed Meg's number Friday morning.

"Yhello," Meg said. "Ten Oaks Kennel."

"Oh, I'm glad I caught you, Meg," Autumn said cheerfully. "I hate to do this, but I have to cancel for tonight."

There was a pause at the end of the line, and then a chuckle. "Ah, it's happening already," Meg laughed.

"What's happening already?" Autumn demanded. "Stop talking in riddles."

"Okay, then. Does this have anything to do with the fact that Ethan Rasmussen is arriving in Finch's Crossing this evening so

Heather can visit Martha?"

Autumn shook her head and marveled at the way news traveled around town, like it had legs of its own.

"Well of course it doesn't," Autumn said, exasperated. "Martha's still uncomfortable around Ethan, and she asked me to come, sort of as a buffer. You know."

"Oh, I know all right," Meg teased.

"Meg, for the last time, Ethan has a girlfriend!" And she clicked off the call, hanging up on Meg for what was not the first time.

That evening, she stood in front of her closet, eyeing her options. She had several nice outfits that she would wear on dressy occasions. She had her working clothes and her casual clothes. But nothing that was in between casual and dressy. Of course, it really didn't matter what she wore. It's not like she was trying to impress Ethan Rasmussen.

"Who am I kidding?" she said aloud. "Of course I'm trying to impress him."

By quarter to six the time forced her to choose something or be late. She settled on a pair of black wool slacks and a light blue merino wool sweater that brought out the color in her eyes. Maybe Meg's prediction that Ethan and Ellen would break up would come true, she thought, then immediately chastised herself. She knew better than to listen to Meg's wild accusations. In fact, Autumn typically dismissed almost fifty percent of things Meg said in any given conversation.

She arrived at Martha's front door precisely at six, a store-bought pound cake in her hands. She had cheated on the cake, but she had made the chocolate buttercream icing herself. Heather answered the door, all smiles and exuberance, and she hugged Autumn so hard around her knees that she almost dropped the cake.

"Here, let me take that."

She looked up to see Ethan's outstretched hands. He was wearing tan khakis and a navy blue sweater over a white button-down with cuffs rolled up at the wrists. He looked as handsome, and as cool and relaxed as the last time she had seen him.

"Thanks," she said, smiling, and she bent down to hug Heather, who tugged her into the living room.

"Want to play Barbies?" she asked.

"Well of course I do," Autumn responded, with a quick glance at Ethan.

"Be careful," he said. "These Barbie sessions tend to go on and on." And he disappeared into the kitchen with the cake.

Autumn sat on the floor next to the coffee table and picked up a doll.

"Are you having fun in New York, Heather?" Autumn's Barbie asked.

The little girl nodded. "We live in a pinhouse, and Ethan makes breakfast for me, but he doesn't know how. And at school I get to paint."

She walked a Barbie over toward Autumn. "Now you have to say something nice to me because I am the most important Barbie in the world," she demanded.

"Why, you are the most beautiful Barbie I have ever seen," Autumn exclaimed, bobbing her doll up and down.

They played until Ethan came out to get them for dinner.

"Wash your hands before we eat, okay?" he said to Heather, and looked at Autumn. "You don't have to wash your hands if you don't want to."

She laughed, surprised that he had a light, playful side and a sense of humor. Perhaps having Heather in his life had loosened him up.

Martha greeted her warmly as they entered the dining room and sat down at the table laid out with a feast that could have fed an army.

"Wow, Martha," Autumn said. "This is a lot of food for four people."

"Well, they're all Heather's favorite foods, you see. We've got fried chicken, macaroni and cheese, sliced baked apples, marshmallow salad with tangerines, deviled eggs…"

"And pizza!" Heather chimed in.

"No pizza tonight, dear," Martha said. "But I've got all your other favorites."

"We eat pizza all the time in New York," Heather informed them as Ethan made a plate for her. "We eat it Monday, Tuesday, Wednesday, and Saturday. You can go to a little restaurant, and they give you just one slice. Or they deliver it, like they do here. They call them pizza pies in New York, and you can watch them make the dough."

She took a spoonful of macaroni and shoveled it into her mouth.

There was an awkward silence as Martha and Autumn stared at Ethan.

"Well, we don't have pizza *that* much," he said.

"Uh, huh," Heather answered as she shoveled in baked apples like she was starving. "You said pizza is easy and as long as we have peppers and onions on it it's like having our vegetables."

Ethan groaned and put down his fork. "Okay, so I'm not doing so great on the cooking. But I'm so busy at work that when I come home I've got too much work to do to cook a lot." He looked at Heather. "Remember that time I made chicken and green beans? That was good, wasn't it?"

"Yes, but you got them from the grocery store, and the lady told you how to turn on the oven."

"I give up," Ethan laughed, breaking the awkwardness with his wide, boyish smile. "Martha, maybe you could give me some of your easier recipes, and I'll give them a try."

"Of course, Ethan. I'd be happy to. And I'll send you home with a big doggy bag on Sunday. It'll keep you for a few days."

After dinner, Martha took Heather to bed to read a story and tuck her in. Ethan and Autumn sat in the living room, each with a piece of cake, and each not knowing what to say to the other.

"So, how's Ellen doing?" Autumn asked, not expecting Ethan to choke on the bite of cake he'd just put into his mouth. "Are you okay?" she asked, watching his face turn red. He was nodding his head yes, and she quickly got him a glass of water from the kitchen, which he gulped greedily.

"She's doing great," he said hoarsely. "Heather really likes her. She took her shopping last weekend, actually. She loves to shop. Heather, I mean. Well, Ellen too…" his voice trailed off.

Autumn imagined the sleek Ellen bounding out of department stores holding multiple brightly colored bags in each hand, like a montage you might see in a movie. Somehow, she didn't quite see how Heather fit into all that.

"That's great. I bet Heather loves to go into all those little boutiques for kids. I just love little girl clothes."

There was an awkward silence, as Ethan realized that when Ellen took Heather shopping, it was more like Ellen took Heather *along* as she shopped for herself. He just smiled and nodded his head.

CHAPTER 11

"How are things really going, Ethan?" Autumn asked gently.

He looked up into her beautiful, open face, her voice full of genuine concern. He loved Ellen, but it seemed like every time he was with Autumn, he instantly and automatically compared the two women, as if it were a competition.

He put down his empty plate and fork. "Honestly, it's going better than I thought it would." He grinned. "Despite the pizza issue."

They shared a laugh.

"And how've you been, Autumn? Martha told me you're a phenomenal artist."

The personal question surprised her. Up until now they had only ever talked about him and Martha and Heather. And Ellen.

"Things are great," she said cheerfully, pulling on her façade. "Getting lots of work done, you know, in the studio."

"I'd love to see your work sometime," he said genuinely.

So would I, Autumn thought. Instead, she halfheartedly offered, "That'd be great. Maybe next time you visit. The studio's a mess right now and not really fit for visitors."

Ethan stared at her a long time. "Autumn, I'd like us to be friends."

"I thought we already were."

"Good," he said, leaning back on the couch. "We didn't get off to a very good start, and I'd like to know that there aren't any hard feelings between us."

Autumn smiled and shook her head. "Not on my part."

"Me neither," he answered, returning her smile.

Autumn was glad they had progressed from small talk, but as soon as they did Martha came down the stairs, and Ethan rose to go, heading back to the Greystone Manor where he had booked a room.

AUTUMN

I wonder if I'll see him again this weekend, Autumn thought as he walked down the steps. As he opened the door to his Jaguar, he looked over his shoulder and gave a small wave. The small gesture surged through her. She waved back, but he was already gone.

CHAPTER 12

THAN WASN'T TIRED when he got back to the Manor, so instead of heading to his room, he took a detour to the bar, where he ordered a light beer, relieved to be doing something distinctly grown-up in a place with no glitter or stickers or markers. Or Barbies. He laughed out loud at the thought.

The man next to him asked, "Care to share the joke? I could use something funny just about now." He stuck out his hand. "I'm Kyle Oswald."

Ethan shook his hand. "Ethan Rasmussen."

"Ah, you're Heather Christianson's new guardian," Kyle observed.

"How in the world did you know that?" Ethan asked, incredulous. "It's not like I'm wearing a sign."

"Everyone knows who you are. The story of you and Autumn

Hamilton in the pumpkin fight is legendary."

"It is?" Ethan couldn't believe it.

"Yep. The way it was told to me was that she broke the headlights and all the windows on your Mercedes by chucking those little decorative pumpkins at it."

Ethan let go with a full-out laugh until he was shaking and almost crying. It felt good to let loose. He wiped his eyes and looked at his companion.

"First of all, it's a Jaguar, not a Mercedes. And second of all, there was no smashing of windows or lights. Where did that come from?"

Kyle jerked his thumb over his shoulder. "Down at Hoffman's Drugstore and the lunch counter. If you want to know what's going on in Finch's Crossing, that's where you go."

"I see. Well, Autumn and I have resolved our...disagreement and agreed to be friends." He took a pull on his beer then asked casually, "So how well do you know her?"

Kyle shrugged. "Not well. I just moved here in September to help the downtown merchants with marketing. The mayor hired me. I see Autumn around town. Sometimes she comes to the evening computer classes I teach." He saw an opportunity and took it. "Do you know Autumn's friend, Meg Overly?"

Ethan shook his head. "Afraid not. Two Finch's Crossing women is about all that I can manage at once, I think."

"Two?"

"Yes, Autumn and Martha," Ethan explained. "Or I should say three, if you count Heather."

"Gotcha. Well, Meg's a handful," he said. "I see what you mean about the women in Finch's Crossing. They're just so..."

"Stubborn?" Ethan offered, not sure where the conversation was going or what adjective would satisfy his new drinking buddy. Kyle obviously approved of Ethan's assessment, and he slapped his hand on the bar.

"Exactly."

"So, what's the story with you and this Meg chick?"

"Nothing. No story. She won't give me the time of day. Heck, sometimes she's downright hostile to me for no reason. Other than that, she's great." He rolled his eyes comically.

They laughed. "You married?" Kyle asked conversationally.

"Nope," Ethan answered. "Long-term relationship though."

"I see. I thought maybe you and Autumn…" his voice trailed off.

"Nope," Ethan said. "We're just friends."

"She's gorgeous, though. And so nice and supportive," Kyle interjected.

Ethan nodded in agreement. He couldn't argue with that. Autumn Hamilton was gorgeous, and the more he got to know her, the more he liked her.

***

Sheriff Buddy Landry sat at the lunch counter at Hoffman's Drugstore, finding himself peppered with questions from the citizens he had sworn to serve and protect. They were rightly concerned, but he had no new information to give them and hated being reminded of that.

"So, no new leads?" Stan asked.

"No leads at all, much less new ones," Connie chimed in for him as she put meatloaf specials in front of the two men. "At least that's the word on the street. Another cup of coffee, Sheriff?"

Buddy nodded and held up his cup. "Well, you're right, Connie. We don't have any leads, but that doesn't mean we aren't doing our best to catch this guy."

"Give us your gut then," Jack Staub asked from a nearby table, obviously following the discussion at the counter.

"Well, Jack, it's hard to say. The burglar's striking in the middle of the day when folks are normally at work, so we don't have any witnesses. Plus, he seems to be finding homes where people are out of town, which leads me to believe either he lives in the vicinity or he has some way of finding out when people are going to be away. And since it's obvious he's being very careful to hide his tracks, I'm guessing that he's a pro."

"What's he taking?" Connie asked.

"Well, that's the strange thing. He's not taking the normal stuff that's easy to turn around quickly, like computers or televisions. He's snatching small stuff, whatcha-call-its, like little statues and trinkets, and sometimes expensive ones, mind you. And also jewelry, but he never takes it all. Just a piece or two here or there. Now that the story is getting out, folks are calling almost every day saying they thought they had just lost something, but now they are convinced it was stolen."

"Huh?" Stan asked.

"Small, artsy objects, pieces of silver, like salad tongs, but never a whole set. Key chains, paperweights, cuff links, letter openers—that kind of stuff. We've checked the pawn shops between here and Pittsburgh, but have found nothing."

"Do you think he'll come into Finch's Crossing?" Connie asked, putting a slice of pie in front of the sheriff. "He's been staying in Mt. Pleasant and Connesville, right?"

CHAPTER 12

The sheriff nodded, wishing that for just a few minutes he could enjoy his chocolate cream pie in peace and not have to worry about the robberies that were foremost in the minds of all the residents of Westmoreland County. He took another bite and swallowed before answering.

"Yep, he's slowly working his way around the county, making a circle around Finch's Crossing, like he's purposely avoiding it, and there's got to be a reason for that, though we've yet to figure it out."

As Sheriff Landry headed back to his squad car, his cell phone buzzed, and he answered it, knowing full well what the caller wanted.

"I'm on my way to see you now, Mayor, and I've got that information you asked for. See you in a minute."

He snapped his phone into its belt clip and crossed Pittsburgh Street, nodding his head at the elderly bailiff who stood at the door of the municipal building during office hours. He wasn't happy with what he was about to do. As a career law enforcement officer, he didn't believe in stereotyping people or necessarily using past mistakes as a predictor of future behavior. But things had come to a head with all of the robberies. And since he was no closer to finding the culprit, he acquiesced to the mayor's request. Technically, as the county sheriff, he answered to the county commissioners, and he could have refused the mayor. But that's not how he liked to play things. He was a straight shooter. He did things by the book, with kindness and respect propping it up like bookends.

Peggy ushered him into her office and gestured for him to sit in one of the armchairs beside her, and she got right to the point, focusing on the folder he had brought with him.

"Is that the information?" She took it from his outstretched arm and flipped through the thick file. "Bottom line it for me, Bud," she requested.

"Well, like you asked, I did background checks on everyone who moved to Finch's Crossing in the past few years. If my theory is correct—that the reason we haven't been hit is because the culprit lives in Finch's Crossing—then we have to find a way to narrow down our suspect pool. As far as new residents, it's not that many people: the Pritchards, those two families from Pittsburgh, a few others. I've ruled a lot of them out because of their work and commuting schedules. And then Kyle, who of course just moved here."

"What are you saying, Sheriff?" the mayor asked.

"I'm not saying anything."

Peggy flipped through the file and pulled out the papers pertaining to Kyle, not wanting to believe what she was reading.

"Good grief, Buddy, none of this came out when I did his reference checks. Everyone had really positive things to say about him and his work. According to them, he was the all-American boy next door." She shook her head. "What are you going to do about this?"

"Do?" he echoed. "There's nothing to do. We don't have any proof to link him to any of the robberies. And besides, you and I both know that just because he's been in trouble before doesn't mean he can't be a hard worker who has impressed folks with his work ethic and talent. I'd like you to remember that, Peggy."

"So, what now? Do we just ignore this information?" Peggy tried not to let the panic she felt show in her voice.

"The best I can offer is to keep an eye on him and see what happens. If he is the thief, and we're watching, we'll catch him sooner or later." He got up and headed toward the door. "And Peggy, we need to keep this conversation just between us for now. And whatever you do, don't let on that you know anything. If he's spooked, he could run, and we'll never get him. You did notice that I said *if* he is the thief? If we wrongly accuse him, we'll be bringing another world of hurt on this young man."

Peggy bit her tongue and didn't say what she was thinking—that it seemed to her he brought that first "world of hurt" on himself.

She nodded as Buddy left and then returned to her desk and sat for a long while looking out her window. She considered the events of the past month. She had wanted to bring the town out of its ongoing slump and attract tourists and new businesses alike. She wanted Finch's Crossing's comeback to be the swan song of her long tenure as mayor. And now she was running out of time. It seemed that instead of moving forward toward her goal, she had taken two very large steps backward, perhaps even endangering the people she was trying so desperately to help. After twenty years in office, she had let matters spin out of her control in a matter of weeks. She slumped forward, letting her head fall into her hands. She sat that way for a long minute, and as she straightened she gave a bitter chuckle as she gathered the wisps of hair that had fallen on her desk blotter. She was literally pulling her hair out.

* * *

As the days grew shorter and the long shadows began to fall earlier, Autumn could see more and more of Martha's house as it emerged from behind the shrinking canopy of falling leaves. Autumn did what she could to keep her friend's spirits up. One evening she packed a light dinner and threw together a colorful bouquet made up of some brave survivors from her cutting garden. They ate on the floor of Martha's living room, picnic style, in front of the fireplace.

"You're going to have to help me up, Autumn," Martha said after they'd eaten. "I'm seventy-two. I shouldn't have gotten on the floor. It's not the sitting down that's the problem, it's the getting up. Once I'm up, I'm fine."

"How are you really, Martha?" Autumn asked softly as the two friends settled on the couch.

There was a long pause. "I'm lonely," Martha admitted, and after another sad, deliberate pause, she said again, "I'm just plain lonely."

Martha reached out and covered Autumn's hands with her own. "Thank you, dear friend, for looking out for me. I hope you know how much it means to me."

"I think there's someone else out there who'd like to look out for you, too," Autumn teased.

"All right, now, let's have none of that this evening. Only time will tell what's going to happen on that front. It does no good to force together two people who don't come together naturally. If it doesn't unfold itself, then it wasn't meant to be."

"Well, it certainly won't help move things along if you continue to refuse to go to Jack's," Autumn pointed out.

"I don't want to talk about that," Martha remarked. "Speaking of not wanting to talk about things, how's your painting going?"

Autumn hesitated for that split second that is just long enough to give you away. "Fine, just fine," she lied.

"I just asked," Martha said, "because it's been a while since I've seen you in your painting coveralls. Used to be whenever I saw you in town or at the market you were wearing those tatty, paint splat-tered old things, just dashing out from your studio for a quick shopping trip." She kept her gaze on Autumn, who didn't have it in her to win a staring contest. "Never mind, honey," Martha said and patted her arm. "You'll tell me when you're ready."

After a game of Scrabble, Martha brought out Denise's baby albums, and looking through them, Autumn couldn't help but notice how tired and drawn her friend had looked holding Denise as a toddler.

"How old were you when Denise was born?" she asked, leafing thought the pages.

"Oh, I was ancient by medical standards. Forty-three." She pointed to a picture of Denise sitting on a Big Wheel, her parents on either side of her. "I remember when that picture was taken. That day I was exhausted. That Big Wheel was a hand-me-down from a neighbor boy, and Denise stayed on it for hours, with me trailing along behind her to make sure she didn't fall off or bash into anything. Having a two-year-old at forty-five is quite different than having a baby in your twenties. Denise was our love child…unexpected, but not unwelcome by any means."

"Hmmm," Autumn said, distracted. "Martha, do you think it's possible that when Troy and Denise made their wills they just assumed that if they died unexpectedly that because of your advancing age—sorry to be so blunt—you might not be in a position to take care of Heather? Or you might actually be gone by then?"

"Well," Martha replied thoughtfully. "I'd never given any of this much thought. But then of course you never expect to outlive your children. I suppose it is possible that was their thinking, and so they simply skipped over me and went right to Ethan."

"It makes a lot of sense," Autumn observed, her thoughts gaining momentum. "Is that something you want to run by Ethan?"

"What, to convince him to bring Heather back to me to live full time?"

Autumn nodded. "Or maybe a shared arrangement?"

"I don't know. Heather seems very happy where she is. You know she calls every night before she goes to bed, and we chat for a few minutes, and she tells me about her day and what she's doing in school. She's full of news. She loves school, and Ethan says her art therapy is working. She misses her parents terribly, but the nightmares have lessened. It's funny. Heather sounds great, full of life. He sounds exhausted—the way I felt when I had Denise. I feel for him. I know what he's going through. Maybe after a few weeks with a five-year-old he would be more likely to talk about a shared custody arrangement."

"Mmm," Autumn responded. "I'm going to be in New York next week to meet a gallery owner for a possible show," she lied, welcoming the opportunity for a distraction from her own troubles. "Would you mind if I popped in and shared my theory with him?"

"By all means," Martha agreed. "I want to do what's best for Heather, but I wouldn't object to shared custody. I don't want her to forget me. And, as you mentioned, I am at an advancing age, and I want to spend as much of the time I have left on this earth with my only grandchild."

After Autumn left, Martha considered Peggy's circumstances and her desire to leave a legacy in Finch's Crossing. *And isn't that what everyone wants?* Martha thought to herself. *To make a mark on this world and be remembered long after you're gone?*

As she locked up and went upstairs to bed, she reminded herself that no matter how bad her struggles seemed, there was always someone worse off.

CHAPTER 13

*S*IR, THERE'S SOMEONE here to see you." Myra's voice squawked through the intercom on Ethan's desk, startling him. "She doesn't have an appointment, but she says she's an old friend from Finch's Crossing."

He had specifically left instructions NOT to be interrupted while he finished preparing opening remarks for his upcoming trial. He was ready to snap at her, but then he remembered Heather's earlier admonishment. The only "old friend" he had from Finch's Crossing had been killed in a car wreck, and he was raising his daughter.

He pinched the bridge of his nose and depressed the intercom button. He was exhausted and irritable. Ellen had insisted they go clubbing the night before, despite his protests, and he didn't get to bed until after two, relieving a rather grumpy Inga. Somehow, Ellen's teasing that he was "no fun anymore" and turning into "an old fuddy-duddy-daddy" struck a chord in him. He had thought he could be a bachelor and a single parent at the same time. But he realized Ellen had only wanted to be with Bachelor Ethan. She had little to no interest in Single Parent Ethan.

"Who is it, Myra?" he asked, trying not to let his irritation show and remembering how small he had felt under Heather's rebuke the last time he snapped at Myra.

"Autumn Hamilton, sir."

His exhaustion vaporized instantly and was replaced by a surge of adrenaline. Autumn? Here? Just outside his office? Not back in Finch's Crossing plotting against him with Martha? He imagined her in the tight jeans and cowboy boots she had worn when they had first met, her long hair flowing, her bright blue eyes staring daggers at him. His eyes darted around the office frantically. His desk was a mess.

"Just a minute, Myra," he said, as he straightened some papers, swept a half-eaten bagel and a dirty napkin into a desk drawer, dropped his Starbucks mug into the trash, and slipped into his suit jacket. "Send her in."

Eagerly, he walked around to the front of his desk to greet her as she came in. Would they hug? He hoped so, and the thought of touching her sent an electric jolt to his brain. Yowza. Or should he offer his hand as if she were a client?

The door opened just a crack, and Autumn stuck her head in the door. "Hello, Daddy," she said, teasing him, and then strolled in looking as cool and elegant as Ellen or any of the lawyers in his firm.

An ice-blue pantsuit with a belted jacket hugged her slim frame, and the color matched her eyes perfectly. Her hair was in some kind of updo, the construction of which would be forever beyond his comprehension. She looked, quite simply, stunning. She was more beautiful than he had remembered. He tried to keep his mouth from hanging open.

"Nice to see you, Autumn," he said eagerly. "Please, sit down." He motioned to the seating area at the far end of the office, and they settled into club chairs opposite each other.

"What brings you this far east?" he asked playfully.

She immediately got back up from her seat and walked around his office.

"I had some appointments with a few gallery owners," she lied.

He knew she was lying because if she were telling the truth she would be looking at him, and she was not. She was here to check up on him.

Disappointed at her motive, but still glad for her visit, he watched as she stared at the diplomas on the wall and then moved to the bookshelves.

"I didn't know you and Troy served together," she said, surprise in her voice as she picked up a photo of them standing together outside their base near Kabul.

"Five years," he said matter-of-factly and rose to take the picture from her. "Why are you *really* here, Autumn?"

She sighed and returned to her seat. "Ethan, Martha misses Heather terribly," she began. "She's seventy-two-years-old. She's worried that she doesn't have all that much time left."

"That's crazy," Ethan balked. "The day before we left she ran three miles, baked an apple pie, and did two loads of laundry that she washed, folded, and put up before Heather and I had even gotten out of bed. She's not going anywhere anytime soon, least of all into her grave."

"Well, anyway," Autumn went on, undeterred. "Martha and I were looking at some family photos last week, and we have a theory about why Troy and Denise left Heather in your care."

"And you've come to share this theory with me?" Ethan leaned back in his chair, stretched out his legs, and observed the beauty in front of him. She was about to outline her case before him like a defense attorney. He would have to listen carefully. It was easy to get distracted around her, and he needed to be on his toes.

"So, no gallery meetings?" he asked.

She shook her head and had the decency to look sheepish. "Not exactly," she said. "What I mean is they aren't the reason I came up, but I will see them. You're the reason I came. I came to see you."

He was surprised at the tingling he felt in every nerve ending as she spoke those words. She was so open, laying her cards on the table. She couldn't even keep up her deception for five minutes. She was the opposite of Ellen, who always seemed to be scheming and manipulating people and circumstances to get what she wanted. And even though he knew Autumn was here to try and handle him, she was perfectly up front about it. With Ellen, you could never be quite sure.

Autumn explained about the photo album and Martha's advanced age when Denise was born. Ethan knew very little about Denise's life before she was with Troy, and he listened politely, having no intention of acquiescing. There was nothing Autumn Hamilton, or anyone, for that matter, could say that would make him change his mind about Heather. There would have to be some sort of disaster before he would break the promises between him and Troy.

What Autumn didn't know, and what he probably would never tell her, was that during their last tour in Afghanistan, on a particularly bad patrol one night in a village not far outside of their small operating base, Ethan and Troy had saved each other's lives in the span of five minutes. And it became an unspoken bond between them that no matter what happened, when one was in trouble, the other would be there. What one requested of the other would be done, without question or equivocation.

The sniper had fired out of nowhere, as they always did, from the rooftop of one of the ramshackle buildings lining the empty market square in the center of the village. The bullet nicked the night-vision mount on Troy's helmet. For a split second, he thought he had been hit. In the next split second, he realized he was trapped out in the open. Troy glanced around frantically, trying to figure out where the shot came from, not knowing which way to run. He was basically a sitting duck. Denise had been pregnant at the time. Ethan, who from his angle could see the sniper, didn't think twice before he rushed out into the open, stood in front of Troy, sighted his rifle, and with a single well-placed shot, took out the sniper. But they must have fired at the exact same time. The sniper fell over dead, but the last shot he fired sent a round through Ethan's upper chest. Another inch or two and it would have hit his heart. But it was a clean shot, through and through, and he was able to stand and run across the open market with Troy to take cover in a dirty alcove and radio for help.

Ethan hadn't seen the second sniper and didn't see him emerge from the shadows until it was too late and the knife was poised to slit his throat. Sometimes the voice still woke him up at night. "It will be my honor to kill an American infidel," the man sneered into his ear. And then, suddenly, he fell away, just barely dragging the knife across the surface of Ethan's throat as he slumped over dead. Ethan saw Troy's Beretta 9mm pistol, a barely visible curl of smoke rising from where he had put a bullet in the insurgent's temple. To this day, he could not remember hearing Troy shoot. But he would bear the scars from that day, from what happened in the space of a minute or two, for the rest of his life. All that he needed to know about honor, love and commitment he had learned that day.

Autumn was winding up her case. "Just think about it, okay?" she was saying eagerly. "It would mean so much to Martha."

Ethan nodded, having no clue what he was agreeing to think about. And then she was standing and readying to leave.

"Wait," he said, surprising them both with the fervor in his voice. "Don't you want to see Heather while you're here?"

"Well of course I do, but I'm afraid my invitation must have been lost on its way to my suite at the Plaza Hotel." She was teasing him in that special way she had that reminded him not to take himself so seriously.

"Consider yourself invited."

He wanted to put his hand on the small of her back as she began to walk out of his office, but he didn't dare. He was afraid of what he might do next. Instead he said, "I'll send a car for you at six, okay? We like to eat at six thirty because it's best if Heather stays on a schedule. The routine is good for her. The Plaza? That's where you're staying?"

"Are you serious?" she laughed. "I was kidding. I'm at the Best Western in Times Square."

His inclination was to pick up the phone and book her the firm's suite at the Plaza, but he knew she would refuse, so he didn't bother.

Barry barreled into Ethan's office as Autumn was leaving, almost bumping into her as she called a farewell over her shoulder. He mouthed something, probably lewd, toward Ethan, and then she was gone. Barry clutched at his heart and pretended to faint. "Whoever that woman is, whatever she wants, just give it to her, man. 'Cause you're gonna end up doing it sooner or later."

If only it were that simple, Ethan thought wryly.

He left the office at four thirty, sailing silently past Myra, who chased him down the hall with a fistful of pink message slips.

"Not now, Myra. They'll have to wait until tomorrow. I'm entertaining this evening. And don't email or text me either. Take the rest of the day off," he added as an afterthought.

He heard Myra's tiny voice as he ran to the elevator bank. "Okay, Ethan…if you say so."

As Ethan rode the thirty floors down in the elevator, he called the gourmet grocery around the corner from his apartment building and ordered a prepared dinner for delivery—a roast chicken, fingerling potatoes, green beans sautéed with garlic. It was fancy enough to impress Autumn but simple enough that Heather would eat it.

"And I'm going to know what to do with these when they're delivered, right?" he said to the girl who was taking his order.

She assured him in a tone that told him he wasn't the first nervous man who had ordered up an impromptu feast at the eleventh hour and had no idea what to do when it arrived. "It will come in oven-ready containers with written directions in the bag," she said. "Do you want any dessert or wine?" she prompted.

"Oh yeah, throw in some dessert. Whatever you have ready is fine. And you'll have it at my house by five thirty, right? No later?" He glanced at his watch, which caused him to lose the legal pads he was carrying.

"Damn," he muttered, as they scattered on the elevator floor. "Sorry, not you," he said to the girl.

"Don't worry," she said. "It's foolproof."

Yeah, he thought, *but is it Ethan-proof?* He remembered his various breakfast disasters and groaned inwardly. By the time the elevator had reached the lobby he was out of breath and leaning against the wall. And was that perspiration on his brow?

By six everything was warming in the oven. The chocolate torte was artfully displayed on a fancy cake plate Ellen had purchased when she had "outfitted" his kitchen. Heather helped him set the table, arranging the place mats and napkins, and waiting for him to place the silverware. When they were done, they stood side by side for a moment, admiring their handiwork.

He didn't tell Heather that Autumn was coming. He wanted to see the joy on the little girl's face when Autumn stepped around the foyer into the living room.

"Ethan?" Heather asked, sensing there was something up that she needed to know about.

"Yes, honey?" he asked distractedly.

"Do you have a fever?"

His hand went instantly to his brow. He was sweating again. What on earth was happening? He was having performance anxiety or stage fright. It was insane. Heather followed him to the kitchen, where he tore off a paper towel and mopped his forehead.

"You're acting weird," she proclaimed, and returned to her *Dora the Explorer* video in the living room.

When the doorbell rang at quarter after six the adrenaline rushed to his ears as it had often done when he went on patrol in Afghanistan. Autumn Hamilton was early and had somehow unleashed a bad case of PTSD on him before even stepping into his apartment. As he smoothed his khakis and shirt, he heard the door open and high-heeled shoes click-clacking down the hallway toward him.

"Hello, hello," Ellen called in her singsongy voice.

Oh, shoot. Ellen had invited herself over for dinner last night as they rode home in the cab. He was so exhausted he had forgotten. He added memory loss to the list of disorders Autumn had given him.

"Hi, Ellen," he called, knowing his voice sounded strained. She kissed him on the cheek and dumped her mink coat, gigantic purse, and several shopping bags on the couch next to Heather.

"Ewee," Heather squealed, as the coat sleeve fell onto her lap, and she shifted away.

"Feed me, darling," Ellen said dramatically, striking a pose in her black silk suit and $400 scarf. "I haven't had a bite all day." Then she sniffed. "Are you actual cooking?"

"Kind of," Ethan confessed. "And we're having company, too. An old friend of Heather's is coming to see her."

Damn. There went his surprise. It wasn't fair to be irritated with Ellen but he was. A lot. He wished her iPhone would start buzzing with an interior design emergency and she would have to run out before Autumn even appeared. As if some cruel being in the universe were reading his mind, the doorbell rang.

Heather leapt to her feet and bounded down the hallway to the front door. She yanked it open and squealed with delight.

"Autumn!" she screamed, and she flung herself into Autumn's outstretched arms.

As Ellen click-clacked her way down the hall after Heather, Ethan quickly laid another place setting. He surveyed the table. He wished he had stopped at the corner market to pick up some flowers. But it hardly mattered now.

Although at the moment he probably could not articulate it, he

AUTUMN

was at the most curious of crossroads. He had to ask himself, was he falling in love with one woman, while falling out of love with another? He couldn't be sure. Exhaustion and stress from trying to hold his life together disconnected him from his feelings. He was so busy trying to stay on track at work, take care of Heather, and appease Ellen that he wasn't sure he knew how he felt about anything.

"So, Ellen," Autumn said conversationally after they had gathered at the table. "Ethan has told us about your interior design business. It must be a lot of fun and very rewarding."

Ellen took a dainty bite of a tiny green bean.

"That's funny," she said coolly, touching Ethan's arm with her free hand. "I haven't heard a thing about you."

Ethan cringed at the unnecessary slight.

Autumn ignored her and turned to Heather. "So, tell us about school today."

"At recess it was..."

Ellen cut her off almost immediately. "Heather," she snapped. "What have we told you about eating with your mouth full?" She lightened her tone. "What I mean, sweetheart, is I'm sure you don't want our guest here to see the inside of your mouth while you're chewing, do you? Now that's a good girl."

Autumn watched as Heather, mildly deflated, abandoned her train of thought and stopped talking. Autumn caught Ethan's eye, stared longer than was polite, attempted a glower, and returned to her chicken.

"El," Ethan said quietly, but not very sweetly. "She's not hurting anything. She was just excited about Autumn being here. Go on, honey, tell us about your day."

For the rest of the meal, Autumn felt Ellen's steel-grey eyes boring into her. *For someone who claims she's never heard of me, she's pretty worried about me,* Autumn observed.

After dinner, Heather and Autumn helped Ethan with the dishes while Ellen returned work calls. Autumn couldn't help but notice the stick-figure paintings on the fridge. They all depicted three tiny, happy figures—a man, a woman, and a child—standing side by side surrounded by huge slices of pizza. The figures were painted with watercolors, but the slices were drawn with thick permanent marker, and the big red pepperoni pieces looked like giant saucers.

"Heather, I just love your paintings. It makes me hungry just looking at all that pizza."

Heather stood next to her and then removed the magnet from one of the paintings and handed it to Autumn.

"If you put this on your fridge then you won't forget me."

When Ethan proclaimed it was bedtime, Heather begged Autumn to tuck her in and tugged her down the hallway toward her frilly pink bedroom.

When he was finished in the kitchen, Ethan walked down the hallway to the back of the apartment and stopped outside Heather's bedroom.

"But I don't like her," he heard Heather say.

"Sometimes," he heard Autumn's soft voice, and he imagined her kneeling in front of Heather as he had seen her do the first day they had met, "we don't like people when we first meet them, but after a while it turns out we do. Remember when you first met Ethan how much you didn't like him? How you used to stick your tongue out at him and steal his keys?"

Heather giggled.

Ethan relaxed against the wall, holding his breath so they

wouldn't detect his presence. He could hear Ellen in the living room yelling into her cell phone, but out of necessity he had gotten pretty good at tuning her out.

"You love Ethan, right?"

Heather's voice was strong and enthusiastic when she said, "Yes!" And it made him smile.

"And you know that Ethan loves Ellen, right?"

"Yeah, but I wish he didn't," came Heather's glum reply.

"But because you love Ethan and you want to make him happy, you need to love Ellen, too, or at the very least be nice to her, okay?"

"Okay. I'll try," Heather said. "But she's still mean."

He heard Autumn rustling the covers to tuck Heather in, and then the light went out. He tiptoed back to the living room, wondering to himself how in the world Autumn, whom Ellen had deftly belittled and slighted throughout dinner, had a heart big enough to tell Heather she needed to love Ellen to make him happy.

CHAPTER 14

AUTUMN WAS GRATEFUL for the warmth she knew would be waiting for her at Power Gallery in Brooklyn, and not just for the reprieve from the cold wind that had turned her feet into blocks of ice despite her sheepskin boots, but also from the chill she carried inside her. It was as if a piece of her had turned to ice the evening before in Ethan's apartment. Perhaps it happened as Ellen stared icily across the dinner table with her fake smile, or as she gazed at Heather's stick figure paintings of the happy family. Whenever it had happened, she now felt a palpable shift inside her. And she didn't like it.

She allowed her heart to soar a little as the cab stopped in front of the gallery, and she admired the sleek, modern sculpture sitting in the front window. She and Frank Power had gone to art school together, and while he was a modernist sculptor, he had connections throughout the art world, and they were good enough friends that she knew he would evaluate her work, on its merits, of course, and recommend her to the right people.

She handed the driver a twenty-dollar bill and hopped out, hugging Frank, who had come out to greet her on the sidewalk. A body-builder standing six feet four, his workman's coveralls and shiny bald head made him look more like Mr. Clean rather than a New York City gallery owner. But he was still a working artist who wielded power tools in the studio like a woodsman with a chainsaw. In fact, he sometimes used a chainsaw. He swallowed her up with a big bear hug.

"I'm soooo glad to see you, Frank," she said, her voice cracking with emotion and muffled by his shoulder. "You have no idea." She pulled back, more composed, and he took her hands in his. "I think you've grown three inches or I've shrunk two since I saw you last," she laughed, instantly regretting the reference to her last visit, which had been two years ago.

"How long has it been?" he boomed, as his voice was as big as he was. "You never come to New York City anymore," he scolded as they walked into the gallery and out of the wind swirling around them. "And you didn't even come when I opened a show with Alonzo Archibald last year, and you loooove Alonzo Archibald."

She took his teasing good-naturedly, as she knew she deserved it. But of course, she couldn't have come to the show. How would she have answered all of the probing questions?

How's your work going?

What are you working on?

Does Scottie Lambert still represent you?

When's your next show?

How could she have faced everyone once they discovered her long, gradual fall from the top? It had been too painful to even imagine attending the show, even though she loved Alonzo's gorgeous creations with large bamboo stalks that he wet so he could manipulate them into amazing shapes. So she had tossed Frank's invitation into the trash and ignored his phone calls and emails. She hoped that maybe he had been so busy with the show that he would have forgotten her rudeness by now. And now, standing in his gallery, after blowing him off, she was about to ask him for a favor she had no right to expect.

"I know, I know," she answered, trying to sound breezy. "I get so busy sometimes. You know how it is."

He held her gaze. "Too busy to return a phone call or email from an old pal?" He was smiling, but she was getting the message that she had hurt him.

So he hadn't forgotten after all. She looked away first and gazed around the room, refocusing the conversation and her mind. The gallery was sparse, and the only art that was not hanging on the walls were these sleek black sculptures that reminded you of tall birds, maybe flamingos, or egrets, or herons, perched atop stark white pedestals at just about everybody's eye level except Frank's. The floor was light pine, and on the white walls hung an assortment of black and white portrait photography of American soldiers in combat, which offered quite a stark contrast to the modern sculptures.

Faces of young men in fatigues gazed at the camera, some smiling and hamming it up, others so serious that their hard eyes sent chills down Autumn's spine as she imagined what they might have just seen. She wanted to absorb each and every photograph, to study them inch by inch, and to know every story they held. They were too dated to have been taken recently in Afghanistan. But as she glanced at them, she realized Ethan could have been any one of these soldiers. And any of these soldiers could have been Ethan.

She broke her gaze from the portraits and looked quizzically at Frank, who recognized and grinned at her puzzled expression.

"Doing a favor for a friend," he said and guided her into his office. "He took those photos in Iraq during the first Gulf War."

Bless him, Autumn thought. *Same old Frank.*

When he had taken her coat and settled her on a small chair with an espresso and biscotti, the inquisition began.

"So, what's up, Autumn? I can tell you're in some kind of trouble. Is it bad?"

She nibbled on a cookie. "How much trouble is your photographer friend in?" she asked, stalling.

Frank laughed, and she warmed to the familiarity of the sound of his voice, feeling suddenly safe in the company of someone she had known for so long—someone whom she hadn't seen or spoken to for two years, but who instinctively knew something was wrong the moment he saw her.

"Johnny Alvarez was a public affairs officer in the Army," Frank explained. "And he loved to take photos. He was part of an armored cavalry regiment. He was the only public affairs officer in that regiment to get a Purple Heart *and* a Bronze Star. He never would tell you this, but he probably saved an entire platoon when an Iraqi soldier tossed a hand grenade into their midst. From what I've read, he made a diving midair catch, and as he hit the ground rolling he tossed it back toward the enemy. Unfortunately, it blew up in midair, and some of the shrapnel caught him on his right side. He wound up losing his leg just below the knee. He's retired now, but he always wanted to have a show of his photos. He's got Parkinson's, and in a few months the doctors think it will get to the point where he won't be able to hold a camera steady long enough to take a picture. Anyway. No one would give him a show, and he was running out of time."

"Oh, my gosh, that's incredible," Autumn said, in awe of her friend, and of Alvarez's courage, as she frantically searched her mind for a cover story for her visit. "Are you getting any interest? I mean, it's a different buyer for the photographs than your regular gallery patrons, right?"

"You would think I wouldn't have any interest," Frank answered, puffing up a little like a proud father. "It started out slow. We had an opening, mostly with his family and friends and people I could convince to come to fill the room. I tried, but I couldn't get even one reviewer here. Johnny said it didn't bother him and that he was happy just to have the show, but I felt like I had let him down. But then this happened."

He handed her a newspaper clipping. "I've had guys from *Stars and Stripes* newspaper, and Johnny was on *Good Morning America*. Word's gotten around, and I've sold more of those photos in the past month than sculptures in the past two years."

Autumn gasped as she looked at the newspaper. It was the front page of the *New York Times* arts section, with photos of not just the Gulf War photography, but also the sleek, black, birdlike sculptures.

Her widened eyes locked on his amused ones. "You got a full-page review. You have to be tight with some VIP to get that kind of exposure. How'd you do it? I mean, not that you don't deserve it."

"Some man who wanders into the gallery from time to time, but never buys anything, heard Johnny's story. Turns out the guy's a World War II vet and a gazillionaire, and he knows someone at the *Times*. That's how they got the story. Who knew? Then he bought five photos and a thirty-thousand-dollar piece as a housewarming gift for his daughter. I had to get ten more photos printed, matted, and framed right away to meet the demand, then ten more, and then twenty more. It just took off. All told, I've hung and sold about three hundred photos in three months. That's why I had to meet you before we open. This place is a madhouse during business hours."

Autumn smiled at her old friend. "You are so awesome, Frank. You did the right thing, not expecting anything in return, and you've been rewarded for your goodness and generosity. Do you know how rare a quality that is in people?"

"I seem to remember a young woman years ago who used to do that for her fellow artists," Frank replied. "I'm convinced that you carried around my slides in your purse for a year until I got my first solo show. And that girl, what was her name, who wore only yellow? She always looked like a fire hydrant?"

Autumn laughed at the memory. "Monica Stanley. She was from Berkeley and was so homesick that she wore yellow to remind her of the sun."

"Yeah, but she painted those dark little paintings with the fine strokes that looked like a cross between hashtags and Chinese writing. I've lost track of her now, but I know you set her up with Scottie, and he got her a solo show somewhere not too shabby if I recall. Not many people would have done that Autumn. And you know it."

"Well, we're just two of kind, you and I, as they say," Autumn said, spinning her new story in her mind as she finished her espresso.

"Well, speaking of you," Frank began, offering her another

espresso from the machine in his office, which she declined. She was not going to take advantage of her friend's good nature, and now knowing he was expecting a crowd when he opened, she wasn't going to take any more of his time. He might be wearing coveralls now, but she knew he would change into a beautifully tailored suit before the gallery opened.

"Oh, I'm just in a bit of a creative slump, nothing major. I just needed an immersion, an artistic shot in the arm. Needed to see people from the time when I was at my creative peak. You know how much I love Finch's Crossing, but..."

Frank interrupted her and rolled his eyes. "I'm surprised you have enough creativity to even have a slump," he teased. He had been after her to move to New York for years.

"Anyyyywaaay," she continued, drawing out the word with a look that said *don't mess with my hometown.* "It helps just to walk the streets and visit the galleries and the museums." She reached across the desk for his hand. "And to see good friends. I just wanted to say hi. And to apologize for missing your show and blowing you off."

"Well," he said. "Apology accepted, I guess. But don't do it again." His voice grew suddenly quiet. "You really hurt my feelings, A."

She cringed at the use of her old art school nickname. They had been good friends, nothing more, though she knew he wanted there to be something between them. Whenever anything resembling a tender moment emerged between them he called her "A."

"I know, and I'm sorry. I just couldn't be around people then."

"People?" he asked, incredulous. "People? Am I just people to you?"

"Of course not, Frank. I didn't mean *you*, and you know it. Stop being so dramatic." They both laughed.

"You know how I feel about you, A," he said in that quiet voice again, and she nodded. "Are you seeing someone in New York? Is that why you're here?"

She surprised herself when she hesitated before she said, "No, there's no one. Still single."

"You still don't feel 'that way' about me, do you?" He knew the answer, but also knew he had to ask it.

She shook her head. "I'm sorry, Frank. Some things just don't happen, and there's nothing to be done about it. The little fire hydrant was madly in love with *you,* and you wouldn't give her the time of day."

"That's because she was five foot one," he protested. "I was fifteen inches taller than she was. At least with you I wouldn't have to pick you up off the ground to kiss you."

Autumn got up and came over to the desk to collect her coat. She stood on her tiptoes and planted a sweet kiss on his cheek.

"I had to ask, A," he said softly.

"I know," she smiled. "And I don't mind."

She left Frank's gallery with a montage of faces and images swirling in her mind. Ethan's eyes joined with those of the other soldiers who stared out from the gallery walls. She saw the smile on Frank's face when he saw her emerge from the cab. Then Heather's joy and Ellen's cool disapproval floated by, jockeying for position. Then she saw the small, lined, and weathered face of Johnny Alvarez, the public affairs officer who had saved a platoon of men by catching a grenade in flight. It was a reminder for her to count her blessings and to remember that no matter how hard her life was, and no matter the problems she faced in her life, there was always someone—many, many someones—whose challenges and obstacles eclipsed her own.

CHAPTER 14

While she hadn't had enough courage to ask Frank for a favor, she had no qualms about keeping her appointments with the other gallery owners and acquaintances from grad school. Her name still carried enough clout to get her in the door.

Three hours later, after tedious meetings with former classmates, she was relieved to be done, though the results were not what she had hoped. They'd all spent the obligatory fifteen minutes or so catching up over coffee and gossiping, speculating over who was now doing illustrations for greeting card companies. And then, after they clicked over to her online portfolio, they all gave her the same polite, perfunctory remarks about her work, but no one wanted any of it. No one could even muster anything more than some bland, meaningless platitudes about "what the market currently supported."

As she rode the train home, she saw the faces of her former classmates as they spoke enthusiastically about looking for the next big original discovery that would take the art world by storm. Meanwhile, instead of advancing, Autumn was spiraling backward into her creative slump, further and further away from anything unique or original that would shake up the art world. Before this dry spell, she had made a very comfortable living from her art. If things didn't pick up, *she'd* be the one drawing hearts and flowers for greeting card companies.

Maybe it was time to do something different with her life, to shake things up a little bit. Was she tapped out in Finch's Crossing? Was geography the problem? She had seen everything that surrounded her thousands of times, over and over. Did she need new surroundings, a new set of stimuli, to bring a new perspective to her work? To her life? Moving to New York might shake things up.

And why had her rebuff to Frank's genuine overtures been so automatic? She loved him, as a friend, and knew he was devoted to her. All she had to do was say the word, and he would come to her. He was handsome and successful, and his kindness to his friends and fellow man was like nothing she had ever experienced before. They had so much in common, too, and he could nurture and support her through this dry spell, and she would emerge stronger and better than before. She allowed herself to wonder if perhaps, just perhaps, Frank might consider living with her for half of the year in Finch's Crossing if she agreed to live in New York City the other half.

And her mind returned to Ethan. She had so looked forward to seeing him and Heather, and secretly, she had hoped the three of them would be alone. Heather was happy there in the city. And although she had her issues with Ellen, she had obviously taken to the woman. Autumn thought of the painting of the three happy stick figures tucked away safely in her purse.

What was it she had told Ethan just a few weeks ago? That Heather was so good at expressing herself through her drawings, and that she would express in her drawings and paintings what she couldn't verbalize, and that he should take his cues from them.

The paintings were speaking loud and clear. And there was nothing left to say. Or was there? She picked up her cell phone and sent Frank a quick email thanking him for their visit and inviting him to visit her in Finch's Crossing.

"In your dreams, darling," he emailed back. "But I want to see you again soon. When are you coming back to New York?"

When indeed, Autumn thought to herself. *When indeed*.

CHAPTER 15

*I*N THE DAYS following her return from New York, Autumn raided every cupboard and box of supplies she could find, looking for the inspiration she needed to save her career as an artist. Enough was enough. If she was going to even consider spending more time in New York, she would have to have something to show for herself, and more importantly, something to bankroll her. She would force herself to do something, anything, no matter how bad it was. She would go on automatic pilot and simply ignore her doubts and insecurities.

She hauled out the watercolors, heavy oils, and even the wax and tried some encaustic painting, applying thick layers of the wax on canvas and then etching designs and collage into the wax. When she'd had enough of the wax, she figured she'd go back to the basics. She clipped a sheet of cream-colored drawing paper to her easel and selected a brand-new graphite pencil out of the pack. And she sat there, absolutely blocked. After a few minutes, she realized this situation was going to require serious help, and she headed to the kitchen. The house was so quiet it was almost painful. She had brought the sights, sounds, and smells of the bustling city back with her, and she wondered if a prolonged dose of its energy would eventually revive her. This painful quietness sure wasn't doing it.

She padded into the kitchen and stood motionless for a moment, intently surveying the recesses of her refrigerator. She knew it was there. She bought a bottle of expensive chardonnay every year or so just for emergencies such as the one she was now experiencing. She could not even remember the brand, but she could remember it cost her somewhere north of thirty dollars. She bent down to extend her view toward the very back of the fridge, and then she saw it, gleaming in the dull glow of the fridge light. She grabbed the bottle and brought it out into the open. It was a vineyard she had never heard of—which was part of the fun—Albemarle Downs, from somewhere in Central Virginia. Mist Kissed Chardonnay, it was called. So Autumn poured herself a conservative glass of artist's block remover and headed back to the studio.

She walked over to her drawing table and stood there looking around at various of her pieces, some finished, some barely started, and took a sip of her wine. Out of the corner of her eye, she spotted a very large floral leaning against the wall. It was a close-up of a magnolia blossom, with a tiny honeybee lounging on one of the petals. She picked it up and laid it on the drawing table. She really liked this piece, and not so long ago, so did a lot of other people. Then she noticed Heather's stick-figure watercolor peeking out from a stack of papers lying on the far corner of the table. She slipped it out of the stack, remembering when Heather had given it to her. Funny how it brought such love and pain at the same time. Heather's recovery and happiness in New York filled her heart with joy, but the smiling trio in Heather's painting gave her a physical ache that she had tried unsuccessfully to wish away ever since her return from New York. She stared at Heather's painting for a few moments, and then she distractedly placed it face down on her magnolia.

As she went to set her glass down on the drawing table, it slipped from her hands and literally bounced off the magnolia. Wine went everywhere. In the split second it took Autumn to realize what was happening, Heather's watercolor, and not to mention Autumn's magnolia, were soaked. Her first reaction was to lift Heather's stick figure masterpiece off of the magnolia and lay it flat on the drawing table. She then ran frantically into the kitchen and returned with a roll of paper towels. As she was dabbing the wine off the magnolia, she noticed something odd.

Autumn lifted the canvas onto its edge and was stunned by what she saw. A light impression, a shadow really, of Heather's three tiny stick figures had transferred to the painting so that it looked like the figures inhabited the magnolia petal, circling the bright yellow center. In the transfer, the figures took on the feel of a prehistoric cave painting. The result was eerie and haunting. Mesmerized, Autumn let the rest of the wine pool around her drawing table.

"Thank you, Heather," she whispered softly aloud, and she went to look for the smallest paintbrush she could find.

For the next week, Autumn experimented with her discovery, first sketching what she could see in her mind, then transferring the image onto the jungle of white floral canvases that had mocked her for months. Taking in hand each brilliantly white and silver floral, she transformed them one by one, painting tiny black stick figures onto one prominent area of the flower. When the white florals were done, she took out fresh canvases of all sizes, and using brilliant colors that heretofore had been untouched, she entered a vortex of sorts, growing stronger and more passionate with each stroke of her brush or charcoal, and the familiar rush of adrenaline returned as if it had never left her. She painted more abstract flowers, and the stick figures looked even better on the new paintings.

If she had looked around her once meticulously clean and organized studio, she would have seen a kaleidoscope of paint tubes and used rags tossed carelessly on the floor and drawers and cupboards left open. But her attention was solely focused on the canvases before her. She wiped her paint-stained hands on her overalls till she looked like she had been attacked by a tiny band of kindergarteners with colored markers. When her cell phone rang for the fourth time in twenty minutes, she opened a window and threw it out as if she were a pitcher on a mound. She had the vague, gnawing feeling of hunger but ignored it as long as she could. Finally giving in, she called for takeout, leaving the money on the front porch with instructions to leave the food outside and ring the doorbell.

After six days of frantic painting, she emerged from her swirling vortex and sat with a cup of tea in the cozy morning room, catching her breath, a pencil and sketch pad in her hand. She gazed out the window at the dark, shadowy trees and bushes and thought of Troy, Denise, and Ethan, and about the terrible circumstances that had led to her rebirth as an artist. If Troy and Denise hadn't died, if they hadn't appointed Ethan as guardian, Heather would never have gone to live with him and would never have given Autumn the unbelievably powerful gift in the form of a little girl painting.

CHAPTER 15

In a roundabout way, she supposed a little begrudgingly, she also owed what she believed to be her revival in part to Ethan, who had enrolled Heather in special art therapy classes to help the little girl deal with the loss of her parents. He reported Heather's progress to Martha in their weekly conversation, and Martha in turn kept Autumn updated. She had been so happy, and relieved, that the little girl had crawled out of the dark spaces and was living a normal, almost happy life.

And she thought of Frank, steady and successful Frank. Then she found herself comparing the two men, making pro and con notes in her sketch pad, then scratching and jabbing with her pencil until a portrait of Frank and then one of Ethan emerged in front of her. Thinking of Frank gave her a warm feeling. She imagined him sitting next to her, sipping tea while they mused over their grad school days and talked about their favorite contemporary artists. It was a cozy and not undesirable scene, but when she saw it in her mind she felt... nothing.

And when she thought of Ethan, she saw his exquisite suits and remembered the steely and rigid way he had carried himself when they first met at the nursery. How happy he had been to see her in New York. At least it seemed that way to her. Sitting in his office he had been visibly relaxed and had opened up to her with genuine kindness. She had not expected that, but rather had prepared to make her case about Martha to a cool, icy lawyer. The heat rose on her face, and she felt the familiar tingling in her stomach when she remembered their last good-bye and the way he had held her gaze for a few seconds longer than was appropriate for a man whose girlfriend was in the other room.

AUTUMN

* * *

After the last dinner seating ended at the Greystone Manor Duncan Olack walked his waitresses, Diane and Gretchen, out to the parking lot. As they exclaimed over the mid-November chill, he watched them get into their cars and drive safely away. Ever since the robberies had started he had been extra careful. When business picked up he would invest in a burglar alarm on the doors and windows. He had investigated the prices and was appalled at how expensive not only the systems were, but their monthly monitoring fees.

As was his custom, Duncan took a mug of peppermint tea to his apartment on the second floor and went to bed. Just after one in the morning, he heard footsteps in the hallway. While that wasn't unusual—he was running a hotel, he reminded himself—every sound unnerved him as he thought about what might happen if someone tried to break into the Manor.

An hour later he still couldn't sleep. He was about to put on his robe and slippers and go down to the kitchen for a snack when he heard a loud bang coming from the lobby then shouts and breaking glass. He rushed downstairs, quickly followed by other guests who were streaming out of their rooms.

"What is it? What's the matter?" he yelled as he ran down the stairs. The first thing he saw was one of the Manor's new guests, Mrs. Lane, screaming at her husband. "Oh, Art. Be careful. BE CAREFUL!"

Duncan followed Mrs. Lane's horrified gaze past the registration counter and down the few steps that led from the dining room into the bar. Mr. Lane, in his late seventies, was brandishing a fireplace poker with one hand while holding on to the wrist of a slight masked figure dressed in black who was swatting at his head. As horrified as he was, the first thought that flew into Duncan's head was, *that guy's fighting like a girl.* Duncan rushed toward the struggling couple, intending to help Mr. Lane hang on to his prize. But it was a bit too late. The masked bandit had slipped free of the elderly man's grip and flew out of the dining room, crashing through the glass in the French doors before disappearing into the darkness.

"C'mon!" he heard Kyle yell behind him. "Let's get him."

Kyle blew past Duncan out through the broken glass doors, followed by Art Lane, who dropped the poker, and scampered after him.

Duncan turned to his guests, most of whom were now huddled at the foot of the staircase in various stages of undress, unsure what to do next.

"Call 911," someone yelled, and Duncan hurried behind the registration desk and dialed.

"What's going on?" asked Miss Dandridge, a latecomer to the scene, in the tight, shrill voice of someone who was not pleased about being awakened in the middle of the night.

"I'm afraid we had an intruder. We may have been robbed," said Duncan, retying the belt on his bathrobe and trying to look official and calming. "Though I'm not sure if he got anything. It looked like he ran off empty-handed."

"Oh my!" exclaimed Miss Dandridge. "We could have been murdered in our beds! I'll never be able to sleep here again."

The Blakes, a hearty couple who came to hike every year, tried to soothe her.

"I don't think it's that bad," Mary Blake said, moving to stand next to the frightened woman. "I'd be very surprised if he came back after being caught in the act and barely getting away."

"I suppose so," Miss Dandridge replied. "But I don't plan to stay here a minute longer than I need to." She turned to Duncan. "Mr. Olack, I will be leaving after breakfast in the morning. Please have my bill ready."

Duncan agreed, disheartened, and watched as she walked over toward the fireplace, picked up the fire poker Mr. Lane had dropped, and disappeared up the stairs.

Kyle and Mr. Lane returned just then, breathless and disappointed.

"I chased him off the property and lost him on Spring Street. It was just too dark to see anything," Kyle said, with Mr. Lane nodding in affirmation.

The rest of the guests sat on the chairs and sofas in the lobby while Duncan tried to assure them of their safety and promising them that he would have a burglar alarm system installed. Though how it could have prevented this burglary, which he was certain this was, he had no idea. The Greystone Manor's lobby was never locked so guests could reach their rooms anytime they wanted. That would have to change.

Sheriff Landry and a deputy appeared in less than five minutes, sirens blaring and lighting up the night sky as they pulled up the long drive and parked at the front entrance. As soon as they came in, everyone started talking at once.

"All right, everyone, calm down," the sheriff said, and Duncan was grateful that someone else was taking control. "One at a time now. I can't understand any of you when you talk over each other like a pack of magpies. Let's start from the beginning. Duncan, you go first."

So, Duncan recounted the sound he heard from his bedroom and the scene he witnessed as he came down the stairs, and then Mr. Lane picked up the narrative, and Duncan went into the kitchen and came back with a bottle of sherry and some glasses.

"It was just after one when we came back from visiting our nephew in Connellsville," Mr. Lane began slowly, still a little out of breath and accepting the tiny glass of sherry Duncan offered him. "The missus and I parked the car out front and came in the front door."

"The porch light was burnt out," Mrs. Lane chimed in. "So it was extra dark, and we walked slowly so we wouldn't trip."

"That's strange," Duncan observed, passing around the sherry to the other guests, whom the sheriff had asked to stick around. "Jack Staub was here just the other day finishing the landscaping, and I asked him to replace all the outside lights. I replace all the bulbs frequently to reduce the risk of them burning out."

"Do you think he purposely broke the light bulb so he could come back and rob the place?" asked Mrs. Lane. She and her husband were first-time visitors from Buffalo.

"That's crazy," Duncan argued. "Jack would never do that. I've known him for years. He does landscaping for all kinds of people in town."

"But you know, now that you mention it," began Dennis Armstrong, a construction foreman from Chicago who was on an extended stay at the Manor. "I've seen him skulking around lately, and a few days ago he was peeking in the dining room windows."

"You're just wrong about Jack," Duncan argued adamantly. "I've known him for twenty years. He doesn't 'skulk around,' and he would never do something like this."

"Then how do you explain the peeping?" Dennis asked, and Duncan just shrugged.

"You never can tell with people," Art Lane offered. "We knew someone at our church who sang in the choir and was an usher once a month, and then, bam, we find out he had been robbing cigarette trucks on the highway and selling cartons for cut-rate prices and making a mint, mostly with prison guards who had a racket going at the state penitentiary in Middleburg."

The sheriff watched him impatiently. "Well, Mr. Lane, while I appreciate your commentary, let's stick with the situation at hand. What happened after you came in the front door?"

"Well that lamp over there," he pointed to the registration desk, "was on, as was the light in the hallway leading to the dining room, so there was enough light to see the lobby. As we were walking across toward the stairs I heard something fall and bounce and looked over at the fireplace, and that's when we saw the guy in black. He had dropped some pieces of silver." He pointed. "Look—they're still there."

The sheriff nodded to his deputy, who put on some latex gloves and retrieved an evidence bag from his pocket. Everyone watched as he picked up a silver salt and pepper shaker set and two candlesticks.

"Do these belong to the Manor?" Sheriff Landry asked Duncan.

"They're from the library," Duncan replied wearily, gesturing behind him with his head.

The sheriff made a note. "Are they valuable?"

"I guess they could be. Maybe for the value of the silver. Let me check in there to see if he got anything else. He could have slipped

CHAPTER 15

some small pieces into a pocket."

The sheriff turned back to the Lanes. "What happened next?"

Mrs. Lane answered. "Well, as soon as I noticed the mask and gloves it was pretty obvious what was happening, so I screamed and startled him. That's when Art grabbed the poker and knocked over the whole set of fireplace tools in the process. The guy was standing with his back to the fireplace and had to run around the sofa to avoid Art, but he wasn't fast enough, and Art grabbed him by the wrist. That's when the vase fell off the table there."

"That's when I came down," Duncan continued. "The robber was swatting at Art and managed to get away and run out the French doors. Or I should say through them. He hurled himself right through the glass."

"Hey, should we check all the hospital emergency rooms for someone coming in with bloody cuts?" Kyle offered enthusiastically.

"Hold on there, CSI," the sheriff responded. "If he was covered from head to toe like you folks are describing, he probably won't have a scratch on him, especially if he ran through the glass as fast as you said. Probably went through it with his side, shoulder first."

The sheriff asked a few more questions then closed his notebook.

"Well, there's not much else we can do now. Duncan, the deputy here will help you board up that French door. We'll canvass the neighbors in the morning to ask if anyone saw someone running away from the Manor. But honestly, we've had a devil of a time catching a break on this guy. He usually strikes during the day when people are at work. No one has seen a thing so far. This was the first middle-of-the-night attempt and his first attempt in Finch's Crossing. He's getting bolder, and we're no closer to catching him."

The guests tittered nervously, and reluctantly went up the stairs and back to bed. The Lanes and a few other couples paused to politely tell Duncan they would be checking out early.

"Can you imagine what our reviews on TripAdvisor are going to say?" Duncan moaned to Kyle after everyone else had gone to bed. "That's three bookings lost in the span of fifteen minutes. And you know there will be more tomorrow. Half of them won't be able to go back to sleep, and after hours of ruminating they'll decide to leave early, too."

Kyle wasn't sure how to respond. Quite frankly, he knew Duncan was right.

"Well, you can't be sure how bad it will be. You might be able to ride it out."

Duncan nodded. "Thanks, Kyle. Let's call it a night. Maybe things will look better in the morning."

Duncan knew he wouldn't be able to go back to sleep, so he fixed himself another mug of peppermint tea and returned to his apartment. He kept seeing the slight figure in black swatting at Mr. Lane. Jack Staub had a slight, trim build. Could it really have been him, as one of the guests had suggested? No. It was impossible. Jack was in his seventies, and the burglar had moved like a young man. But then again, Mr. Lane had to be around the same age, and he had managed to partially subdue the robber and then sprint after him with Kyle. And as much as he didn't want to admit it, he, too, had seen Jack looking in the windows lately. As he tossed and turned, he tried to decide what motive Jack Staub could possibly have for trying to rob the Greystone Manor.

As he had predicted, more guests checked out ahead of schedule the next morning, expressing their sympathy but adamantly protesting that they would never be able to sleep in a place that had just

CHAPTER 15

been robbed.

The weekly edition of the *News-Observer* hit the stands two days after the robbery. It was, of course, front-page news, with the dramatic middle-of-the night burglary attempt recounted in lively, over-the-top detail with quotes from distraught guests, all of whom had left early. The article went on to describe the string of unsolved burglaries and concluded with the thought that "a dangerous criminal lurks among us, and we must all remain vigilant until he is caught." By the next week, business was down by fifty percent. Duncan broke down and read the reviews online. More bad news. How he hated social media and the Internet.

* * *

It was almost eleven o'clock at night a few days after the Greystone Manor had been robbed when Kyle searched his room frantically for his messenger bag. It contained all of his notes from his meetings with the merchants. Silently cursing himself, he realized that he had left it downtown earlier in the day. He had met with the mayor in the late morning then sat on a bench in Gazebo Park to rearrange his file folders. When Stan Brilhart came along he tucked his bag under the bench to make room for the large man to sit beside him.

He'd have to go downtown to retrieve it, and he hoped it would still be there. He drove his van through the darkened and deserted residential streets, turning on Pittsburgh Street, where the storefronts were silent and stoic under the soft glow of the street lamps.

This is what Finch's Crossing will be like if I fail, he said to himself, imagining the merchants standing outside their empty shops, longing for customers. He shuddered at the thought as he parked and almost ran to the bench, unable to contain his impatience any longer.

He breathed a sigh of relief as he pulled his bag out from under the bench.

From his office on Spring Street, just a block away, Sheriff Landry saw a van with Ohio license plates crawl along Pittsburgh Street and stop at Gazebo Park. Now this was an interesting turn of events that piqued his interest considerably, and he rose from his desk to stand by the window, where he had a perfect view of the empty street and park. It surprised and disappointed him to see Kyle Oswald step out of the van and pull something out from under a park bench then get back in his van and drive away. What did he pick up, and why was he doing it in the dark of night? Was it a stash of stolen goods? He had eliminated Kyle as a suspect because he had been present at the Manor robbery. But perhaps he had a partner who burgled homes while Kyle dumped the bounty somewhere, selling it for quick cash. He returned to his desk. What on earth would he tell the mayor, he wondered, finally concluding that the best course of action was to do and say nothing for the time being. He might have an opportunity to talk with Kyle and could casually work what he had seen into the conversation. After all, he reasoned, there could be a perfectly reasonable explanation for what he saw.

CHAPTER 16

WHEN HE WASN'T working, Ethan was either with Heather or Ellen, rarely with both, and more often with Heather. Ellen hadn't been shy about expressing her displeasure with this arrangement. He tried to think of things the three of them could do together, but Ellen either declined or, on the rare occasion that she agreed, typically cancelled at the last minute.

On a Saturday morning in mid-November Ethan was surfing the Internet looking for something the three of them could do together while Heather happily munched her cereal and played with her Barbies in the kitchen. He was only half listening to her little girl chatter until he realized that the Barbies represented herself and Ellen.

"Don't chew with your mouth open," the larger Barbie instructed the smaller one. "Ladies do not eat with their mouths open. Don't slurp your soup. Cut your chicken into smaller bites, and don't cram it in your mouth."

"I'm sorry," said the smaller Barbie in a meek little voice. "The soup is so yummy I want to eat it fast, and I love salsa chicken."

"Don't be a bad girl," was the nasty reply.

Heather walked the two dolls around the kitchen island until the bossy one fell over.

"Ouch!" she exclaimed. "Why don't you ever put your toys away? I just tripped over your stupid doll furniture. Now hang up your coat, put your backpack away, and do your homework!"

"No!" screamed the meek Barbie, no longer holding back. And to Ethan's surprise, the little Barbie whacked the mean Barbie, sending her tumbling to the floor, where she landed with a "twack." He watched as Heather sat the victorious Barbie in front of her and began singing a song from *Sesame Street*.

Dumbfounded, he wasn't sure what to do. Had Ellen really said all those things to Heather? Sure, she wasn't a natural with children, but had he been so distracted that he hadn't noticed how Ellen and Heather interacted? He thought back to the dinner with Autumn and the way Ellen had seemed to scold the little girl. He had intervened, he remembered, and Ellen had backed down. Apparently, however, that intervention had not been enough to persuade Ellen to soften her demeanor toward Heather.

* * *

Kyle sat on the smooth red vinyl seat at the luncheon counter at Hoffman's Drugstore and studied Sandra, the waitress. He knew her 1950s-style waitress uniform, complete with the little paper cap on her head and the eyeglasses that seemed to have wings on the edges, were not something she did to fit into the décor. He was convinced she was still living sixty years in the past.

"So what'll it be, sweetheart?" she asked, cracking her gum and smiling with heavily painted red lips. "The usual, or do you need to burn rubber, in which case you'll need it to go?"

Kyle smiled to himself. She even spoke 1950s. He had ordered a grilled cheese, potato chips, and a soda and settled in with a magazine when he heard a voice behind him that he thought he'd never hear again: Andy Potter. The slap on his shoulder felt like a clamp, slowly grinding into him, and he squeezed his eyes shut, hoping, for just a moment, that perhaps he had imagined the figure he felt hovering behind him.

"Wow, Kyle, what a coincidence running into you here, of all places. Man, it's great to see you. Mind if I join you?" Andy took the empty stool to Kyle's right, and Kyle slowly turned his head to watch as Andy ordered a cup of coffee and winked at Sandra.

"What are you doing here?" Kyle hissed.

"What? Can't an old friend look up another old friend?"

"We aren't old friends," Kyle protested vehemently. "I want you to go. Now."

"Go?" Andy asked, smiling that nasty smirk Kyle had stared at for longer than he wished to remember. Andy stirred sugar into his coffee and took a sip. "But I went to so much trouble to find you."

Kyle squeezed his eyes shut as his heart began to sink. "What do you want, Andy?" he whispered. Maybe if he just gave Andy whatever he wanted he would go away.

"Well, you see, the thing is…" he cut himself off as he saw Meg strolling along the walk on the other side of the plate glass window. "Now who is that beauty?"

Kyle couldn't ever remember seeing Meg around town without Autumn. He wondered what was going on. On any other occasion, Kyle would have wanted to see Meg, but today he prayed she wouldn't come into the drugstore. And to his relief, she just walked on by.

Andy swiveled on his stool as Sandra returned to take his order. "I'd like to introduce myself," he said smoothly. "I'm Kyle's friend, Andy Potter." He extended his hand, and Sandra shook it.

"Andy, meet Sandra," said Kyle, rather unenthusiastically. Kyle forced himself to smile and nod as Sandra welcomed Andy to Finch's Crossing, asking him where he was from and how long he was going to stay. Andy was one of those men who were too good-looking for their own good. He resembled a Nordic god with a complexion like sand, and he had the wardrobe of a Calvin Klein model. *It was probably all stolen*, Kyle thought to himself. Suddenly he realized Andy and Sandra were both staring at him.

"Sorry. What?"

"Andy was just asking if you could put him up for a few days," Sandra said.

"Oh, of course," Kyle responded automatically, knowing what would happen if he said no.

"I'm just here for a few days, so I don't need to go to the trouble to get my own room. It would be time to leave by the time I got settled in."

Kyle knew that was code for "I don't have any money," and he realized the reason Andy was here. He wanted Kyle to give him money. His head snapped back to Andy. He heard him say, "We were roommates for a while in Ohio. We were taking a self-improvement course while Kyle here was in college. It was one of those required team-building things, you know, all for one and one for all."

He looked slyly at Kyle, who suddenly understood. If he didn't give Andy what he wanted, Andy would blow his cover.

Kyle threw some money on the counter to cover his uneaten lunch and Andy's coffee and Sandra's tip.

"Thanks, Sandra, but Andy and I haven't seen each other for a while. There's a lot to catch up on." He steered Andy out of the store, calling "Bye, Sandra," as he went.

She smiled and picked up the money, calculating how much her tip would be and wondering why she felt so creeped out by Andy Potter.

* * *

Scottie Lambert scooted through town in his fire-engine-red Mini Cooper. He did not like making house calls, especially when it involved leaving Pittsburgh for the nether regions. But Autumn had been one of his best clients, and despite their professional separation, they had become good friends. For the past few weeks she had not returned his phone calls or emails, so he had little choice but to force a face-to-face meeting, whether she liked it or not. He had a feeling she was in trouble.

"Yoo-hoo," he called as he poked his head in the side door that led into Autumn's kitchen. She hadn't answered the doorbell, and the door was unlocked, so he let himself in.

"Dear sweet Jesus," he said aloud, surveying the mess around him. Pizza boxes and takeout containers littered the island, as if Autumn had just fed a football team, but the dried-up pieces of sausage and Chinese fried rice made it perfectly clear that the containers had been here a while. Dishes were stacked up in the sink, and there was a stack of unopened mail on the counter.

"I promise, as God as my witness, that I will stop eating Twizzlers," he said to himself as he wandered back toward the studio. "Just please do not let her be dead."

As he approached the closed door he was half afraid that he would smell that horrible odor of a decomposing body, but only the pungent scent of paint and turpentine met his nostrils.

He knocked on the door, and when she didn't answer he just barged in.

"Autumn, you have had me frantic with worry," he began. "I half expected to find you dead on the floor..." he cut himself off as he surveyed the canvases around him.

"Geez, Scottie, you scared me out of my mind," Autumn reproached him, as he circled the room, his eyes feasting on her work. "What are you doing here?"

Scottie didn't answer her as he approached a canvas with a silvery-white geranium stalk poised beautifully in a glass vase. Walking in a tight circle, weaving in and out of the petals, was a tiny army of matchstick people, marching in a row like a colony of ants.

He stepped closer and cupped his chin in his hand and eyed the painting from two inches away.

"If you would answer your phone, dear friend, I would not have had to seek you out and disturb your work." He turned to her. "This is brilliant, Autumn. I've never seen anything like it."

For the first time in weeks, Autumn actually took a long, deep breath, feeling a weight lift off of her shoulders.

"Do you really think so?" she asked tentatively.

Scottie turned to look at her and really saw her for the first time.

CHAPTER 16

"Good grief, Autumn. When was the last time you took a shower? No offense, but you look like one of those homeless witnesses hauled in to talk with Benson and Stabler on *Law & Order: Special Victims Unit*."

Autumn fiddled nervously with her shirt and tried to pat her hair back. "I've been in a sort of vortex," she said. "I can't explain it. I've been blocked for so long, and suddenly it all came rushing out, and I couldn't stop. Do you really like it, Scottie? I mean, really, as in you think you can sell it?"

"Sell it? Darling, it's going to sell itself. It's incredibly striking and strong, and the childlike vulnerability of the tiny stick people is jarring because it is so unexpected. It's like a child took a black crayon to a museum masterpiece. It's haunting. I can't take my eyes off of it. How many more of these do you have?"

Autumn walked out of the studio, and Scottie followed her up the stairs. Lining the wall on the second-floor foyer were a dozen more of the magnificent floral paintings with the tiny stick-figure motifs, each one that much better executed than the next. He was scrambling for words he couldn't find when he heard the front door bang and Meg's voice calling, "Where is she? Is she dead? What the hell's going on?"

"We're up here, and she's not dead," Scottie called cheerfully. "Definitely not dead."

"Meg, what are you doing here?" Autumn asked, trying not to sound irritated, and hoping there wasn't anyone else on the way over. Her mind irrationally jumped to an image of Ethan in his office looking at her wild hair and insane artist's outfit.

"Geez, what is that smell?" she complained. "Who are you, and what have you done with my best friend? Autumn, you look terrible."

"Thanks, best friend."

"I called her on my way over," Scottie explained, glancing thankfully at Meg. "I didn't know what I was going to find, and I asked her to meet me here in case it was your corpse."

"So I guess I'm not the only one you've been blowing off," Meg said, her anger receding as she swiveled to take in the paintings.

"Wow," Meg said, pivoting to take it all in. "These are so weird, but I like them, you know."

When she didn't respond, Meg and Scottie turned to look at their friend. She was sitting on the top stair, tears streaming down her face. Meg went to her side instantly.

"Oh, Autumn, what's the matter?"

"I was so sure I was dried up," Autumn hiccuped. "You can't imagine the terror I felt for the past year. I don't know how to do anything else but paint, and the thought that I wouldn't be able to do that anymore..." her voice trailed off, and she looked at Scottie. "Anyway, I didn't want to call you because I was afraid it wasn't real. I had to make sure that it wasn't just a fluke."

Scottie sat down next to them. "Baby, it ain't no fluke. When I get done with you the whole world is going to know who Autumn Hamilton is."

Autumn grinned. "I thought they already did."

"Only half the world, hon. This will seal the deal with the rest of them."

"What do you mean the terror you felt for the last year?" Meg demanded. "I don't remember you mentioning anything about any terror during the, say, thousand times we've seen, phoned, texted, or messaged each other in the past 365 days."

"That's because I didn't want anyone to know. I was too

ashamed."

"Ashamed of what?"

"I don't know, exactly. That I was tapped out. A failure. That I was so lonely and empty that there was nothing left inside of me worth painting about."

After Scottie had left Meg insisted that Autumn take a shower. "And for your own sake, and mine, shave your legs," she commanded. "I don't even want to think about what kind of forest you have growing on your calves."

Autumn emerged thirty minutes later, clean and refreshed, and found Meg bagging up a sack of trash in the kitchen.

"You sure you didn't have a frat party in here?" she asked good-humoredly, throwing the mostly empty cartons of Chinese takeout into the trash bag.

Autumn went to the stove and put the kettle on for tea. "It was better than a frat party," she answered.

"Why didn't you tell me this was happening to you?" Meg asked gently. "I had no idea. I feel so stupid that I couldn't see that you were suffering."

"I didn't want you to know," Autumn admitted, as she waited for the water to boil. "I hid it from you, from everybody. I'm sorry about that."

"I just don't understand, Autumn," Meg said, accepting a mug of tea from Autumn. "I know I'm not the most sensitive of people. But I'd like to think that you feel you can trust me with this type of thing."

"Well," Autumn said slowly. "You are kind of difficult to approach, even for me sometimes."

"Am not."

"Are too."

"Am not. Now help me get this trash out. The kitchen's starting to smell as bad as you did."

* * *

Sheriff Landry, as promised, had canvassed the neighborhood following the burglary attempt at the Greystone Manor, but as one might expect, no one had seen anything out of the ordinary.

And Duncan, unable to stand by and do nothing, decided to make a quick visit to Jack's nursery a week after the robbery. It was against his better judgment, but the words of his guests echoed in his mind, reminding him that Jack had been seen at the windows a lot. He chided himself the entire way, telling himself he was making a big mistake.

When he got out of the car at the nursery, he surveyed the garden center, which was neat and tidy as it always was with wreaths, pine roping, and Christmas trees artfully arranged. He walked inside, past the tables filled with poinsettias and boxes of Christmas tree lights. Jack was nowhere to be seen, so he called out his name.

"Over here," was the muffled reply, and he followed the sound of the voice to the back of the shop where Jack was standing on a ladder, rearranging boxes.

"Hey there, Duncan," Jack said when he spotted him. "How about giving me a hand down?" he asked. "I'm a bit stiff in the knees today."

Duncan moved to the ladder and anchored it with his weight while Jack made his way down slowly. He stared at the old man's face and hands but saw no fresh scratches or marks.

"What can I do you for?" Jack asked when he stepped off and

limped over to the cash register counter, where he made a few notes in a ledger. "Something wrong with the landscaping?"

"Ah, oh, no, no, it's great," Duncan stammered. "I just needed, ah…" He cursed himself for not coming up with a cover story. Jack turned to stare at him as he stumbled along. "I'm thinking of putting an arbor out near the back patio. Just wanted to see what you had along those lines."

Jack looked at him with a strange expression. "Well, Duncan, with the snow on its way any day now I'm not sure now is the time to start planning a flowering arbor or trellis. You really should wait till spring."

"Oh, right," Duncan replied. "I was just planning ahead. That's all."

"Ahuh," Jack responded as he went back to his ledger. "Anything else you need?"

"Oh, no, that's it really. Just wanted to think about future projects, you know, for spring." Duncan wanted desperately to change the subject. "So, did you hurt yourself or something?"

Jack looked at him quizzically, and Duncan motioned toward the ladder. "No, just get stiff sometimes," he said. "Can't move like I used to. I think I overdid it last week on some special projects. Joints burning a bit these days, but I'll be all right. Thanks for asking."

"Okay, then," Duncan said. "Well, you coming out this afternoon to finish with the boxwoods?"

"I'll be there unless somehow you changed your mind from what we talked about yesterday."

"Oh, right. I forgot. No, we're good."

Jack hung the ladder back on the wall hooks.

"You feeling all right, Duncan?" he asked, peering at him in that hard way he had about him. Duncan nodded, said good-bye, and walked out to the Greystone's passenger van, wiping his clammy hands on his khakis. He was about to open the door when he heard Jack calling after him.

"Wait a second, Duncan. There's something I forgot to tell you."

Duncan turned as Jack came to stand beside him.

"I've been keeping an eye on some of your indoor plants from the first-floor windows." He chuckled and looked down at his boots. "Didn't want to muddy up your rugs. Anyway, you need to move that fig tree in the lobby to one of the south-facing windows in the library. And if you let up on watering the Christmas cactus it will bloom before too long."

Duncan stared at him, dumbfounded.

"You sure you're okay, son?" Jack was staring at him, hands on hips, a perplexed look on his face.

"Yeah, Jack," he said, shaking his head at himself in disgust. "It's all good. See you later today?"

Jack nodded and watched Duncan drive away. *Couldn't be drugs*, Jack thought to himself, *but there was definitely something squirrely about Duncan.*

CHAPTER 17

*M*ARTHA HAD INVITED Autumn and Meg to join her at the Greystone Manor for the Thanksgiving meal, and they readily accepted, eagerly anticipating the Thanksgiving brunch that was the stuff of legend. When they were seated at a cozy table next to a roaring fire, Autumn glimpsed Kyle sitting by himself at the bar and watching a football game.

Meg followed Autumn's gaze, and she locked her eyes on hers. "Don't you dare," Meg commanded. "I know what you're thinking."

Autumn just smiled. "Have you looked at the website he did for you yet?"

"How did you know about that?" Meg asked, surprised.

"You told me, remember? And so did Kyle. So, have you looked at it yet?"

"I've just been so busy, you know, with all the pregnant dogs."

"Uh huh," Autumn answered, disbelieving. "So, let me rephrase: do you *plan* on looking at it?"

"I'll get around to it."

And Autumn knew she would, eventually. Meg did everything in her own time, and there was nothing she or anyone else could do to budge her when she had made up her mind about something—or even when she refused to make up her mind about something.

Meg changed the subject and asked Martha, "How are Ethan and Heather doing?"

Much to Autumn's surprise, Martha's face lit up at the mention of her granddaughter. Autumn had expected to see sadness since Ethan had not brought Heather for the holiday.

"She is doing so well," Martha enthused. "She takes that art therapy class, and Ethan's trying to talk her into violin lessons, but she says she can't because her dolls and teddy bear need her full attention at the moment. Apparently, they are moving from one side of her bedroom to the other, and she has a lot of packing to do."

"That child has quite an imagination," Autumn laughed, pleased that Ethan was trying to nurture the creative side of her.

As an afterthought, she asked, "And how does Ethan seem to be coping?"

Martha laughed. "I think his adjustment period is going to be longer than hers. Kids are really resilient, but us adults, well, we're stuck in our ways, especially a bachelor like Ethan. His biggest challenge, he said, is the morning routine, getting Heather dressed, fed, and out the door on time. He's given up on a hot breakfast, though he says he gives her hot chocolate made with those instant powder packets on particularly cold mornings."

"Oh, no!" Meg interrupted before Autumn could respond. "He's seen us, and he's coming over."

Kyle, wearing his typical dark jeans with a crisp dress shirt, cuffs loose, joined them at the table.

"Happy Thanksgiving, everyone," he said cheerfully.

Autumn introduced Martha, and with a Cheshire cat grin for Meg, Martha asked him to join them.

He looked at the empty fourth chair. "Well, if you don't mind. Just for a minute. I've already eaten," he motioned toward the bar.

"Well you can at least have a piece of pie and coffee while we eat our dinner," Martha insisted, and he sat down as the waitress came by with a place setting and he ordered apple pie à la mode and coffee.

"Are you ready for the big day tomorrow?" Autumn asked. "Biggest shopping day of the year."

"I better be," he laughed. "They're counting on me. Actually, I am ready. I've whipped that group into shape. You saw how well they did at the Halloween pet parade. I'm expecting at least to double that."

Autumn tried to steer the conversation toward the subject of Meg's website. "How many websites did you end up creating for the merchants?" she asked, not looking at Meg, but feeling a swift kick under the table.

"Last count it was eleven." Then he smiled at Meg. "And counting yours that's twelve." He played with his coffee cup and asked, "Have you had a chance to look at it yet?"

"Not yet. It's not at the top of my priority list right at the moment," Meg responded blandly, adding, "I'll get around to it."

Kyle stared at her, disbelieving. Had she really just said she was actually going to look at it? True, she said it with as much enthusiasm as if she were talking about flea dip, but she had said it, and he felt his heart flutter as a wide smile spread across his face.

"Well, I think you'll really like it when you have a look. I hope you will, anyway." He turned his attention to Martha and Autumn. "Can I interest you ladies in some mega shopping tomorrow? I can tell you where all the hot sales are."

"We'll be there," Martha promised, and Autumn nodded her agreement, then forcibly nudged Meg's shoulder and looked at her expectantly.

"Better count me out," Meg offered, not *too* unpleasantly. "I've got two Shepherds about ready to birth and three others that are sick. Plus, the canine unit from Buffalo is coming for a pickup. Can't believe I let Sammy off for the holiday. Don't know what I was thinking. You won't see me for the next two days at least. And don't bother calling because I won't be answering the phone either."

"Okay, then," Autumn responded. "That will give me a chance to pick up your Christmas present from Stan's 'everything's a dollar' bin at the hardware store."

As they ate their dinner and listened to Martha's stories about Heather and Autumn's plans for an upcoming exhibit in Pittsburgh, Kyle snuck sideways glances at Meg and wondered how a woman could look so darn gorgeous in a plaid flannel shirt, blue jeans, and Doc Martens. He had noticed that this uniform of Meg's did not change regardless of the occasion. Martha was wearing a chocolate-brown pantsuit, and Autumn wore black dress pants and a beautiful russet-colored merino wool sweater with a silk scarf tied around her neck. No doubt about it, Autumn was beautiful and chic, but Meg had that natural, girl-next-door beauty that enchanted him. He half expected that she was the kind of woman who didn't know how beautiful she was. And he seriously hoped he would have the opportunity to take her into his arms and tell her some day.

During the meal, Autumn was pleased to notice that Meg had been almost nice to Kyle, passing him the sugar packets without rolling her eyes and remarking on how the revival of the commercial district was so important to the town. *That was as close to a compliment as Meg would give*, she thought.

* * *

Meg knew her expectant mothers would be fine without her. Dogs have been having puppies on their own for eons. But she so enjoyed the process, to be right there when it happened. She was a sucker for the little cuties, and she wanted to make sure there were no complications.

She sat there in a padded folding chair, utilizing the mirrors Sammy strategically hung from the kennel ceiling. From her vantage point she could see directly down into the two facing kennels. Meg had made sure there were no other dogs anywhere near the two mothers-to-be and spread big, fluffy beach towels and old bed comforters on the floor in case either one felt the instinctual need to make a nest of sorts. The shepherd moms were both lying on their sides, one seeming much more nervous than the other, panting and whining.

"Okay, girls," she said, completely out of earshot. "I'm ready when you are. Fancy don't let me down. Neither one of you."

As she was waiting for the pups, Meg picked up her laptop and on a whim decided she would finally take a peek at whatever atrocious and unnecessary website Kyle had forced upon her. She couldn't remember the web address, so she scrolled down her emails until she found the one from Kyle and read, "The site's not live yet, but you can still visit all the pages and click on all the links. Hope you like it. And make sure you scroll down to the very end of the 'Contact Us' page." He ended with a smiley face emoji.

Really? What guy uses emojies?

She clicked on the link in the email and immediately thought she was on the wrong site. This was so professional! Then she realized it was very much the right site. There was a picture of her, holding Spike! Wow. She recalled Kyle incessantly following her around at the dog parade, taking her picture against her will, over and over, and how angry she had been at him. Now, looking at a picture of her hugging Spike to her chest, she was flooded with mixed emotions.

She clicked on the "Our History" tab and was blown away. There were pictures of her parents when they first started out, of Ten Oaks itself, of the early kennels, and even a picture of her when she was about ten years old. How on earth did Kyle get that? There were links to old newspaper articles and testimonials from customers. There was a list of former and current customers. Meg couldn't believe how long the list was.

She thought to herself, *if people see this, my business is gonna go through the roof! I'm gonna have to hire more staff. At least make Sammy full time.*

Remembering Kyle's email, she clicked over to the "Contact Us" page and scrolled down. At the bottom of the page, in bold red letters, were the words "Meg, Click Here." She did and was immediately taken to the video of an old ABBA concert, with the singers belting out one of their old hits, "Take a Chance on Me."

She watched the video, stunned at the gesture. He must have remembered that she was listening to ABBA the night he surprised her. At the end of the video she clicked replay and watched it again. This was the nicest thing anyone, aside from her parents, had ever done for her. She felt like she might either burst into tears or break her face smiling.

She glanced up at the mirror just in time to see a new puppy in the kennel. She snapped her laptop closed and rushed in to comfort the new mom, with Kyle very much on her mind.

* * *

Ethan dreaded spending Thanksgiving with Ellen's very stiff and formal, not to mention boring and pretentious, family in Connecticut. He was particularly torn because he worried that Martha would resent him for not bringing Heather home for the holiday. But he had promised her they would be together for Christmas, and that seemed to satisfy her. If Martha had to choose between the two, Christmas would be her choice. He had agreed to go to Connecticut to appease Ellen, to do something proactive to work on improving their relationship, which quite frankly, had not been that great lately. And he was going to have to do something about how she treated Heather. And soon.

Convincing Heather to leave her Barbies at home, Ethan piled all her other little girl stuff in the car. They picked up Ellen and were on their way to Connecticut. Ellen had not even greeted Heather, Ethan observed, inwardly seething. It was becoming more and more apparent to him that he might have to sacrifice his relationship with Ellen for Heather's sake. And, perhaps, his own.

Dinner was served by a housekeeper in a cold, formal dining

room with highly polished sideboards and sterling-silver serving dishes and table settings. Ellen's mother tried to put Heather at a "children's table" in the kitchen with the live-in housekeeper's ten-year-old son. Appalled at the suggestion, Ethan had refused, and another place setting was laid for Heather, who tentatively took her seat, unsure of what she had done wrong.

And things just got worse from there. After dinner, Ellen's father took him into his office and had a "what are your intentions with my daughter?" conversation, which Ethan deftly navigated with generalities and some successful attempts to change the subject by flattering the man, who he knew loved to talk about himself.

As he left the office to find Heather and Ellen, he stopped in his tracks as he heard Ellen's voice coming from the dining room, where she and her mother were finishing dessert. Heather was playing with the housekeeper's son in the kitchen, he suspected, because Ellen was talking about boarding school.

"I'm just at the end of my rope, Mother," she complained in a whisper that Ethan could hear. He had tiptoed to the door of the dining room and lurked outside. "Ethan is spending less and less time with me, and I'm afraid I'm losing him. If I can talk him into sending Heather to Beacon Academy she would be close enough for regular visits, but far enough away that she won't be part of his regular routine. Of *our* regular routine."

"Do you think he'd even consider that?" Ellen's mother whispered back.

"You sent me when I was eight. Heather's five. That's not much different. And look how well I turned out!"

Ethan couldn't help it. He snorted a laugh and, having revealed his presence, had to make an entrance into the dining room, pre-

CHAPTER 17

tending he hadn't heard the conversation.

"Ready to go?" he asked.

The drive home was quiet. Heather slept, and Ethan, still taken aback by Ellen's yet to be proposed plan for Heather, was forming his thoughts for the conversation he'd have to have once Heather went to bed.

"It's not working, El, for either of us," Ethan began as they sat on the couch with brandy after he had tucked Heather in bed. "And I think you know that, too. You're not cut out for this. And I totally understand that you didn't sign up for this when we first started dating."

"You're breaking up with me?" Ellen screeched. "You can't be serious. After four years you're just cutting me loose? That's absurd. You owe me, Ethan. I gave you some of the best years of my life."

Ethan was silent as she raged on.

"I can't believe you're going to let a five-year-old child dominate your life. She's a child, Ethan. You can't make your decisions based on her."

"And I can't believe you would even consider sending a five-year-old child to boarding school," he said coldly. He was trying to be gentle and kind, but he hadn't expected her venomous reaction.

Ellen sat up straighter and picked imaginary lint off her skirt, not meeting Ethan's eyes.

"So now you're eavesdropping and spying on me?" she demanded accusingly.

"No, I just happened to be coming out of your father's office and walking down the hall when I accidentally overheard your conversation," he replied calmly. "You must know, in your heart of hearts, that I would never send Heather to boarding school, even if she hadn't just experienced a horrible tragedy."

At that moment, they both turned toward the noise coming from the long hallway that led to the bedrooms, where Heather stood crying and hiccupping, wondering what she had done to make Ellen so mad at Ethan.

Ethan was at her side in an instant, and as he comforted his precious cherub, he heard Ellen's high heels clicking across the hardwood floor to the front door, where she let herself out.

Holding a sobbing Heather, who was apologizing for making Ellen angry and promising to be good from now on, Ethan knew, without a sliver of doubt, that he had made the right decision, and he chastised himself for not doing it sooner.

CHAPTER 18

*K*YLE WAS UP, dressed, and walking on Pittsburgh Street by 7 a.m. on Black Friday, riding high on the success of the Halloween pet parade shopping bonanza. He felt like it was the first day of school, or like he was sending his child off to college. Whatever it was, he knew he was nervous, and excited. He had worked so hard for this day, and once the mayor saw what he was capable of, perhaps the daily anxiety that plagued him might lessen.

"Oh, Kyle," he heard Miss Elsie call to him as he passed her shop. "Come help me for a minute? There's a dear," and she held her shop door wide open. He stepped into a store transformed. Fully decorated Christmas trees, at least five of them, sat throughout the shop, twinkling and sparkling at him to the point where he thought he might go blind if he didn't look away. Garlands, bows, wreaths, and candy canes were placed throughout the shop. While it was stuffed to point of exploding, it was charming with its cozy and welcoming ambiance. He could already smell spiced apple cider wafting in from the kitchen, and on each table, was a three-tiered plate holder, each stuffed with tiny cakes and cookies. She must have been up all night baking. He stared at her, openmouthed.

"There, on the top," he heard her say.

"What? Ah, sorry, Miss Elsie. Sorry, I was so dazzled by your decorations, I didn't hear you."

"Oh, that's all right, dear. I'm pretty dazzled myself. I was up all night. But I can't reach the tops of the trees, and I'm not sure I should go up on the ladder. Be a lamb and put the stars on the tops, please? Oh, and keep your fingers off of the cakes, mind you. I want to make sure I have enough for the shoppers."

He heard someone behind him and turned to see Andy come into the store.

"Why Andy, love, it's so nice of you to come and help your friend. Here, take a star and place it atop that tree by the register. You're tall. You won't need a ladder. Just watch you don't knock anything down."

As she bustled away and disappeared into the kitchen, Andy gave Kyle a smirk.

"Dude," he said. "You didn't think I would abandon my friend on his big day, didya? Everyone's been talking about 'Kyle said this' and 'Kyle said that.' You got these people loving all over you, man."

When Andy had disappeared after a few days of hanging out in his room at the Greystone Manor, eating his food and watching on-demand movies on cable, he thought he had seen the last of him. How calculated of him to return today of all days. Was he going to choose today of all days to ruin everything for him?

"Just put the star on the tree and get out of here."

Kyle watched as Andy walked to the back of the store then pointed to the register and laughed.

"They are eating out of your hand, man. You could take anything you wanted from under their noses, and they wouldn't even notice."

"Hey," Kyle hissed. "I don't do that, and you know it. Mine was a special circumstance."

Andy mimicked him and walked out of the shop, and Kyle watched as he headed for the IGA with one of his twenty-dollar bills in his pocket.

With Andy out of sight, Kyle left Miss Elsie's and continued his rounds down Pittsburgh Street, amazed at what the merchants had done. Stan had ordered an immense quantity of less than twenty dollar tools geared toward "lady shoppers," as he called them, looking for gifts for fathers, husbands, grandfathers, and uncles. He and Kyle had gone back and forth on that decision.

"I just don't know about laying out all that cash up front like that," Stan had told him. "It's a big risk, especially with January and February being so slow and all."

"Just trust me," Kyle had told him. "I know what I'm doing." And together they had written posts, tweets, and Facebook ads geared toward female shoppers. It was a brilliant strategy, and Stan had been giddy with anticipation.

Kyle stopped to admire Stan's display—boxes of electric drills, screwdriver sets, socket sets, and various versions of two-in-one tools—that towered above him.

"Wow, Stan, this is a little over the top, don't you think?"

"Well, I thought about what you said, and I decided to double the order." Stan patted Kyle so hard on the back that he thought he would fall into the display. "I just thought what the heck! Kyle knows what he's doing. I'm all in!" And he moved around to the other side of the display to stack more boxes.

Teppy Eicher had created a type of scavenger hunt for shoppers as an incentive to visit multiple merchants. The more shops they visited, the more discounts and gift cards they received. With Kyle's help, Teppy adopted a white Christmas theme in her Christmas boutique, dressing the entire shop with white and silver ornaments and decorations. In the window, she had placed a dressmaker's form dressed in a white tutu and streams of white and silver ribbons and bows. Yards of white velvet draped elegantly behind it, and white Christmas lights hung from the folds. The result was stunning. And with Kyle's help she displayed her merchandise in the shop to show that all the white items were available in multiple colors.

The Merchants Association had decided that the shops would open at nine in the morning in order to catch the shoppers when they completed their big-box raids. Santa would stroll and greet shoppers from eleven to one, and the high school choral singers dressed as carolers would sing their way around town from four to six in the afternoon. Stores would stay open as long as there were shoppers on the streets.

Kyle felt as if he were making his directorial debut, waiting to pull open the curtain and step onto the stage. At nine sharp Mayor Brightwell joined him on the sidewalk in front of the Burnt Orange Antiques Emporium. A few minutes later he watched as Andy, holding a can of soda and a huge candy bar, sauntered up and joined them.

"Hi there, Mayor," he said, not offering his hand. "I'm Kyle's friend from way back, Andy Potter. You must be so proud of him."

The mayor looked at Kyle. "He just came to see me today, you know, for moral support," Kyle lied, not knowing what else to say.

"Yeah," Andy echoed around a mouthful of chocolate bar. "Where we come from, we helped each other out all the time. It's better that way. You know?" He hugged Kyle around the neck. "When you've been through what we've been through together, well, that creates a kind of bond, you know?"

The mayor, in fact, did know, having asked Sheriff Landry to do a background check on Andy. What she couldn't understand was what his intentions were with Kyle. She chose to ignore what he had said, looking away from him to take in the street. Laughing, Andy walked off.

That was one problem gone, for now, Kyle thought.

But he had bigger ones on his hands. Where were the crowds? He had flooded the market with social media, advertising, and radio spots. Only people living in caves would not have heard about Finch's Crossing's holiday sales and the day's extravaganza. Painfully aware of the mayor beside him, Kyle watched miserably as a few cars appeared and the shoppers dribbled in like a slow leak from a faucet. They sauntered in and out of the shops, some making purchases, some just browsing. All he could see in his mind was the massive amount of food Miss Elsie had prepared for the anticipated crowds of shoppers. He thought of her tiny frame, standing at attention by the front door in her flashing antler headgear, waiting to welcome the shoppers that weren't coming nearly fast enough.

At noon, a van from the retirement home deposited a small group of seniors for their weekly shopping, and they headed straight for the IGA and drugstore. The afternoon was better. Done with the big-box stores, a tiny fraction of the number of shoppers Kyle had expected straggled along Pittsburgh Street in a pitiful stream.

Mayor Peggy had driven around town rousting people from their homes, as she sometimes did on Election Day, asking them to get over to Pittsburgh Street to do their part to support their town.

She returned around five to find Kyle sitting alone in the gazebo, his head in his hands.

"It was a disappointing turnout," she said, trying not to sound angry with the young man on whom she had hung the town's hopes.

"That's a nice way to put it," he replied dully. "It was nothing short of a complete disaster. And do you know what's even worse? I can't explain it. I have no idea how this happened. It simply makes no sense whatsoever. I optimized their websites and showed them how to use social media. I set up online advertising, wrote their press releases, and set up radio interviews."

She patted him on the back. "With this crew, what doesn't make sense to you now might make perfect sense in the grand scheme of things. There's an explanation out there among them. I'm certain of that. Even if they don't know it."

"Huh?"

"Are you sure they followed all of your directions?" she asked.

"Well, I set everything up for them and showed them what to do; I just assumed they would actually do it."

Peggy raised her eyebrows, so he continued.

"I went through everything with each one of them in preparation for the pet parade, and that *was* a success, remember? They watched me, and I made sure each one of them took a turn at the computer. Then I left detailed, step-by-step instructions in a sort of cheat sheet." Kyle was waving his hands wildly. "And they were simple instructions—I made sure of that, too. With examples. And screenshots. That was part of my mission here, not just to do all the projects myself, but to show the merchants how things worked so they could assume the tasks after I'm gone."

The mayor nodded her head in agreement. The more he talked, the more he realized it didn't matter what he said, because it didn't matter what he had done. It obviously hadn't worked.

"If I were you, I'd do a little checking up on them," Peggy said when he was done explaining.

"I'm too embarrassed to face them," he muttered. "What must they all think of me? They trusted me. They put their livelihoods in my hands, and I let them down."

"Well, if it makes you feel any better," Peggy offered, "it's better than last year."

"Yeah, but their financial investment this year is greater, and if they don't make enough in return, they won't even break even, much less get ahead."

She couldn't argue with that.

"Listen, son," she said, as if she were speaking to her boys. "Why don't you try to find out what happened, and then let's talk. There might even be something you can do to turn this around before Christmas."

She watched as Kyle rose and walked away in the opposite direction of the commercial district. He was taking the long way back to the Greystone Manor, she guessed, to avoid seeing anyone. She couldn't blame him. They were very much in the same position. It was she who had brought Kyle on. If he failed, then by default, she failed. She thought back to the file Sheriff Landry had shown her. He had been right. There was nothing there to tie Kyle to the burglaries. But there had been plenty to be concerned about then. And there was even more to be concerned about now. Had he actually done what he said he would do? She had no way of checking on him since she knew so little about the kind of work he did. Maybe he had slacked off his responsibilities because he was involved with a burglary ring. She hated thinking that way, but she was the mayor after all, and it was she who had to look the facts hard in the face and make the tough decisions.

Back at the Greystone Manor, Kyle sat in front of his computer and accessed every social media account and website he had set up in the past weeks. With each click he sank deeper and deeper into despair. He couldn't believe what he was seeing. He had been so careful with them, but obviously setting them free to do their own work was like letting children loose in a candy store unsupervised.

Somehow Teppy, whose Et Cetera Boutique and Christmas Shop was perhaps the most important shop in town, had managed to knock her website down completely. Stan seemed to have disabled all of his social media accounts, and when Kyle searched, he could not find one of the Facebook ads he had so carefully written to attract Stan's "lady shoppers." Somebody went behind him on Miss Elsie's website and rewrote all of his carefully worded prose designed to put her shop at the top of Google's search results. He called the local radio station only to learn that when the news reporter had phoned at the prearranged times for interviews, the merchants had put him off, not understanding that their interviews had been carefully scheduled for a certain time slot. Only Stan had been ready at the appointed time, but he was so nervous and tongue-tied that his interview lasted thirteen seconds, and the station was forced to go to commercial due to "technical trouble."

Then he looked at their tweets. He had carefully given them a list of keywords to use in their tweets. And with the alert system he had set up, they could tweet back to people who expressed interest in the area or in products or services they offered. It was foolproof. Or so he thought.

Some of them had forgotten that they only had 280 characters. They must have kept typing until they had finished their message and not seen that only the first 280 characters made it onto the screen. He clicked over to Miss Elsie's Tea Room's Twitter page and looked at her last tweet. She hadn't even made a point by the time her 280 characters were used up. And no one used the hashtag phrases he had given them.

And it just got worse and worse. He forced himself to take extensive notes as he reviewed the wreckage of his work. The only saving grace was that at least it was not all his fault. He may have been dealing with adults, but from what he could see, he would have to hold their hands and keep his eye on them as if they were kindergartners.

The next day he knew he had to face everyone, but was secure in the knowledge that the disastrous shopping day had not been completely his fault. He grabbed his messenger bag and headed out.

Despite his trepidation of the conversations to come, he enjoyed the walk from the Manor and through the quiet residential streets clustered around the commercial district.

His first stop was Miss Elsie's. He had to wait while she finished waiting on a group of ladies wearing gigantic red hats, so he took a seat by the window and powered up his laptop. One of the young girls who worked there part time, brought him a soda and a plate of cookies, giving him a sympathetic smile.

The wind had picked up, and the weatherman had said it would be extremely cold that night. Looking at his reflection in the window, he reminded himself how lucky he was, despite his recent failure, that he had a warm place to live and enough food to eat. Just a year ago he had been living in his van. He had been laid off from his job in a warehouse distribution center where he worked nights and was forced to choose between paying rent on his apartment or paying his tuition for his last semester at the technical college in Cleveland. It wasn't that bad being homeless, he told himself at the time, especially since he had *chosen* to be homeless. And he had his van. He still had enough food to eat and looked clean and presentable every day, thanks to the showers in the college's fitness center. His van's license and registration were up to date, and as long as he parked it in a different spot in the student parking lot every day he felt safe. For a long time, campus police never suspected anything. He stayed late studying at the library until it closed at 11 p.m. He knew that the campus police finished their rounds by one in the morning, so he moved his van down the street and waited then moved it back to the campus, hoping no one would notice. It had been freezing through March, though. Some nights he wore every piece of clothing he owned and slept under five blankets and comforters he had bought cheap from the Goodwill, and still he nearly froze.

When Miss Elsie joined him at his table, she was wiping her hands on a dish towel.

"Sorry for the wait," she apologized. "The Red Hat Society ladies meet here once a month, and it's all hands on deck. Between you and me, I think they're multiplying." She folded her hands and put them on the table in front of her. "So, what did you want to see me about?"

Kyle looked around the tea room, which was still as stuffed with decorations as the day before.

"What did you do with all that food?" he asked, barely able to

CHAPTER 18

cough out the words that only made him feel more miserable.

"Oh, don't you worry about that. Stan took it over to the men's shelter in Mt. Pleasant. It won't go to waste. Live and learn, that's what I say. Live and learn. Now don't take this the wrong way, dear, but I knew all this SEO business wasn't going to work, but I wanted to support the mayor."

"But, Miss Elsie," Kyle began, needing to tread delicately, "you see, there were a lot of problems with the way you and all merchants handled the things I set up."

"Oh?"

He plunged on. "I'm not saying it's your fault or anything."

"Well I should hope not," she responded, straightening her tiny frame in the chair and jutting her chin out.

"Well, let's look at your tweeting, for example," he said cautiously.

"Oh, yes," she chimed in. "I am tweeting several times a week just like you said. It's actually fun."

"I'm sure it is, but here's the thing, Miss Elsie. Your tweets aren't really getting any useful messages out there." He hated to see her smile turn so quickly into a frown. "But don't worry," he rushed to say. "We can totally fix this." He turned his computer around so they could both look at it. "For example, this tweet here."

Miss Elsie read aloud, "'Hello My Dear Current, and hopefully new, Customers. This is Miss Elsie and I'd like to introduce you to my little shop, Miss Elsie's Tea Room....' Well, what happened to the rest of it?" she asked, incredulous. "I had a whole bit there about coming to Finch's Crossing and relaxing with tea and cider after a long day of shopping."

"Remember what I told you about the 280 character limit?" Kyle prompted.

"Well, yes," she bristled. "But I didn't think you were serious. That's the stupidest thing I've ever heard."

"Okay," said Kyle. "Well, all that aside, you *really* only have 280 characters—that means letters and punctuation—so you have to be succinct and get to the point." He gestured at the next line of text. "Here, I've written an example of a good tweet."

Again, Miss Elsie read aloud. "'Holiday sales this wknd, Finch's Crossing, shop then relax with hot tea/cider at Miss Elsie's, Pburgh St.' Well that's not even grammatically correct," she complained. "And all those abbreviations, no one is going to know what I'm talking about."

Kyle reached out his hands and took Miss Elsie's gnarled fingers, hoping she wouldn't snatch them away. He had to find a way to reach her.

"Miss Elsie, will you just trust me on this? Just try it my way for a few weeks and see what happens. Okay? This time, I won't leave you alone. I will be with you every step of the way."

Miss Elsie smiled and squeezed his hands. "Well, all right, Kyle," she replied. "We'll try it your way. But only for a little while. Now, if you will excuse me, I need to catch up on my correspondence."

"Oh?" Kyle asked hopefully. "Like your email?"

"Don't be ridiculous," Miss Elsie shot back. "I'm talking about good old-fashioned letter writing. Putting pen to paper and letting people know that you care enough to pick out a card just for them, write a heartfelt note, and take it to the post office."

Kyle imagined Miss Elsie sitting with the Red Hat ladies in the large banquet room at the back of the restaurant, sipping tea and writing letters.

CHAPTER 18

After he left Miss Elsie's Kyle had practically the same conversation with the other merchants. Confident that he had them all straightened out, he headed back up Chestnut Street and to the Greystone Manor to fix the rest of the problems they had caused.

I wonder if this is what it's like to have kids, he thought to himself.

CHAPTER 19

*K*YLE HAD THREE weeks to pull off the biggest retail recovery Finch's Crossing had ever seen. He knew exactly what he had to do. He just wasn't sure how he was going to do it. And between dodging Natalie's advances without losing her as a client and keeping track of Andy, he was mentally exhausted.

Using some of his own meager income, he invested in social media ads and Google pay-per-click ads. Within just a few days he was seeing more and more traffic on the merchants' websites, and his heart soared, just a little, with hopeful anticipation. He set up his own Twitter alarm for about fifty keywords and spent long hours into the night responding to tweets from people looking for Christmas bargains, holiday outings, and fun things to do. He would get the shoppers into Finch's Crossing one by one if it came to that.

After an exhaustive day spent on the social media project and

CHAPTER 19

designing ads to run in the *Westmoreland Gazette*, all he wanted was to finish a few press releases and then eat a quiet dinner in front of the television. He had some great ideas for news stories, and if things went as planned, Miss Elsie would be featured in the *Pittsburgh Post-Gazette* in a few days. It turned out that she had been giving her restaurant's leftovers to the homeless shelter in Mt. Pleasant for thirty years. If that wasn't worth a holiday story, he didn't know what was. He had taken a lot of photos of her tea room, all trussed up in its holiday splendor, and sent them and his newly written release to the Westmoreland County reporter at the *Pittsburgh Post-Gazette*. He had promised Kyle that he would take a look, and if it seemed like a good story, he'd be out to interview Miss Elsie. Kyle would be sure to have the mayor on hand as well. It would be an even more interesting twist if the reporter had known that he himself had been homeless at one point, and ate leftover food from a garbage can, but that he would keep to himself. He knew he would eventually have to tell the mayor about his past if he wanted to stay in Finch's Crossing. Even if no one discovered his secret, he knew he couldn't keep it hidden for ever.

Satisfied by his efforts, he made himself a sandwich and stretched out on the bed to watch the news. After only one bite he heard the familiar scratching at the door, and he felt the hairs on the back of his neck stand up at the sound. Andy had come back. He hopped off the bed and opened the door to a very disheveled-looking Andy with a nasty black eye and a cut lip. Andy didn't even say hello. He pushed past Kyle, plopped down on the bed, and picked up the sandwich.

"Hey," Kyle protested. "That's mine. I just made it."

"Well it's mine now," Andy grumbled and took a huge bite. "I need a soda or something."

Kyle tossed him a bottle of water from the tiny fridge and leaned against the bureau, bracing himself.

"What are you doing back here?" he asked coldly. "I've given you all the money I can. If I give you any more I won't have any for food." Kyle gestured at the sandwich Andy was devouring. "Like my dinner, for example." Fortunately, Andy had not caught on that Kyle didn't have to pay for his meals in the Manor restaurant.

"C'mon, man, can't you see I'm in trouble here?" Andy pointed at his eye.

"Yeah, you're trouble all right. What do you want, Andy?" Kyle was tired of playing this game with his former cellmate. Andy knew all about his story, having listened to the conversation he had had on a phone not far from the cell. He knew all about Kyle's shame and was using his pride to blackmail him.

"I just need a place to crash, okay? Just for a coupla days."

Kyle crossed his arms over his chest. "That's what you said last time, and now you're back."

Andy stood up and walked over to Kyle's desk, which was covered with papers, designs for ads, and his notes and photos. He ruffled through the papers. "Why do you care so much about these people, man? It's just a little hick town with nothing going on." He laughed. "Except maybe that tasty blonde we saw walking down the street last time I was here. Right? Remember?"

Oh, Kyle remembered all right how Andy had leered when he saw Meg walk past the drugstore where they were having lunch. He had to clench and unclench his fists to keep himself from punching the nasty grin off Andy's face.

"Hey, take it easy, man," Andy laughed. "I was just kidding. You look like you're gonna pop an artery or something."

CHAPTER 19

Andy stayed for a few days, eating his food, renting pay-per-view movies, and walking around town. When he came back to the hotel room, he loved to tell Kyle who he had spoken to and what they had said about him. And what he had said about Kyle. And then he just disappeared. One evening Kyle came home from a meeting with Teppy Eicher and Andy's things were gone, as well as the full contents of his fridge and eighty dollars Kyle had taped behind the mirror over the bureau. As relieved as he was to see him go, Kyle knew he would be back. He would always come back.

In the days that followed, Kyle continued his own rounds down Pittsburgh Street and through the residential neighborhoods, so beautifully decorated for the holidays. He had finally found a place to call home, and now, because of Andy, he was miserable again. And if things continued as they were, with Andy popping up every time he needed money or a place to stay, he'd have to move on and leave Finch's Crossing, and Meg, behind.

* * *

If she had to eat one more disgusting greasy hamburger, Natalie thought, she was going to puke, but the lunch counter at Hoffman's Drugstore had proven to be *the* place to pick up key information about the string of robberies everyone was talking about. It was here that she had learned a few weeks earlier that the sheriff suspected that the daytime burglar, as they were now calling him, was actually from Finch's Crossing, because he had broken into houses in a perimeter around the town, never hitting any homes in the community.

And today, the information she gleaned was no less informative. She sat boldly beside Sheriff Landry and Jack Staub, trying to balance on the stool despite her tight pencil skirt, munching on a cheeseburger, the grease dripping on the plate into a little pool.

"Any news on the burglaries, Sheriff?" she asked sweetly. "Any closer to catching him?"

Bud Landry had known Natalie her whole life. He had played golf with her father, Judge Prescott, and he knew the spiteful troublemaker she had been as a teenager.

"Any theory we did have was blown wide open when the Greystone was hit," he said. "We thought the culprit was one of us, seeing as he stayed away from here, but now I'm not so sure. I'm back to looking up toward the northern county, maybe up past Somerset, too. Haven't investigated there yet."

"Shame," Natalie said sweetly. "All that work gone to waste, and now you're back to square one." She slipped off her stool. She knew exactly which place she would hit next. "Nice talking to you, Sheriff."

Natalie walked jauntily down the block, thinking again of the Texas businesswoman whose creative business model had solved her own cash flow problem. She silently thanked the woman who burgled the homes of wealthy women during the day, stealing clothes, shoes, and accessories to sell in her consignment shop. Business hadn't picked up at the atelier, but with her new venture in play, Natalie could now pay the rent and keep the lights on. And she could hold her free poetry readings and avant-garde concerts, unconcerned if people came just for the free food. She was exposing them to the finer cultural offerings, and that was a start. It irked her that some people left after loading up on the food, but enough people were decent enough to stay. She did take some of Autumn's advice and scaled down on the fancy food, ordering sandwich platters from

CHAPTER 19

the IGA and cookies from Miss Elsie's. When word spread that she had changed the menu, attendance doubled. Now about twenty people came.

The woman in Texas had been stupid enough to steal too close to home and sell the stuff in her shop just five miles away. Natalie, with a self-satisfied smirk, determined that she was infinitely smarter than that dope because she hit places out of town and sold the goods online to people out of state. She'd even been lucky enough several times to come across stashes of cash. Now her steady reconnaissance of Sheriff Bubba had paid off, and she could continue hitting places closer to home. She was getting weary of all that driving. The gasoline bill was cutting into her profits. Besides, no one was looking for her here. In fact, no one was looking for *her*, much less a *woman*. Everyone assumed the thief was a man.

Natalie had observed that Meg Overly's house had been dark for the past three days as she drove past on her way out of town. Plus, she hadn't seen Meg in that time either. The Overlys weren't rich, but they were comfortable middle class and were bound to have sufficient bounty.

At eleven that evening, Natalie donned her black clothing and face mask. She drove the first two miles out of town, down Homestead Avenue, where she parked on the street, making the last quarter of a mile on foot, slipping silently through the night. Ten Oaks Kennel was located just far enough from the neat residential neighborhoods for her purposes. By the time she had walked up to the driveway, the thunder and sleet had begun. She ran, giving a wide berth around the perimeter of the property to avoid the kennel and waking up the dogs

This is just too easy, she smiled to herself as she lifted a first-floor window and slipped silently into the house. *There's no reason I couldn't keep doing this for the rest of my life.*

CHAPTER 20

*I*T WAS THE thought of Meg alone at the big kennel with all those dogs and no electricity that swayed Kyle's wavering mind. The storm came on quickly, and the impressive amount of lightning eventually did its thing, knocking out the power. Recalling what Meg had said at Thanksgiving dinner, about being alone with two pregnant dogs, he decided he would extend a helping hand even if it was the middle of the night. She might be stubborn, but she wasn't stupid. And besides, maybe she had looked at the website by now. He packed a few flashlights and extra batteries and headed out, undeterred by the spitting sleet, flashes of lightning, and fierce thunder that accompanied his short drive across town. Pulling into the long driveway at Ten Oaks, he encountered a fallen tree and had to hoof it the rest of the way up the driveway toward the kennel.

He called Meg's name as he approached the kennel so as not to startle her, remembering the awkwardness of his last visit. She emerged immediately from the building, shining a powerful flashlight in his face.

"What the hell are you doing here?" she accused him angrily. Before he could respond an angry clap of thunder clapped around them. "Geez," Meg muttered. "What a night. Well, since you're here, I could use a hand."

Kyle laughed aloud at the absurdity of her comment, as if he happened to be in the neighborhood in the middle of the night.

"I thought you might need some help," he said, following her inside.

"Well, for once you're right," she responded, leading him through the runs. "The generator is out."

"The dogs aren't scared?" he asked, surprised to see them lying calmly in their cages.

"No," Meg answered. "That's part of their training. They have to learn to be calm in all sorts of situations. That's what we do here, make sure their temperaments are suitable for law enforcement, and then they go off for advanced training elsewhere. Here we are." She stopped in front of a larger run with the door open.

"I only have one pregnant shepherd left." Meg swiveled to face him as she sat down next to the panting dog. "Hold the lantern up so I can see," she ordered, and Kyle did as instructed.

Twenty minutes and eight puppies later Kyle was sitting on a stool watching Meg as she loving placed more blankets around the new pups.

"I could have done it without you, but I appreciate you coming," Meg said almost nicely. "It was thoughtful of you to check on me."

Kyle grinned broadly. He couldn't help himself. Then he shone his flashlight directly on Meg's face so he could see her expression.

"Aha!" he declared as the light illuminated her face. "I knew you could smile!" Then just as quickly he switched off the light. "What the…" he whispered, craning his neck and stepping around Meg, who whirled around to face the same direction. The two looked out the window and watched as a slim figure, illuminated by the moonlight, slipped across the yard toward Meg's house and then hoisted himself through a window.

"Oh my goodness," Meg whispered excitedly. "I don't believe it. It's that burglar everyone's been after. This is so cool!"

And she took off running out the kennel door and toward the house.

"Meg," Kyle hissed. "Get back here. At least wait for me to call 911."

She sprinted ahead, totally ignoring his pleas. She had made it all the way onto the front porch, her right hand beginning to twist the front door knob, when he finally overtook her. He reached around her, grabbing both wrists simultaneously, and dragged her forcibly off the porch and into the yard.

"Geez, are you trying to give me a heart attack?" he demanded. "You can't just go tearing in there. What if he has a gun?"

Meg considered for a minute. "Okay, that's a valid point. But it might take the sheriff a while to get here, and I don't want him to get away."

"Okay," Kyle agreed. "But we'll go in together. Follow me." He forcefully positioned Meg behind him as they crept up toward the house and back up onto the front porch. Tiptoeing behind him, a feeling of being safe and protected washed over her.

"The front door's unlocked," Meg whispered.

"Are you serious?" Kyle asked. "Isn't that a little...dangerous?" he gestured to the side of the house where the burglar had entered.

"No one locks their doors," she said. "Now when you get inside, go down the hall and take the first doorway on your left. That's the dining room, where all the silver is."

The two crept inside, and sure enough, there was a soft glow of a flashlight coming from the dining room. They could hear the clatter of things being dropped into a bag. Meg tugged on the back of Kyle's jacket so he would stop. She used hand gestures and rather comical facial expressions to indicate that he should go into the dining room and that she would go around to the kitchen and the open window where the thief had entered. He nodded his understanding, trying not to laugh and incredulous at how calm and in charge she was. Meg crept away, and after he had given her enough time he stepped into the dining room and clicked on his flashlight, illuminating a slight figure in a ski mask holding a duffle bag.

"Stop!" he yelled. "I've called the cops. They're on the way."

The burglar dropped the bag and flashlight and as Meg had predicted bolted in the direction he had come, with Kyle and Meg close behind. It was a competition now to see who would catch the intruder. There was a loud thud, and then Meg's triumphant voice yelled, "Gotcha!" followed immediately by a loud groan.

Turning into the kitchen, Kyle shone the light on the figure Meg had pinned to the floor. He watched as Meg lifted off the ski mask with her free hand.

The severe black chin-length bob was revealed first, partially obscuring the face.

"Unbelievable," Kyle exclaimed, speaking first. "It's a woman!"

"It's not a woman," Meg replied. "It's Natalie Prescott. My how the mighty have fallen."

"Oh, shut up, Meg," Natalie hissed from the floor, her eyes looking around madly for an escape route.

"Don't even think about it," Meg said, and then the sound of a siren in the distance began its fast approach. "You're sunk."

* * *

A sleepy Autumn parked her Jeep in front of the sheriff's office and slipped inside the quiet building, so strange without the typical hubbub of daytime. She reviewed in her mind her brief conversation with the sheriff just moments ago, but still couldn't believe what he had told her. Natalie, the burglar? It just didn't seem possible.

"Why did you call me, of all people?" Autumn yawned, approaching Buddy.

"She said she didn't have anyone else to call," he answered, as he led Autumn into a small room where Natalie sat at a small table. She had been crying, and without her makeup she looked like a lost little waif.

"Natalie," she said gently. "Is it true? Did you break into Meg's house?"

Natalie nodded miserably.

"But why?" Autumn prodded. "I know business has been bad, but you should have asked for help instead of resorting to stealing things."

Natalie snapped her head up. "I did ask for help, remember?" she practically snarled. "A lot of good that did. And besides, you were the one who told me to do it. You said I needed to do whatever it took to save my business."

"Obviously, I didn't mean you should rob people!" Autumn answered, trying to keep her cool. "I meant you needed to do anything *within reason*, Natalie. You know very well what I meant, and you have to take responsibility for your actions and not blame someone else."

"Oh, she needs to take responsibility, all right. A lot of it," she heard the sheriff's voice behind her. "She's a real cat burglar, this one. She says she's been sneaking into people's houses while they're at work and lifting jewelry and silver. And since we can't find any trace of the items in the pawn shops, I'd bet my last dollar that she's selling them online."

They turned to look at Natalie, who had started crying again and looked like she was about to say something, but Autumn stopped her in time.

"Don't say anything more, Natalie," she commanded. "We need to get you a lawyer before this goes any further. I'll call Ethan Rasmussen first thing in the morning."

Autumn glanced at her watch, tempted to call Ethan on his cell phone. But the late hour, and the thought of waking Heather dissuaded her. Looking at Natalie, she secretly hoped she had some kind of mental disorder or compulsion that had led her down this path. Maybe she was a kleptomaniac and could get probation and mandatory treatment instead of prison time. In the same instance, she wondered why she even cared what happened to Natalie.

When the sheriff stepped out of the room, Autumn leaned across the table and gave Natalie her best "I mean business look." Natalie stared back, her red-rimmed eyes hard and flashing with anger.

"There's just one more thing," Autumn said. "Why does Meg hate you so much? What did you do to her?"

Natalie sighed a heavy sigh and yawned, as if she were bored to death. She looked straight at Autumn, shaking her head. "It's no big deal. Meg blew it all out of proportion. It was just an art exhibition. I didn't mean anything by it."

"Blew what out of proportion?" Autumn pressed, leaning back and crossing her arms over her chest. She wasn't sure if she wanted to hear this.

"They were just some pictures I took of Meg and her roommate... you know? For my senior art show."

"No, I don't know, Natalie," Autumn said hotly. "I guess you're going to have to spell it out for me." She paused. "Unless, you're saying, the photos are somehow compromising? Intimate?" Her voice trailed off.

"That's exactly what I'm saying," Natalie responded.

Autumn laughed, making Natalie cringe. "You know what, Natalie? I don't believe you. Not for one second."

"You can see for yourself. I still have the photos."

Autumn gaped, mouth open. "What? Where are they?"

Natalie just shook her head and smirked, her black bob a slick helmet on her head that made her look like a tiny Lego person.

"I don't have to tell you, now do I? They are my intellectual property. And besides, it's not like I'm going to do anything with them."

"Then why do you still have them?" Autumn spat out at her, unable to contain her temper any longer. "And as for 'you don't have to give them to me,' you're right. You don't." She got up from her chair and headed toward the door, looking over her shoulder. "And I don't have to help you."

"Wait!" Natalie said, almost pleading. "You're right. I don't need them. You can have them and the negatives."

"Where are they?" Autumn demanded.

"In the office in the back of my atelier. Second drawer on the left in a large envelope that says "Meg Overly."

Autumn's stomach dropped at the sound of Natalie speaking her best friend's name.

"I'll need the keys," she demanded.

Natalie again shook her head. "No, you don't. The back door's unlocked." Then she started to laugh a hollow, bitter laugh. "Of all people, *I* should know better than to leave my door unlocked."

"Karma's a beast," said Autumn, as the sheriff stepped back into the room. She was thinking to herself that there was just about no one in Finch's Crossing who would want to steal anything from Natalie's atelier.

The sheriff took Natalie gently by the arm, helping her up from her chair, about to lead her into the jail cell that would be her home for a while. He called to Autumn, "She'll be arraigned first thing in the morning. You should come back about nine."

* * *

At precisely eight the next morning Autumn dialed Ethan's office number. When Myra answered, she tried to explain as succinctly as possible, apologizing for interrupting.

"I know he's very busy, but if I could just speak to him…"

Myra interrupted her. "Am I correct that this is Miss Hamilton calling from Finch's Crossing?"

Surprised that Ethan's assistant recognized her voice, she answered in the affirmative.

CHAPTER 20

"I'll put you right through," Myra said. After Ethan's behavior the last time Autumn Hamilton was in town, there was no doubt in Myra's mind that Autumn was special and Ethan just needed a little nudging in her direction. She never could understand what he saw in the awful Ellen person. After she had transferred Autumn to Ethan's phone, she picked up the line she had put on hold.

"Terribly sorry to have kept you waiting, Ellen," she said smoothly. Ellen had been calling incessantly lately, and Ethan had refused to take her calls. Myra suspected they had broken up, a prospect that made her quite pleased "I'm afraid Mr. Rasmussen will be in a meeting for the rest of the morning and can't be disturbed."

As she expected, Ellen mumbled something rude and hung up without saying good-bye.

In his office, where he was, in fact, *not* in a meeting, Ethan hung up the phone, stunned. Strong, independent Autumn was calling him for help. He couldn't believe it. He depressed the intercom button.

"Myra," he said excitedly. "Call the school. Tell them I'll be there to get Heather in thirty minutes, and then call Inga and ask her to pack Heather for a weekend trip. Oh, and you better tell Martha we're coming and book me into the Greystone Manor."

"Gladly!" Myra responded, and she picked up the phone to dial the number for Heather's school.

CHAPTER 21

WHERE ARE WE going?" Heather asked, as she skipped along beside Ethan to the parking garage.

"It's a surprise," he said, smiling down at the little girl who had won his heart.

"The park?" she asked.

"Better," he teased.

"Pizza?"

"Nope. What's better than pizza? Think."

"Finch's Crossing?"

"You got it!"

"Yippee!" she yelled, and began running, racing him to the car. He had to break into a run himself to keep up with her.

As she buckled herself into the car seat, she began chattering about all the things she needed to tell Nanna and the new pictures she wanted to draw for Autumn.

She surprised him with what she said next, although by now, he realized, nothing that came out of her mouth should surprise him.

"I think I like Autumn better than Ellen," she said then dipped her face down into her *Scooby-Doo* coloring book.

He didn't reply. He wasn't ready to say it out loud, but he was thinking it, too. No. Not thinking. He knew.

After he deposited Heather at Martha's he headed straight to the jail in the bottom of the courthouse to meet his new client, who had been arraigned, denied bail, and returned to her cell.

"Where's Autumn?" he asked, looking around the small police station, disappointed that she wasn't there.

"She had to run a few errands," the sheriff replied, letting him into the examination room, where a tiny, dejected woman in an orange jumpsuit sat waiting for him. "She said she'd catch up with you later."

After his meeting with Natalie, Ethan was elated to see Autumn's phone number as his cell phone rang.

"How about I buy you lunch?" her cheery voice asked. "It's the least I can do."

"You don't owe me a thing, but I'll take you up on a late lunch. I'm starved, and Heather's with Martha, so I have all the time in the world."

Autumn felt that now familiar and delightful rush of adrenaline in the pit of her stomach. Her feelings for Ethan were snowballing quickly, and before long, she told herself, she wouldn't be able to deny just exactly how strong they had become.

Ten minutes later they were comfortably ensconced in a booth at Miss Elsie's.

"So how are you doing, after all this?" he asked when they were settled.

"Just tired, I guess," she answered. "It was a long, emotional night. I barely slept. I just can't believe Natalie resorted to robbing people's houses to find things to sell on eBay."

"It happens all the time, and usually the perpetrators are caught." Then he added, "It is sad," not really feeling sorry for Natalie, but not wanting to appear callous in front of Autumn, whom he desperately wanted to impress more and more every time he saw her.

"I wish she had felt like she could have come to me," Autumn said regretfully. "But I'd been too busy lecturing her about her snobbery. Which *is* an issue, mind you. I guess she just felt like she couldn't confide in me."

"Autumn," he said gently," taking her hand in his across the table, "this isn't your fault, or your responsibility. You can't take this on. Natalie is a grown woman, responsible for her own actions and decisions."

Autumn was stunned, almost speechless, at the sight and touch of his skin on hers. It was such a simple gesture, but at the same time it was telling her what she had longed for these past few weeks.

"You're right, of course," she stuttered, not wanting him to let go of her hand, but knowing that they shouldn't be holding hands in public. What if Heather saw? Or Ellen? For all she knew Ellen could come strolling into the tea room and catch them.

"I just hate to think how alone she must have felt, how desperate." Autumn thought about her own loneliness and weeks of desperation when it seemed her painting days might be over. "What's going to happen to her?"

"I'm really not surprised that the judge didn't grant her bail. She was pretty notorious and, well, the notorious…" his voice trailed off, and Autumn picked up the thread.

"So she'll have to stay in jail until her trial?"

"I'm afraid so, unless the district attorney offers her some kind of deal, which I doubt he will."

Autumn paused for a moment. "Sheriff Landry says that the prosecutor wanted to make an example of her because she's made a fool out of the department, flummoxing them for so long. If she hadn't miscalculated her last move, she'd still be out there robbing everyone blind. She didn't know that Meg had two pregnant dogs and a few that were sick and so she was staying in the barn."

"I guess that's that then," Ethan replied. "Her trial will probably be set for after the holidays. No judge I know likes to start a new trial this close to Christmas. It's a cut-and-dry case. She confessed. I won't need long to prepare, and hopefully I can get her out on time served and probation—and, of course, restitution."

"You!" Autumn exclaimed, perplexed.

"Well, isn't that why you asked for my help?" he asked gently.

"Yes, I guess," she answered. "But just to get her through the first stage and explain what was going to happen to her. It's really generous of you to take her case. You know she can't pay you."

"That's all right. My firm does its fair share of pro bono work," he answered evenly, knowing all too well that Barry would flip out if he told him he had taken on *this* crazy case pro bono, with no justification other than wanting to please Autumn.

"Well, let me repay you. Why don't you bring Heather and Martha over for Christmas dinner?"

When he hesitated, she plunged on, not wanting to give him the opportunity to say no.

"It's a widows and orphans dinner," she explained. "It's been a tradition since my sisters moved away and my parents died. All of us single people, spinning in our own orbits, coming together for a festive meal. Just think about it. It'll be one of the best Christmas dinners you've ever had," she promised. "It's potluck, and you haven't lived until you've tried Jack's sweet potato casserole." She added as an afterthought, "Of course, Ellen is more than welcome, too,"

He stared at her for a moment too long. Of course. She couldn't have known that he and Ellen had broken up.

"Ellen and I broke up," he blurted. "A few weeks ago."

"Oh, I'm so sorry," Autumn replied with a poorly veiled lament, when in fact, she was not one iota sorry. "Do you want to talk about it?"

It felt strange to be holding his hand across the table while talking about his recently decamped ex-girlfriend, but she couldn't bear the thought of him withdrawing his touch.

He shrugged and sighed. "There's really not that much to tell. Unfortunately, having Heather in my life was just a little too much for her. I'm not sure if she just doesn't like children or if it was more a matter of having to compete for my time. Probably a little of both. In any event, it's over." She felt him squeeze her hand as if conveying a secret message as he continued. "And to be honest, I don't think she was really good for Heather."

Autumn nodded, remembering the conversation she had with Heather as she tucked her into bed during her visit to New York.

"Breakups are always hard no matter what the reason," she replied, wondering who broke up with whom.

"It was the best thing for Heather," he said. "Ellen as much as said so." He paused then looked her square in the eye. "And it's the best thing for me, too. We were committed to each other, but the relationship wasn't going anywhere. If it were we would have been married by now. Four years is a long time to be in a relationship that doesn't move forward."

Autumn didn't know what to say, so instead of responding she reluctantly removed her hand from his and took a bite of her sandwich. Four years *was* a long time, and she couldn't help but wonder if he still had feelings for Ellen.

She must have sighed aloud in her musings, because Ethan asked her what was wrong. His voice surprised her. She was so busy imagining what it would be like to kiss him she had almost forgotten he was there.

"Nothing. I was just thinking, that's all," she said, hoping he couldn't read her thoughts. "Well," she continued, changing the subject and returning to the original topic. "I hope you and Heather and Martha will come for dinner, then."

He smiled in return. "I can't think of any place else I'd rather be," he said warmly, and after hesitating for a moment he continued. "Autumn," he said haltingly. "I want to tell you that my feelings…"

Before he could get out the words to tell her that he had developed feelings for her—intense feelings—and that he couldn't stop thinking about her, they were interrupted by Miss Elsie as she made her customary rounds to each table to check on her guests.

"Hi, Miss Elsie," Autumn greeted her warmly. "I'm not sure if you've met Ethan Rasmussen. He's Heather's guardian."

"No, I haven't had the pleasure," Miss Elsie responded, shaking his hand. "I've heard Heather is doing well. I'm glad. Is there anything you two need?"

Ethan shook his head. "Thanks for asking, though. You have a lovely restaurant."

Miss Elsie beamed, and he saw out of the corner of his eye that Autumn was reaching for her coat. The moment he had hoped for had passed. Maybe there would be an opportunity over Christmas, he told himself, as Miss Elsie greeted another customer and Autumn rose to leave.

They walked side by side to their cars, with Autumn's shoulder occasionally brushing his, giving him chills. He thought about continuing the conversation, but he decided he didn't really want to reveal his feelings for her standing on the sidewalk. They stopped at Autumn's Jeep, and he opened the door for her, wanting so badly to take her into his arms and show her how much she had come to mean to him, how much he wanted to be with her. But there were too many people around.

"So, you'll definitely come for Christmas?" she asked as she slid into the Jeep.

Ethan smiled. "Definitely."

Autumn pulled away from the curb, a vision of Ethan in her eyes and the words to "Joy to the World" zipping away in her brain. She decided this would be a good time to head to Town and Country Nursery to invite Jack for Christmas dinner. It would give her the opportunity to play Cupid and perhaps get the ball rolling on the budding, yet stalled, romance between him and Martha.

As she drove she thought back to the exchange with Ethan right before Miss Elsie had interrupted them. What had he been about to say? She knew what she *hoped* was the answer to that question.

"I want to tell you that my feelings," he had said. His feelings... what? Maybe that his feelings about Heather's living arrangement hadn't changed. Or was he talking about his feelings for Ellen? Or

CHAPTER 21

could it possibly be that he was talking about his feelings for her? She just knew there was *something* between them. She could see it in how he held her gaze just a moment longer than necessary and in the way he had responded when she called him to help Natalie. And then, out of the blue, an image of Frank standing in his gallery with an exhibit of her paintings on the walls popped into her head. She shook the vision away as if she were a wet dog shaking off water. Where in the world had that thought come from? She put both men out of her mind when she arrived at her destination, now ready to focus on Jack.

"You coming for dinner?" she asked, as she watched Jack cut the thick, sappy stems from pine boughs and rope them to each other, making garlands, the aroma of needles fresh in the crisp air.

"Yep."

"Gonna bring your sweet potato casserole again this year?"

"Yep."

"If I recall," Autumn said, "Martha was particularly fond of that dish last year. I believe she had seconds."

Jack ducked his head and smiled into his greenery as he bent down to grab another piece. He had remembered that. She had raved about it, and when it was time to go home, he noticed that Autumn had wrapped up the leftovers for Martha to take home. He'd have to make more this year. He might even make a small dish just for Martha and present it to her when she was about to leave.

"Will Martha be there?" he asked nonchalantly.

"You can count on it." Autumn grinned at him and squeezed his arm. "Okay, I'm off to the IGA," she said. "I'll see you around town."

The pungent smell of pine had put Autumn in her annual Christmas baking mood, and she walked up and down the baking aisle at the IGA restocking the staples she would need for hermits, orange cookies, cranberry noels, and of course the traditional decorated sugar cookies. She spotted Kyle at the end of the aisle looking at the coffee.

It had been a long time since someone new had joined the widows and orphans Christmas extravaganza, but Autumn thought if anybody qualified as a lonely orphan, it would be Kyle.

"What can I bring?" he asked after Autumn had invited him. He was suddenly very excited about Christmas. He hadn't planned to go home, not wanting the expense of a plane ticket or a long drive, and he was dreading a lonely Christmas turkey sandwich in his room at the Manor.

Autumn consulted her list. "That depends. Can you cook?"

Kyle had to laugh. He hadn't had time to cook while he was working full time and attending classes at the technical college. And by the time he was homeless and living in his van he was eating out of garbage cans. The snack bar in the student commons threw out the breakfast biscuits, lunch sandwiches, and various salad items when it closed for the day. When Kyle crept back to campus at night and parked his van behind the garbage area he went dumpster diving and always found enough to feed himself the next day. Could he cook? No.

"Sorry, no," he said. "But there must be something I can contribute."

"Mmmm," Autumn agreed. "You can buy the rolls. Mrs. Parker's in the freezer section. Better get three dozen. They're really popular, and they only sell them around the holidays. By the way," she cooed, with a wink obviously implied in her laugh, "they're Meg's favorite."

"Sometime I want to talk with you about Meg," he said boldly.

"And sometime I'd like to hear what you have to say," Autumn replied, scratching rolls off her list. "But right now, I've got a million things to cook and bake. I'll see you Christmas afternoon. Come around one thirty so we have time to defrost the rolls and heat them."

He nodded distractedly. He was already looking forward to that conversation about Meg. Maybe Autumn could help interpret her friend for him. Sometimes, Meg was a foreign language that needed translating.

* * *

That afternoon, Meg and Autumn heaved one of the two Christmas trees out of Meg's truck and carried it into Autumn's living room, placing it in the stand in the bay window. They put the smaller of the two in the dining room, where it fit perfectly in the alcove in front of the French doors. This tree was always Autumn's favorite to decorate. During their globe-trotting, Autumn's parents had purchased Christmas decorations from each country they visited. Every year, the Hamiltons had always had two trees, and Autumn had always continued the tradition. The large tree in the living room was decorated with traditional ornaments, like glass balls, ribbons and bows, strings of popcorn, and tinsel. The "alcove tree" was always and only adorned with the various Christmas treasures from all over the world. The sisters always delighted in the family's increasingly eclectic international ornament collection.

Autumn had brought the boxes of international decorations down from the attic in early December. She couldn't wait any longer. Now, she pulled out her collection of Christmas CDs, brewed a pan of hot mulled cider, and sorted through the ornaments with

Meg. She couldn't decide which she loved more, the Peruvian angels pressed from tin, the reindeer and bells from Sweden, or the small, hand-carved wooden ornaments from Germany featuring little drummer boys, Christmas trees, and sleighs.

Meg pulled out a small box of straw ornaments and inspected the little rattan baskets, hats, and longboats with brightly colored tassels on the bows.

"These don't look very Christmassy," she declared, threading each with a small hook and finding places for them on the tree.

Autumn just smiled.

Instead of tinsel or gold garland or strings of red or gold beads, Autumn threaded long strands of knotted wool material from Tibet through the boughs.

"Why do you think you don't like Kyle?" Autumn asked suddenly, hoping that if she caught her off guard she might get an honest answer. Meg had always been so closed off. It was hard to coax her into talking about her emotions.

Meg didn't answer, instead picking up some tiny glass-blown Santa Clauses and hanging them near the top of the tree.

"Who says I don't like him?" she finally answered.

"C'mon, Meg. I've known you forever," Autumn said. "I can read you like a book."

"He's too young. We've already been through this. That doesn't mean I don't like him. Just not interested. At all."

"Is that the only reason?" Autumn threaded the garland and sipped her cider while she observed her best friend.

"Why does it even matter?" Meg asked, taking a break from decorating and flopping down on the couch.

"Because I think you *want* to like him," Autumn replied. "I just don't understand why you won't let yourself. He's crazy about you."

"I could ask you the same thing about Ethan," Meg said evasively, glancing back sideways, not sure what kind of reaction her comparison might elicit.

"We're not talking about me and Ethan," Autumn replied.

"Why not?" Meg eyed her coolly. "I saw you with him this afternoon outside Miss Elsie's, and you were making goo-goo eyes at him. And was that drool I saw on your chin? You were so grateful to him I thought you were going to jump in his lap so he could scratch you behind the ears." Meg laughed out loud, knowing Autumn wouldn't.

Autumn rolled her eyes. "Your dog metaphors are really stupid, you know that?"

"Are not."

"Are so."

"Are not."

"I want to talk about you and Kyle."

"Well I don't," Meg almost snapped, then apologized quickly. "Look, I'm sorry. I don't mean to be nasty, but I just wish you'd leave it."

Autumn put her mug down on the coffee table.

"What's wrong, Meg? I'm worried about you."

Meg felt the softness in her friend's voice. She knew her concern was genuine. But this was a private matter that Meg needed to, and would, figure out herself.

"There's nothing to worry about, okay? I'm fine." She knew she wasn't fine, but how could she tell Autumn that the reason she didn't like Kyle was because he had discovered her secret living arrangement, and she felt vulnerable? She barely knew him, so how could she trust him? True, he had never given her any reason to mistrust him. He had always been more than kind, more than generous. And he had kept her secret from Autumn. So far. She had totally expected him to tell Autumn that Natalie chose to burgle her house because it had sat empty for so long, but he hadn't. She had to admit that this did elevate him in her esteem, if just a tiny bit. But there was still the problem of Natalie. True, she was sitting in jail, but that might make her more likely to lash out at her since it was Meg who put her there.

"Does your permanent bad mood have something to do with these?" Autumn asked, reaching into the drawer of a side table and producing a manila envelope that she handed to Meg.

"What's this?" her friend asked, puzzled.

"Open it," Autumn responded, adding, "I got them from Natalie."

Meg hesitated and looked at her friend as if to ask permission to open the envelope.

"It's okay," Autumn said softly. "Natalie told me the whole story."

"I doubt that," Meg snapped. "She told you her version, which has nothing to do with the truth."

"Aren't you going to open the envelope?"

Meg shook her head and put the envelope on the coffee table. Sighing, she sank back into the sofa.

"Don't need to. Believe me, with Natalie back in town my mind conjured up those images as if I had just seen them yesterday."

"Tell me about it," Autumn urged.

"What do you know already?" Meg asked.

"Natalie told me that she had taken some compromising photos of you at Briar Rose and used them as part of her senior photography exhibition."

"Yeah, that last part is right. And the whole school saw them. But they weren't compromising, only Natalie made them look like it. She even titled the two photos 'Secret Love' and 'Secret Love II.' She ruined my whole last semester of college. My roommate, Maria, moved out, and the whole floor gave me dirty looks every time they saw me because Natalie told them I had taken advantage of her. It was horrible."

"Oh, Meg," Autumn interjected when she paused to take a breath. "I never knew. Why didn't you tell me?"

Meg shrugged. "There wasn't anything anyone could do. And after I graduated and Natalie went off to graduate school I figured I could put the whole thing behind me. Besides, I didn't want the whole stupid, sordid story following me home."

"Sordid?" Autumn asked, puzzled.

"You didn't look at the photos?" Meg asked with surprise.

Autumn shook her head. "Natalie told me where to find them in her office, in that envelope. I figured if you wanted me to see them you'd show them to me. I just wanted to give them back to you. The negatives are in there, too."

Meg sighed and reached for the envelope, withdrawing two photos and placing them on the coffee table in front of Autumn, who studied them intently.

"It looks like you're about to kiss her," Autumn said, pointing to the dark-haired girl in the pictures.

"It sure does, doesn't it? Natalie never stopped to consider that what she thought she saw wasn't in fact what she saw. Okay, so here's the story. My grandmother died just before spring break my senior year. I was heartbroken, you know? My grandmother was like a second mother to me. She's the only person, besides you, who accepted me the way I am. Anyway. I got the phone call when I was in my room, and Maria, my roommate, was there. I was bawling, and she came over and sat next to me on my bed and gave me a hug. And along comes Natalie, skulking around campus looking for scoops, and she snapped her camera as she peeked inside my dorm room door, which wasn't shut completely."

"And it just so happens that the exact moment Natalie came along with her camera, the two of you pulled away from the embrace," Autumn said.

"You got it," Meg said, growing agitated. "She captured an image that looked like we were about to kiss. And when Natalie came back to town the first thing that came to mind was that she was going to haul out the pictures and hang them in her stupid atelier. I don't think I could have dealt with that, you know? I'm all for tolerance and live and let live. You know that about me. But she crossed a line and depicted me in a private moment. Even if I had been with a guy in that situation I would have seen it as an invasion and would have been just as angry."

Autumn was nodding. "I'm going to throw out a wild guess here that one of the reasons you're staying away from Kyle is that you're afraid he might find out about the pictures. Am I right?"

Meg nodded. "And it didn't take long for Natalie to set her sights on Kyle. I could just see her showing him the pictures to spite me because he was interested in me and not her."

"Well, I wouldn't put that past her. But it's all in the past now, and the photos are out of her hands. What are you going to do with them?"

Meg rose from the couch and crossed the room to the fireplace, picking up a box of matches from the mantle.

"May I?" she asked as she turned to Autumn.

"Great idea," Autumn answered with a smile and helped her

friend stack some kindling in the fireplace, and they watched together as photos crackled and hissed in the flames, then disappeared for good.

"How do you know Natalie won't say anything about this to Kyle or anyone else? Just because the photos are gone doesn't mean she can't launch a smear campaign. And she might have made copies."

Autumn grinned. "Believe me, you don't have to worry about Natalie anymore. I got Ethan down here to take her case, and he's representing her for free. She owes me, and she knows it."

"Ah, Ethan," Meg teased. "We're back to where we started before you pulled out those stupid pictures."

"Actually," Autumn corrected, "we were talking about you and Kyle."

Meg ignored her. "Every time you talk about him you get this glint in your eyes and you can't stop smiling. It's pretty obvious that you're crazy about him. Quite a contrast from a few months ago when you hated him!"

"Obvious?" Autumn asked, appalled. "What makes you say that?" She was completely embarrassed. Who else suspected?

"Obvious to me, that's all. Don't worry, your secret's safe…until the two of you declare your never-ending love for each other and get married."

Now it was Autumn's turn to roll her eyes.

CHAPTER 22

HE BOXWOODS, GREENS, magnolias, and hollies in Autumn's yard received a Christmas pruning every year. Their deep greens, waxy leaves, and vibrant berries would end up arranged masterfully on her mantle and along her banisters. As always, she had bought a dozen poinsettias from Town and Country Nursery to put around the house. She had tried to get Martha to come along with her so she could see Jack, but Martha was still stuck on that embarrassing interaction she had had a while back when she had bought those stupid screwdrivers and walked out without them. Martha knew she would have to see Jack at Christmas dinner, and she hoped that Jack would be so distracted with all the conversations and festivities that he would not recall her embarrassing overture.

When the phone rang a week before Christmas, Autumn was elbow-deep in greenery—blue spruce, cedar, white pine, hemlock, and all varieties of evergreens—from Jack's nursery. She was working on the centerpiece and fit the phone under her chin as she continued fussing with the arrangement in the low-slung silver vase that had been her grandmother's.

"Hello, merry Christmas," she said cheerfully, feeling unusually chipper and upbeat—until she heard her sister's voice on the other end of the line. "Win. What a surprise."

"What, can't I call my sister to wish her an almost merry Christmas?" Win's cheery voice was fake and had the hard knife edges that Autumn had come to dread, for they were typically pointed at her.

"It's just I haven't heard from you in a while," she answered, thrusting some holly down into the vase, just a little too hard, and she knocked out the boxwood.

"Darn it," she whispered under her breath, and she gave up on the decorating to concentrate on the conversation.

"Well, you know how busy I get with work," Win explained. "But I have another surprise for you. I'm coming for Christmas! Isn't that great? I've finally decided to take a few days off to visit. I bet you're up to your ears in decorating…poinsettias in every room, fresh pine boughs everywhere. Maybe a little mistletoe? Piles of gold pine cones?"

Autumn had to fight hard to keep her real feelings at bay. "That's great, Win, but why the sudden change of heart? You hate Christmas, remember? That's why you never come."

"Yes, but I love my sisters. When are Spring and Summer arriving?"

"They're not coming this year," Autumn replied, wincing at the thought of not having her other sisters as buffers to Win's stinging sarcasm and cutting digs. "Spring has a shoot the day after Christmas in Paris, so she'll be there for the holidays. Summer's been working as an au pair, and the family is going to the Caribbean."

"Good grief, when is she ever going to get a real job?" Win groused angrily. "It's time she grew up and stopped all this nonsense. Last year she actually worked as a chauffeur, remember? A *driver*. It's insane."

"That's just Summer." Autumn felt compelled to defend her baby sister against Win's frequent bouts of hostile criticism. They had only been on the phone for five minutes, and Win had already started in on her. "Anyway. When are you arriving?"

"I'm taking the twenty-third off, and I thought I'd drive in Christmas day and head back that evening."

Autumn chastised herself for being relieved at Win's interpretation of "taking a few days off." In the past, even a one-night stay had been enough for her to do plenty of emotional damage to her sisters. But Autumn had developed the ability to skillfully ignore Win's biting comments. By pretending the words had never been spoken, she gave them no power over her. She would just have to steel herself for the criticism that would begin as soon as Win walked in the front door. She would just have to let it all roll down her back, like water on a duck. She loved that image. Shining droplets shimmering and sliding off the colorful feathers—harmless, inconsequential, largely unnoticed.

She surveyed the dining room, taking in the silver bowls full of glass balls, the red candles standing at attention in all the candle holders, the pine cones painted gold (Win had guessed correctly). She could predict Win's assessment with pinpoint accuracy: "Don't you think it's a bit much, Autumn? You always overdo it with all these trinkets. It's positively suffocating in here."

"You still doing that ridiculous widows and orphans dinner on Christmas afternoon?" her sister inquired mockingly. Win was laughing, almost guffawing, as she asked. She simply had no inkling of how abrasive and nasty she had become.

Autumn had walked to the back of the house to grab more glass balls. In for a penny, in for a pound. She would go all-out this year, and not just because it galled Win, but because she loved how she felt as she walked from room to room in her home and glimpsed the familiar decorations she brought out year after year. She loved the rhythm of it all. She loved that Christmas had its own time of the year. Every year. And she so valued the fond memories she held of her childhood Christmases.

"Sure am," she answered. "We've got quite a collection this year and a few newcomers." She held the phone behind her back and mouthed, "That you will find fault with immediately."

"Just as long as Jack Staub isn't there. He creeps me out. He just sits there like a statue and barely says anything," Win complained. "Speaking of creeping me out. Who else is going to grace us with their pathetic presence? Anyone interesting?"

Autumn resisted pointing out that Win herself was gracing the gathering with her presence. "Martha will be here with Heather and her new guardian." As she spoke the words, she knew that as soon as she saw him, Win would latch on to Ethan.

"How's Meg? Still knee-deep in dog doo-doo?" Win asked, changing the subject.

Autumn couldn't stand the constant criticism any longer

"Look, Win, I just saw the UPS truck pull into the driveway," she lied. "I'll see you Christmas day. Maybe we can go to the midnight service? Try to make it in time for the dinner. Jack will be sooooo disappointed if he doesn't get to see you." This time she laughed.

Win scoffed at the idea of cramming into a church pew with a bunch of people she couldn't stand, as Autumn knew she would, and then rang off.

Autumn walked into the living room and picked up one of her favorite family photos. The four sisters were standing in front of a lopsided sand castle on the Outer Banks the summer she was eight. They had their arms draped around each other and were grinning from ear to ear, sand sticking in their hair and to their damp bathing suits, brightly colored shovels and little pails scattered around them. They had been so happy together then, always playing together, laughing, and having fun. They'd play card games like Go Fish and Old Maid or the board game Candy Land, their favorite. On Christmas Eve, they used to play dress-up and perform funny plays for their parents before they went to church. She couldn't remember exactly when Win had transformed from the sweet little girl in the photo at the beach to the nasty, bitter woman she was today. Sighing, she put the picture back and turned up the Mormon Tabernacle Choir's rendition of "O, Come, All Ye Faithful" emanating from her iPhone. She refused to let Win dampen her Christmas spirit.

* * *

On Christmas morning, Autumn awoke to see thick white flakes fluttering earthward, covering everything with a fluffy down blanket. From her bedroom window, she noticed the pine and hemlock boughs beginning to bend under the weight of the collecting flakes. It would be a white Christmas after all!

While she luxuriated in bed she thought of the many blessings in her life. She had revived her art career, although she was not sure how much credit she could take for the revival. Certainly, there was the universe to thank, and divine intervention, and of course, Heather. She was back in the studio every day working vigorously like the young, hungry art student she had been fifteen years ago. Her life was full to overflowing with friends she cherished and work she loved, and she had a beautiful home that seemed to have the spirit of an old friend. The only thing missing was someone to share it with.

Before Ethan announced that he and Ellen were no longer together, Autumn had not allowed herself to take out and really examine her feelings for him. But there was nothing stopping her now, and she imagined how the house would feel with the energy of a happy couple and the exuberant enthusiasm and giggles of a little girl. What would it be like to have him come home to her every evening?

But of course, this was just wishful thinking. Ethan's life and work were in New York. Just because he was no longer with Ellen didn't mean that he didn't have ties to his home and his work. He was a partner in a law firm, and she knew people just didn't give up those types of positions.

I'm no different than Martha, Autumn thought to herself. *I keep telling her she'll have to make the first move with Jack, but here I am in the same boat, acting exactly like she is.* She had a sudden empathy for her older friend. *I know exactly how she feels,* she thought wryly.

Ethan had made a lot of progress since that scene in the pumpkin patch just two months ago, she realized. The patience and tenderness he now showed Heather, not just with his words, but by accommodating the needs of a fragile little girl, had surprised Autumn at first.

But she saw firsthand tender proof of Ethan's love for Heather displayed throughout his apartment, from the five different kid-brand cereals on the kitchen counter to the pink Hello Kitty pillow chair positioned smack-dab in the middle of his sleek and modern décor. She laughed as she imagined Ellen gritting her teeth every time she saw the eyesore destroying her "aesthetic."

During the evening Autumn spent at his apartment, she had noticed a big basket in the living room filled to the brim with little girl toys. Naked Barbie dolls, not something one typically sees in a New York lawyer's bachelor pad, were positioned around the bathroom sink. Heather made it clear that they were awaiting their baths. Autumn had even noticed what she was sure were the stubborn remnants of permanent-marker stains on the custom blonde wood floor beside the big-screen television.

It was undeniable. Ethan had come far, and by all appearances, without many battle scars, if any. She wanted to tell him how proud she was of him and how grateful she was that he had embraced Heather and welcomed her into his life, giving her the love and security and stability she so badly needed.

She would invite him to dinner when she saw him later today, she decided. Yes, that was a good idea. A dinner date made sense instead of hurling all of her feelings at him lock, stock, and barrel standing on Pittsburgh Street or Martha's driveway. She knew Martha wanted to spend as much time with Heather as possible, and during their short visit Ethan would most certainly have plenty of free time. She'd take him to the Mezzeluna Cafe, her favorite Italian restaurant in Pittsburgh. Not many people knew her in Pittsburgh, and the possibility of interruptions by the likes of Miss Elsie would be minimized.

* * *

Meg arrived late morning, dressed in a red flannel shirt, black cords, and her ever-present Doc Martens, carrying three pie boxes, which she dumped on the counter.

"Merry Christmas!" she said, followed by an equally festive "Bah humbug!"

"Careful," Autumn scolded her as she opened the boxes.

"Just as you ordered, madam," Meg said, hanging up her coat in the hall closet. "One pumpkin, one mince, and one apple. I had to drive all the way to Mt. Pleasant to get those, I will have you know."

Autumn inhaled the tangy scent of the mincemeat then put the lids back on the boxes and stored them in the pantry. "That's because, as usual, you forgot to call in the order to Miss Elsie's, am I right?"

Ignoring her, Meg rolled up her sleeves. "Where should I start?"

Autumn pointed to the pile of potatoes on the island. "Peel, boil, mash. In that order."

Meg settled on a stool with the potato peeler while Autumn checked on the turkey.

"Win's coming," she said casually, as she basted the bird and then slid it back into the oven.

Meg's hand slipped, and the peeler grazed her knuckles. "You could have warned me," she accused.

"Well, while we're at it, I invited Natalie, too."

"Well, this keeps getting better and better," Meg declared, keeping her eyes on her peeling. "I thought she was still in the clink."

"Well, she was. Is. Ethan filed a motion to grant bail, and so I invited her in case she got out," Autumn said simply.

"You should have told me, Autumn. You know I don't like surprises."

"Why?" Autumn asked. "So you could make up some excuse not to come today? I think you need to forgive Natalie, and what better opportunity than on Christmas? Besides, she's not coming."

"Just so we're clear, I will never forgive Natalie for what she did. And you better not have seated me next to Win either. Or Kyle," Meg shot back petulantly. She glanced past the door into the dining room to see if Autumn had arranged the place cards yet.

"I don't want to talk about Natalie anymore," she declared. "What does Win want this time?"

"She didn't say, and I didn't ask."

"The last time she came to visit she wanted you to agree to sell your grandparents' farm. Remember that? She bullied you into agreeing to list it, remember?"

Autumn nodded. "But I didn't sell it, did I? I stood up to her. Eventually."

"I hate the way she treats you, and I don't understand why you won't call her on it. She's mean to you, Autumn. Downright nasty."

"She's hurting inside, Meg. Show some compassion. Besides, she's mean to everyone. Not just you and me."

"Hurting? Miss Perfect? Get over it. She's been like this her whole life. She's just a snake trying to manipulate you. She thinks you're stupid because you stayed here. Remember? Last year she said you had wasted your life because you didn't move to New York. And she's always ragging on Summer. The only person she's nice to is Spring because she thinks she can use Spring's international connections to pick up new clients. Manipulator, pure and simple."

Of course, it was all true, but Autumn was determined to ignore her sister's hurtful nature, to rise above it—way above it. She took the turkey out of the oven and basted it again for good measure as Meg put the potatoes on to boil. She would make the gravy right before serving the meal, and her "pathetic" guests would bring all the predetermined sides. By early afternoon, they were dribbling in with cheerful greetings and gratitude for coming into the warmth of Autumn's living room.

When Kyle arrived, he negotiated around Meg at the stove to put the rolls into the oven. Autumn smiled as she watched Meg telling Kyle how to wrap up the rolls in foil and threatening him with bodily harm if he burned them.

Autumn walked into the living room and watched the snow as it fell in thick, wet flakes over the entire neighborhood. It had gathered momentum in the last few hours, and it looked like at least ten inches had accumulated. Had Ethan changed his mind? Did he decide to stay at Martha's instead of venturing out in the bad weather? Certainly he could manage the fifty yards or so from Martha's house to hers. Or had the snow delayed his and Heather's arrival from New York? She briefly considered calling Martha, immediately deciding Martha would see right through that and sense the desperation in her voice. She felt a pang of worry coupled with a knot of disappointment. She had been so looking forward to seeing him. She looked down at the formfitting red wool dress hiding under her apron. She had picked it up in Pittsburgh the last time she had visited Scottie's gallery. On an impulse, she had darted into the chic boutique next door and bought the expensive dress to wear on Christmas Day. For Ethan.

Jack arrived and delivered his sweet potato casserole and looked around for Martha without saying a word, and Scottie blew in with the green bean casserole, which he deposited on the counter, and then drifted into the dining room.

"Gorgeous, darling," he exclaimed dramatically as he rearranged the place cards. "Nice try," he yelled as he took Win's place card and put it at the other end of the table, as far away from him as possible, and moved the lovely Martha next to him.

"I hope you're not doing what I think you're doing," Autumn said, as she brought in two little plates of butter patties. She had sliced the butter sticks into quarter-inch squares, chilled them, and used a tiny heart-shaped cookie cutter to cut each square into a heart, and then she transferred them onto the rim of the plates, the points of the hearts all pointed at the geometric center of the plate. She used holly leaf and berries as garnish in the center of the plates.

Scottie whistled as he turned to look at Autumn and pointed to her and raised his eyebrows for the benefit of Jack, who had come into the dining room looking for Martha.

"Well, I declare," Scottie mused. "I must admit that for a long time now I have wondered if you had legs, seeing as though I have never actually set eyes on them. What's up with the getup? Which, by the way, is absolutely stunning."

Autumn blushed. "It's Christmas," she said simply, shrugging slightly. "Look at you—you got all gussied up, too, with your sport coat and red and green bow tie."

She stood at one end of the dining room table and, in a cross between a comical and official voice, announced to everyone but to no one in particular, "I have strategically placed everyone. All seats are final."

She then placed a butter plate at each end of the table and picked up Martha's place card and returned it to the seat next to Jack's. Satisfied, she went back into the kitchen.

Scottie grumbled and wandered in behind her. "Well, if you're going to make me sit next to the Ice Queen, you'd better give me a drink pronto," he complained and then, noticing Meg mashing potatoes at the stove, called out pleasantly, "Hey, Meg."

"Hey, yourself," she answered.

"Don't overcook those mashed potatoes," he warned, smiling and reaching for the bottle of shiraz and the oversized glass Autumn had set out on the counter for him. He poured himself a generous serving while Meg raised her eyebrows at him.

"What?" he asked innocently. "Liquid courage."

Then he walked to the stove and proceeded to instruct Meg on how his mother used to make the absolute best mashed potatoes one could ever hope to experience.

Kyle introduced himself, standing vigil by the stove, determined not to burn Meg's favorite rolls.

"Why does everyone assume I can't cook?" she complained, oblivious to how obvious the answer to that question was to just about everybody else.

"Well, can you?" demanded Scottie.

"That's beside the point," Meg responded, refusing to relinquish her potato masher to Scottie's outstretched hand. Squish, squish, squish. She continued undaunted.

Win arrived next, her fur coat draped over her arm as she strolled in, without presents, as usual, Autumn observed. Perhaps they were in the car. She could have at least gotten something for Heather.

"Hello, family and friends," Win announced as she entered the kitchen. "Why is it so hot in here?"

"Well, we *are* cooking," said Autumn. "Nice to see you, too, Win."

Win gave her sister a limp hug and an air-kiss on her cheek. "Well, of course I'm glad to see you, sis. Do you really think I would drive all this way, in treacherous conditions, I might add, for anyone other than you?"

She glanced at Meg.

"Hello, Meg." And Meg grumbled a greeting back in her general direction. "Oh Scottie, you're here. Good. At least we'll have *some* culture with our turkey," she exclaimed as she held out her hand, expecting him to pour her a glass of wine.

Autumn shot Meg a warning glance from the sink, and Meg rolled her eyes in return. Autumn didn't know it, but Meg had switched Win's place card as soon as she had arrived.

Martha, Ethan, and Heather were the last to arrive, and Autumn let out a sigh of relief that she didn't realize she'd been holding in. She stripped off her apron, declaring, "It *is* hot in here."

Ethan trailed behind Heather and Martha, loaded down with presents and stomping the snow off of his shoes. Martha brought her cranberry sauce and chestnut stuffing into the kitchen, calling, "Autumn, I declare, that turkey smells like a dream," and stopping a little short when she saw Win but recovering nicely. "Well, hello. What a nice surprise," she declared as she popped the stuffing into the oven beside the turkey. "I didn't know you were coming."

Win couldn't tell if she was being genuine, but she really didn't care anyway.

"Yes, here I am in all my glory," she responded with another limp hug and air-kiss.

Autumn could hear Heather's delightful laugh and "oohs" and "aahs" coming from the living room as she admired the twinkling tree and instructed Ethan on the precise arrangement of their presents under it.

"No, that one goes there, out in front, and Meg's goes over there."

Autumn imagined him on his knees complying dutifully with the wishes of the little girl he seemed to have come to love as his own.

They emerged from the living room hand in hand and entered the kitchen, echoing Martha's comments about the delicious, savory aromas emanating from the oven. Heather ran to her, and Autumn scooped her up in her arms.

"Look. Win's here, too," and Heather gave Win a little wave and a smile. Heather seemed to be the only person Win was cordial to, which was a relief.

"Hi, Winny," she called, and Win waved back at her with perfectly manicured red-tipped fingers.

"Hi, sweetheart." She made no move to hug the little girl she had known since she was born.

Autumn greeted Ethan with a smile as he stood in the doorway between the kitchen and dining room, and barely resisted the urge to fling herself at him. His smile was as warm and genuine as the one he gave her in his office in New York and then again at Miss Elsie's.

"Ethan, I'd like you to meet my sister, Win."

He turned his gaze, following Autumn's gesturing hand, horrified at what he saw. Horrified. Leaning on the island with a glass of wine in her hand was the woman he had met in a hotel lounge five years ago. He hadn't even known her name. Was that really her? Ethan liked to think that he lived an honorable life, one that never caused him any regrets. And he had, except for that one time, that one-night encounter with the woman standing before him. Frozen in the doorway as the reality of the situation burned into him, regret multiplied exponentially in his mind. All he could think of was Autumn. Sweet, honorable Autumn. She would despise him. This wasn't something that even a woman like Autumn could forgive.

"Oh, but we've met," Win purred. "That night in Chicago five years ago. Don't tell me you've forgotten." She laughed with a fake twinkle and a wink.

"Hello," he said tightly, his mouth suddenly feeling as if it were filled with cotton. There was no way he could pretend she had him mixed up with someone else.

Autumn felt her smile drop, just as a stone dropped in her stomach. She quickly readjusted her expression to hide not just her shock, but the wave of hurt, envy, disbelief, and utter disappointment that swept over her.

"Oh," she said, trying to sound breezy. "You two know each other?"

"We most certainly do," Win declared, moving to the doorway and offering hand. "We know each other *very* well. I'm Winter Hamilton, Autumn's older sister. Nice to see you again."

Ethan, reeling, did not hold out his hand to return her handshake, so she dropped her hand back to her side, laughing. "Oh, no need to be shy. I won't bite you. This time."

Ethan was grateful that Autumn took Heather out of the room. He suspected she had wanted to get as far away from him as possible.

There was an awkward silence in the kitchen as Meg and Scottie, who had mouthed silent "OH MY GODs" to each other, struggled to steer the conversation away from Win's attempts to flirt.

"Ethan," Scottie said. "Can you please help me with the fire? I think it's gone out."

At the stove, Meg snickered into her mashed potatoes.

In the living room, Autumn was grateful for Heather's chatter as she admired the decorations, picking up the glass balls and gingerly fingering the figures in the crèche, Autumn willed her heart to stop pounding and blinked back the tears stinging in her eyes. She couldn't believe what she had heard. Was it possible that she had misunderstood? No, she concluded. This was exactly the kind of thing Win would do, and then she'd throw it back triumphantly as a conquest that she wanted the world to know about. She wasn't surprised by what Win had done. But Ethan? How could Ethan have done such a thing? Had they been a couple? Autumn had often wondered what he had seen in Ellen, besides the fact that she was gorgeous. But now it dawned on her. He preferred women like Ellen and Win. Women who were so different from her it was almost laughable.

Suddenly, she felt stupid in her tarted-up red dress. This wasn't her. She had planned to wear black wool trousers and a simple red silk blouse. She looked down at the dress that hung above her knees, a modest slit up each side. Next to sophisticated Win, in her meticulous designer cream wool pants and matching cashmere sweater, she looked like the proverbial country mouse.

The only saving grace was that she knew five years ago he was not in a relationship with Ellen, and so he probably had had this one-night stand as a single man. When Ethan and Scottie wandered in to gaze at the blazing fire, Autumn stared at Ethan's back as if boring her eyes into him would produce an explanation that would dispute what she had just heard. He did not look at her as he came into the living room.

Probably mad at me, trying to figure out how to get rid of me now that he's reconnected with my gorgeous, successful sister, she told herself.

She returned to the dining room with Heather. As the little girl played with the set of glass angels arranged on the sideboard, Autumn plucked up Ethan's place card from the seat to her left and switched it with Kyle's, who she had originally placed at the end of the table next to Meg.

I'll figure out another way to set those two up, she promised herself, and went back into the kitchen to make the gravy.

Ethan did not make eye contact with Autumn throughout the meal, keeping his eye on his plate or helping to cut Heather's slices of turkey. He had seen the surprise on her face when she realized what had happened, and he couldn't bear to see the hurt, disgust, and disappointment that he knew blazed in her eyes.

Unaware of the tension triangle at the table, Kyle, Jack, and Martha carried the conversation, with Meg and Scottie steering it away when Win maliciously started talking about her trip to Chicago five years ago. At one point Scottie found it necessary to kick her under the table.

"Ow," she howled. "Geez, Scottie, watch what you're doing."

"Sorry, Win," he offered with a crocodile smile, "my foot must have slipped."

After dinner, Autumn served coffee, cider, and pies in the living room as everyone gathered to exchange presents.

"Oh," Win declared, as she accepted packages from Autumn, "I didn't know we would be exchanging gifts or I would have brought something for our special guest." She was looking at Ethan as she spoke the words. Ethan ignored her and watched as Heather tore into her pile of gifts.

He felt his blood boiling in his veins as he realized that Win would have known that this was Heather's first Christmas without her parents, and he marveled at her selfish, cold-hearted behavior. He risked a glance at Autumn, who was serving and passing slices of pie around to her guests. She was such a caring, attentive hostess and had done so much to make this a special holiday for Heather. Just the week before she had emailed him for a list of gifts he thought Heather might like, and gathering from the large pile of wrapped packages under the tree, he guessed she had purchased all the toys and books he had suggested. The contrast between the sisters amazed him, and he realized with a sinking heart that whatever chance he might have had with Autumn was now gone.

He stole glances at her when she was occupied, looking anywhere but at him. Each time he saw her, she became more beautiful to him, and the regret of his night with Win grew more and more stifling. Sitting next to the tree with Heather, her legs tucked under her, Autumn was the only gift he ever wanted. He realized that now.

It figures, he thought, *as soon as I decide what I really want, I can't have it.*

As her guests were leaving, Autumn gathered coats from the hall closet and almost knocked Heather over as she made her way back to the living room. The little girl had followed her to the coat closet.

"Here," she said shyly, holding out a painting. "I drew you another picture."

Autumn shifted the armful of coats and took the painting, another depiction of Heather, Ethan, and Ellen, smiling happily in front of the Statue of Liberty. "It's beautiful," she said gently. "I love it. You are very talented, Heather. Your drawings of Ethan and Ellen look just like them, too."

Heather scrunched up her face, perplexed. "That's not Ellen," she said. "That's Inga. I never drew Ellen. She was too mean." And with that, she hugged Autumn around the knees and scampered away.

Fate was a cruel master, Autumn thought to herself as she settled on the couch in front of the fire with a cup of cider and Heather's painting. Realizing that Ethan and Ellen hadn't been the loving, happy family she had assumed they were, it was too late. Ethan had ignored her for the rest of the afternoon and only offered a quick wave as the trio left to return to Martha's. There would be no date at Mezzeluna in Pittsburgh. And no proclamation of love.

CHAPTER 23

"OU KNOW YOU need to talk about Ethan," Meg instruct-ed a few days after Christmas as the two friends de- deco-rated Autumn's house. "I know you're upset because you never take the decorations down before New Year's."

"There's nothing to talk about," Autumn responded. "Sure, it was an awkward moment, but these types of things happen. And I'm not surprised in the least about Win. This is just the kind of thing she would do."

"Yeah, I know. She's a sleaze ball. But what about Ethan?"

"What about him?" Autumn responded, desperately wanting to get away from the conversation. "There's really nothing to tell. He had a one-night stand with my sister, five years later they hook up again, and he ignores me and leaves without saying good-bye."

"Don't be stupid," Meg almost yelled. "He didn't 'hook up' with

Win. They went their separate ways. And besides, Ethan wasn't ignoring you. He was ashamed to look at you. Seriously, I thought he was going to have a heart attack at the table and fall face down into the cranberry sauce. Which, by the way, was really good. I love how Martha uses those slivers of ginger..."

Autumn cut her off. "It really doesn't matter. What's done is done."

"It's not done between you. I saw the way you looked at each other in front of Miss Elsie's a few weeks ago. You're as far away from being done as from here to Alaska."

Autumn snapped the lid on the last plastic container and slid onto the floor, her back against the couch.

"You're right, but only sort of," she said quietly. "Yes, I do have feelings for Ethan. And I'm almost positive he does, too. I felt it too that day in Miss Elsie's, and I thought he was about to tell me how he felt, but we were interrupted, and the moment passed."

"So, make another moment," Meg commanded. "Pick up the phone and tell him that you're not mad about Win. And tell him you're in love with him."

She picked up Autumn's cell phone from the coffee table and began to scroll through her contacts. With a few clicks she had dialed the number and handed the phone to Autumn, who immediately ended the call and pocketed her cell phone.

"Why do you always have to be so aggressive?" she snapped. "I can't believe you sometimes, Meg. What if he had picked up? I'd either have to talk to him or look like a complete idiot."

"That's the whole point, to talk to him. And by the way, you are acting like a complete idiot. But it's your life."

CHAPTER 23

* * *

The month following Christmas was such a whirlwind that Autumn didn't have time to dwell on her feelings for Ethan. She just had to accept the fact that feelings just don't turn on and off by themselves. What surprised her was that she felt as strongly about him as she did prior to Win's little surprise. Was Meg right? Should she contact him? Maybe it wasn't him she had the issue with. After all, he was a single man and could do as he pleased. Maybe it was Win's behavior she had to face and confront.

As promised, Scottie had secured her a show in a major gallery in Pittsburgh at the end of January, and her time was consumed with the frantic preparation. Galleries typically planned their exhibitions months, even a year in advance, but this gallery owner had insisted he wanted the show as soon as possible because he was determined to be the gallery that premiered her new work. Autumn was more than happy to oblige.

In another major coup, she would have a solo show at a New York City art gallery in the fall, which made her think of Frank—sweet, dear Frank—and how easy it would be to be with him, living their lives side by side as fellow artists. And every time she thought of Frank, she couldn't help but think of Ethan.

Scottie had become a regular guest in her studio, apparently having abandoned his distaste for the "nether regions," as he liked to call just about any place other than Pittsburgh.

As she was putting the finishing touches on one of her paintings, he came strutting in calling, "Yoo-hoo. Where are you?"

"Don't you ever knock?" Autumn teased, and he ignored her, of course.

"How much do you love me?" he asked. "I mean, seriously, do you know the things I do for you?"

"Of course I do, Scottie. You're not only my agent, but you're a dear friend."

"Well, dear friend, I am speaking to you as your agent. Let me ask you this. What is one of the most important events in an artist's life?" he continued.

"Hmmm…important events?" Autumn mused. "A New York City solo show? But I already have that, thanks to you."

"Think bigger. Better. Think worldwide exposure among collectors and curators."

Autumn blinked. "No!" she almost yelled, her eyes widening and her mouth open as she jumped from her chair and hopped around, suddenly vibrating with new found energy. "You are not serious? The *New York Times* art section?"

"The one and only, and you can thank me later," he answered triumphantly. "The reporter will be here tomorrow to interview you, and he's bringing along a photographer. Girl, you better fix yourself up," he said appraisingly. "Do you have time to get your hair done?"

Autumn just laughed. "Don't worry, I'll make myself presentable."

"And clean up this studio, too, but not too much. You're a working artist after all."

A pang of longing in her gut surprised her. Yes, she was a working artist again, thanks to Heather, and maybe the universe, and certainly divine intervention.

Scottie was still talking. "Didn't I tell you I'd make you famous? Everyone wants a piece of your new work. It's a sensation. And it's only going to intensify. Brace yourself, baby."

CHAPTER 23

As was his custom, he blew her a kiss as they exchanged good-byes, and then he was gone.

Autumn walked to the enormous glass window that overlooked her garden, still dark and dormant in winter's gloom. Hugging herself and smiling, she couldn't believe that this was happening to her. It was perhaps the most significant moment so far in her career, and she had no one to share it with. Oh, she could call Meg, of course, who would be over the moon and then launch into some conspiracy diatribe about how the press couldn't be trusted, and especially the *New York Times*.

Autumn longed to share her good fortune with Heather, to tell her the story of how her painting had transformed her work. Her life. But would a five-year-old understand the impact her little painting had caused? Probably not, but Ethan could have explained it to her. She had loved watching his love for Heather develop. It was clear that he adored her, and maybe more importantly, that Heather adored him. But Ethan had deserted her, and that was that.

Still, she would tell the reporter the story of spilling the wine and the stick figures on Heather's paintings transferring to her own painting. She told herself it was important to give credit where credit was due. A part of her, too, wanted Ethan to see the article, to read about her success—the success of the woman he had so far given up on.

* * *

Kyle sauntered proudly along Pittsburgh Street and took his usual place at the lunch counter at Hoffman's Drugstore, no longer afraid to come face to face with the merchants. He had triumphed after all, bringing in droves of shoppers during the three weeks before Christmas. The article about Miss Elsie had done the trick. Shoppers came out to support her just because of her long-standing charity work. The pictures of the tea room, with its five Christmas trees and other decorations stuffed to the rafters, didn't hurt either. She had truly created a whimsical, sparkling winter wonderland. And once she had the shoppers in her tea room, Miss Elsie very sweetly, but adamantly, insisted that they visit her very dear friends at the other shops on Pittsburgh Street. Kyle had watched her in action, making her rounds from table to table, checking on everyone. She asked each person who they hadn't bought gifts for yet, and putting her finger to her chin, would say, "Well, let me see." And she would proceed to direct them to one of the shops where she was certain they would find the perfect gift.

He smiled as he remembered Stan telling him he had sold out of all his "lady gifts," and Lila Geyer had to do a rush order to her distributor for matching mother-daughter Christmas Eve pajamas to meet customer demand. Even the Pritchards, who owned the Number One Wok, had seen an upturn and had to hire a part-time helper during the rush.

But now that his work was done, Kyle had to face the fact that he had to figure out his next step. The mayor expected his full report at the end of the week, and he suspected that at that time she would end his contract, which, of course, he had expected all along. He planned to present his proposal that he would open his own marketing firm in Natalie's vacated building, and for a small fee from each of the merchants, he would stay on and continue his work for them, while taking on new marketing and public relations clients. All he needed from the mayor was a small retainer to get him started on rent and utilities. In exchange, he would take on the responsibility of promoting the next Fall Festival.

But first, there was Andy to deal with. Kyle knew that as long as he tried to keep his past a secret he was vulnerable to Andy's demands. And as long as Andy knew where he was, he would never stop sniffing around, trying to make trouble for him. The only solution was to tell the mayor and the merchants the whole story and hope they were understanding and sympathetic. He figured with the hugely successful Christmas season they had all had, and despite the dismal Black Friday performance—which wasn't his fault at all, he reminded himself—the merchants would be on his side. And maybe they would put some pressure on Mayor Peggy.

Kyle asked Duncan if he could hold a meeting in one of the vacant upstairs dance parlors and was relieved when Duncan quickly agreed. He invited all the merchants, plus the mayor, Sheriff Landry, and of course Meg and Autumn to a special evening merchants meeting on a Sunday evening when all their shops were closed.

When they had all gathered, filling up the chairs he had put out, he stood in front of them, wiped his clammy hands on his slacks, cleared his throat, and began to speak.

"I'm not the person you all think I am," he began. "I lied to you all about my past and my experience because I thought if you knew m secret, you wouldn't hire me. And you just don't know how mu needed this job."

The crowd sat in stunned silence. Only Miss Elsie spoke.

"Go on, son. It can't be as bad as all that."

Kyle laughed self-consciously and shook his head in affirmative.

"I'm afraid it is, Miss Elsie. And I wouldn't blame y of you, if you hate me by the end of the evening." He addressed the mayor. "Mayor Peggy, the references you checked were all fake. You talked to a friend of mine who pretended to be the different people you talked to."

Peggy just nodded, not at all surprised by what she was hearing. But the crowd around her tittered.

"You see, when I was in college…" He stopped as he saw the sheriff stand and join him at the front of the room.

"It's all right, son," he said. "You sit down now. Let me take care of this."

Kyle sank into the chair vacated by the sheriff, not sure what he was up to.

This is not going to end well for me, he thought, half expecting the sheriff to clear the room so he could haul him away.

The sheriff waited until everyone was quiet.

"Do you all remember, about thirty years ago, a young man who came to this town, with a record a mile long? Reckless driving. Disturbing the peace. All sorts of nonsense." He looked over the crowd at some of the nodding heads. "And do you remember what you all did for him, those of you old geezers who have lived here forever?"

Many of the people nodded their heads.

"You gave him a second chance, despite all his past transgressions. You let him prove himself to you and gave him the opportunity to be part of this community." He gestured at Kyle. "This fine young man came to our town to help us. Would you agree that he helped this town for the better?"

The crowd called out in unison, "Yes," and let the sheriff continue.

"During his last year in college, Kyle ran into some trouble. He lost his job and only had enough money for rent or for tuition. He chose to pay the tuition because he wanted to finish his education and make something of himself. He tried to find a job, but it was hard because you need an address for a job, and he didn't have one. So he lived in his van for almost a year. Imagine that. Living in a van parked on the college campus, showering in the college gym day in and day out. Eating food from the dumpsters."

Kyle sat, like stone, flabbergasted at what the sheriff knew about him. How in the world did he find this out? And how long had he known about it?

"He was very careful and respectful," the sheriff was saying, "but the campus police became suspicious, and they called the local sheriff. Kyle was arrested for vagrancy and spent a couple of nights in jail." He turned to look at Kyle. "I suspect that's what you didn't want us to find out about, isn't it?"

Kyle nodded, managing a hoarse, "Yes, sir."

The sheriff turned back to the crowd. "But that's not the end of the story. When the college president heard Kyle's story, he went down to the jail and convinced the sheriff to drop all the charges and expunge them from his official record."

There were many approving murmurs from the crowd.

"And then the college found some emergency financial aid for him, and he was able to get a small apartment and a job at a fast-food restaurant. He graduated and then ended up here, with us. Is that about it, son?"

He turned to Kyle, and before Kyle could thank him the crowd was upon him, hugging and kissing him, telling him, "Bless your heart" and "We love you" and "We're so sorry this happened to you."

He took the hugs and kisses, all the while scanning the room for Meg and Autumn. Finally, he saw them, standing away from the crowd. Autumn was smiling at him. Meg, of course, looked sullen, but, to his surprise, she gave him a little wave. And that's when his tears came.

Later, in Peggy's office, she and the sheriff explained how they had known about his past, and the mayor pulled out the folder Buddy had given her as part of his investigation of the robberies. She handed it to him.

"I don't think we'll be needing this anymore," she said, smiling.

Kyle was afraid to look but opened it anyway. It was the police report and a few other related items, including a copy of the letter the college president had written to the police department. He looked up at them in wonderment. "You've known all this time, and you didn't say anything?"

Peggy and Buddy looked at each other and smiled.

"Do you remember that young man I spoke about earlier, in the meeting?" the sheriff asked, grinning. Kyle nodded. "That young man was me, son. Everyone deserves a second chance."

Kyle could only grin, giddy with relief and, suddenly, anticipation. He remembered his conversation with Eric, who also said he deserved a second chance. He was starting to believe it himself. His confession had also freed him from the hold Andy had over him. The next time he popped up and learned there was no way he could hurt Kyle, he wouldn't stick around. That part of his life was over. And he knew that better times lay ahead.

When Kyle and Buddy had gone, Peggy got up from her desk and walked to the window to look out onto the quiet buildings that waited in the shadows of the streetlights for the next shopping day to begin. She was proud of Kyle and admired the strength it took to come forward with his secret. And she knew she should follow his example. She would make her announcement soon. But not yet. She wanted to bask in her recent success and enjoy it for as long as she could. She knew people suspected that something was wrong—her wig wasn't *that* good—but they had respected her privacy, and for that she was grateful. If she could just hang on until fall, she thought, she would see the rebirth of the Fall Festival. And she would have one last Christmas with her beloved Bob and a little time to straighten out her boys.

* * *

On a lazy Sunday in New York, Ethan and Heather were tucked in the apartment against the cold and the snow. Heather, having moved on from Barbies to include Ken dolls, was staging a fashion show on the island in the kitchen.

"Today is fashion week," she declared. She had fashioned a runway out of cereal boxes stacked on their sides into a long line. "You can't look until it's time for the fashion show," she commanded Ethan, who had just settled into his leather recliner in the living room.

He looked aimlessly through the *Times* front and metro sections, half reading the articles, half listening to Heather instruct her dolls as to who would wear each outfit and why, even though all the dolls looked alike to him.

"You have blonde hair," she was saying, "and you like pink."

As he laughed at her little girl logic he turned to the arts section. His stomach clenched, like a fist squeezing a tennis ball, and he could suddenly hear his heartbeat in his ears. There, on the page in front of him, Autumn Hamilton stared back at him from an oversized photo of her in her studio. At least he assumed it was her studio, never having had the chance to see it for himself. Her long auburn hair was pulled back in a high ponytail. Her face was perfection, with her porcelain skin and large, azure eyes that held his gaze now, the same way they had a mere few weeks ago. The photographer had not only captured her outer beauty, as her slim frame leaned against a counter, her feet crossed at the ankles, but the inner beauty he loved came across in her expression and brilliant smile.

"Well that was fast," he said aloud, as he imagined how Autumn must have thrown herself into her work following the scene at Christmas, forgetting all about the tender moment they had shared—or almost shared—at Miss Elsie's. He could hardly blame her, he reprimanded himself, and he read the article from start to finish. The beginning of the article was a review of her work, which the writer described as "haunting" and "the most original work this reviewer has seen in two decades."

He studied the paintings, mesmerized by the tiny matchstick figures parading on perfectly rendered white flowers. Ethan was not much of an art critic and at first was put off by the stick figures. But he found himself looking closer at the pictures and seeing how the little men were not placed haphazardly, but to form parts of the petals, leaves, and stems themselves. He wondered how anyone could create something that was so bizarre yet compelling at the same time.

He found the answer as he read on. In a long quote from Autumn he learned how a spilled glass of wine on a little girl's painting had changed the course of her work forever. She went on to describe the circumstances in detail, naming Heather, and even mentioning Ethan as her guardian, going only into the briefest of detail about the death of Heather's parents and the art therapy that was helping her to deal with the grief.

Ethan felt a mixture of stunned awe, sadness, and a distinct feeling of pride surging within him. That he even played the slightest role in Autumn's life made him love her even more. He was the guardian of the little girl whose inspiration had changed the course of her work! She could have credited Heather without mentioning him. He took the paper into the kitchen, interrupting Heather's fashion show.

"You go back to your seat and wait. Fiona is naked."

"Okay. I will in a second, but do you want to see something special?" he asked, adding, "About Autumn?" And then he spread the paper out on top of the cereal boxes.

The mention of Autumn's name got Heather's immediate attention, and she abandoned her fashion show and exclaimed, "Lemme see, lemme see."

"It's here, sweetie, in the paper." And he pointed to Heather's painting, the paint faded and the figures distorted as if they had melted. Autumn had framed it in a thin silver frame and it hung prominently in her studio.

"That's my picture," Heather said in wonderment. "How'd it get in there?" And then she exclaimed loudly, "Eww, that's not what it's supposed to look like."

"There's a story in this newspaper about it. Autumn put your picture here. Do you want to know how she did it?"

Heather nodded, resting her head on his shoulder for a closer look.

"It's Autumn," she said excitedly, pointing to the newspaper.

And Ethan began to read, his voice strong with the pride he felt for the woman he loved. When he was done, Heather looked at him quizzically.

"I did that?"

Ethan nodded and pointed again to the newspaper.

"See, here is your name in print, and mine."

"Cool," Heather said, already returning to her dolls. "She must like us if she put us in the paper."

Ethan was taken aback with a jolt, impressed, as always, with a little girl's innocent wisdom. Was it possible that Autumn did have feelings for him after all? Was this her way of reaching out to him?

Heather interrupted his musings.

"But if she really, really liked us, like ice cream or cookies, she would have put our names in more times, and in red or pink, and with little hearts."

Of course, he concluded sadly, Heather was probably right. A passing reference in an article that pretty much *had* to mention Heather didn't really mean anything.

Why did it have to be, when it came to Autumn Hamilton, he always found himself at a dead end?

CHAPTER 24

MARTHA KNEW WHAT was waiting for her when she woke up the next morning: five inches of snow and more on the way. There was no sense in going out there to clear it until it warmed up, so she got herself a cup of coffee and slipped back under the covers to watch the news. When she headed down for a second cup of coffee, still in her bathrobe, she was surprised to see that her driveway and sidewalks were clear. There was even a path from the front door to where she had parked her car.

"What in the name of heaven?" she said aloud. She went to the front door to look through the peephole and saw Jack Staub put his snow shovel in the truck bed. She wanted to call out to him, to thank him or even to invite him in for a cup of coffee, but she was in her nightgown and robe, and that is not how she envisioned their first date.

When Jack had finished with his work, he just sort of stood around the truck, as if waiting for something.

Martha realized he was waiting for her! She flew up the stairs and grabbed the clothes she had worn the day before out of the hamper. She nearly lost her balance putting on her underwear, and then her slacks, and thought she would dislocate her shoulder trying to get into her bra so quickly. She remembered her mother's admonishment when she was a child. "The faster you go, the behinder you get," and willed herself to slow down, just a little bit. She ran her fingers through her hair and went back down the stairs and flung the front door open just in time to see the tailgate of Jack's truck as it chugged down Loucks Avenue and turned onto Grove, disappearing from sight.

"You're going to freeze to death standing there with the door open," she heard a familiar voice say. It was Peggy Brightwell from across the street, retrieving her newspaper from her front porch. "Is everything all right?" she asked.

"I don't know," Martha said. "I think I need a little dating advice."

"I'll be right over," Peggy said. "Just let me get my shoes on."

Martha poured them each a cup of coffee, and the women sat across from each other in Martha's cozy kitchen. It hadn't been re-done in thirty years, but Martha loved the familiar avocado-green appliances and parquet floor.

Peggy looked tired, and she was wearing a very attractive wig that was surprisingly similar to her own color and style.

"Tell me how you're feeling," Martha said gently.

"Oh, you know, good days and bad days." She gave a brave smile. "Today is a good day, and I'm going to eat that casserole you sent over the other day for lunch. You really don't have to do so much for us," Peggy continued. "It must be wearing you out. All those meals for Bob and the boys."

"You forget I had a household full of teenage boys for a while," she reminded Peggy.

"Oh no, I remember quite well," Peggy laughed. "They were a handful."

"And they were eaters. Like vacuum cleaners they were, sucking up all the food in sight and asking for more. I couldn't keep up with them." She grew quiet. "It was different with Denise. She ate like a little bird…" Her voice trailed off. "Anyway, I know what it's like to have two growing boys who eat everything in sight. I'm happy to do it."

"Well they love your cooking," Peggy said. "In fact, I've been instructed to tell you that their favorites are your pot roast, spaghetti sauce, and chicken pot pies."

Martha beamed under the compliment. It was nice to be needed.

"What do the doctors say?" Martha asked gently.

Peggy shook her head. "They won't say anything until after the chemo's done." She shrugged. "I'm not going to borrow trouble. So, what was Jack Staub doing here so early in the morning?" Peggy asked.

Martha blushed. "Well, not what you're thinking."

"Mmm, that's too bad," Peggy replied slyly.

"Peggy!" Martha exclaimed, startled.

"What? You can't enjoy a man's company because you're old?"

Martha didn't know what to say.

"Well, no. I mean, yes. Oh, I don't know what I mean." She buried her head in her hands, and her whole body shook with laughter. "Everything gets so much more complicated the older you get. The good things slow down, and the bad things speed up."

"I don't see why it has to," Peggy said. "The basics haven't changed, you know."

"Oh, I don't mean that," Martha said, laughing. "What I mean is, when I was younger, women just didn't approach men and ask them on dates. I was taught that you wait for the man to come to you."

"Hmm. Well if you're going to wait for Jack Staub to make the first move, you might as well give up."

"That's what Autumn said," Martha replied distractedly.

"But then again," Peggy said.

"Then again, what?"

"Oh, never mind. It's just a silly thought."

"Please, Peggy, at this point I'll take any bit of advice, no matter how silly it is."

Peggy held out her cup, and Martha poured a refill.

"Did you ask Jack to come this morning and plow and shovel?" she asked.

Martha shook her head.

"I didn't think so," Peggy replied triumphantly.

"What does that have to do with anything?"

"I think you can interpret that as Jack making the first move," Peggy said excitedly. "It makes sense, don't you think? Everyone knows when it comes to women he's too shy to make any direct move, but this was his way of telling you that he cares about you. I doubt he's in the habit of going around randomly to people's houses and clearing snow for the fun of it, especially when he's got so much land to clear at the nursery. Just think how long it must take him to shake the snow off all of those azaleas."

"But he didn't even wait to see me after he was done. At least not long enough. By the time I threw on my clothes and walked out the door, he was gone."

"Exactly," Peggy said. "In his mind, he didn't have to wait for you. He'd already said what he needed to say by clearing your driveway. I watched him for a little while. He even put deicer down at the end of the driveway where it usually ices over. If I were you, I'd be ready for him the next time."

* * *

The weeks after Christmas had been difficult for Heather. The weather in New York had been cold, grey, and windy. Heck, even folks who had not lost both their parents were depressed. She missed them terribly, but being back in her routine of school and going to her art lessons, she perked up some. She saw Dr. Abernathy once a week, who had promised Ethan that Heather was making progress, even if some days it didn't seem like it.

She had yet to make any real friends or be invited for a sleepover or "play dates," as Ethan had gathered these kid get-togethers were called. But a concerned call to Dr. Abernathy one afternoon set his mind at ease. Basically, Heather just needed time to heal slowly, until she felt like she could do more normal things. This normalcy would come incrementally, and probably in fits and starts. It hadn't even been six months since the tragedy that took Denise and Troy, and Dr. Abernathy promised Ethan that Heather was making remark-able strides considering her circumstances.

February was particularly busy at the firm, and Ethan, in a way grateful to have something to get his mind off Autumn, was trying back-to-back cases by the middle of the month. He was harried, frazzled, and distracted. And he hated it. He soon realized that no matter how busy and exhausted he was, Autumn was there, in his daydreams and in his night dreams, and to his great dismay, an image of Win would always barge in and obliterate everything.

One afternoon, Myra slipped into the room where Ethan was conducting a deposition. He hated to be interrupted, especially during these meetings. She slipped a piece of paper in front of him, and he read it with a growing sense of horror. *Heather's school called. No one has picked her up yet.*

He froze in place, feeling the blood draining from his face and arms until he thought perhaps he wouldn't be able to move. But he turned his head to look at the clock on the wall and realized, in horror, that he was supposed to pick Heather up from school two hours ago. Inga had called him at ten that morning. She had broken a tooth and was able to get an emergency dentist appointment at two thirty, so he had agreed she should go get her tooth fixed. She instructed him about the pickup policy and told him what time to arrive. She had even texted him at lunchtime to remind him.

"Excuse me, ladies and gentlemen," he said calmly, even though he felt that every organ in his body was about to burst open. "Ms. Blenco will be taking over the deposition from this point forward."

He gestured to the young associate on his left. She was one year out of law school and as green as they come. But he didn't have a choice. They had already postponed the deposition twice, and with the approaching trial date it would be suicide to cancel now. It was those types of tactics that got you in trouble with the judge. He gathered his papers and grabbed his suit coat from his chair.

"I have every confidence that Ms. Blenco can move this deposition forward to its conclusion." He didn't look at her. He couldn't.

He had just dumped a major assignment into the lap of a first-year, and he would hear about it later. He said a silent prayer that the deposition wouldn't reveal any major surprises.

He flew out the conference room door and into his office, re-trieved his briefcase, and bolted toward the elevators. "Call the school," he called to Myra. "Tell them I'm on my way."

"Already done," he heard her say as he stepped onto the elevator.

How could he have been so careless and irresponsible? In what world does someone forget their kid at school? He rested his head against the wall. In his mind he saw Heather, sitting hunched over on the sidewalk, her Hello Kitty backpack clutched in her lap, tears streaming down her cheeks.

It was rush hour when he emerged from his building, and it took forever for him to find a cab. By the time it screeched to a halt in front of the Dalton School, dusk was falling. He threw the cab-bie a fifty, the smallest bill he had in his wallet, and bolted up the front steps to the front entrance. When he found it locked he began pounding as if his life depended on it. At that very moment, he felt as if it did.

He heard footsteps scurrying down the hall and saw the head-mistress, Mrs. Waterford, rushing to him.

"Mr. Rasmussen," she said to him in that principal voice he re-membered from his school days. "You do not need to use your fists to get my attention. I was waiting for you in the library just down the hall." She opened the door, and he rushed in, frantic.

"Where's Heather? Is she all right? I am so sorry. I have no idea how I could have forgotten—the nanny had an emergency, and I was in a deposition…"

Mrs. Waterford, in her tweed suit and sensible shoes, was peering at him with her owl eyes and interrupted him with a stern, "Mr. Rasmussen, that is quite enough!"

He stopped talking immediately.

"I don't care if you were having tea with the president or were traveling to England to be knighted by the queen herself. There is NO ACCEPTABLE EXCUSE for forgetting to pick up your child."

Ethan was defeated. And he knew she was right.

Her voice softened a little as she continued. "Now, I know there are extenuating circumstances here, and you and Heather are in an adjustment period. But I'm sure I don't have to remind you, Mr. Rasmussen, of the abandonment issues Heather already faces due to the death of her parents. I found her forty-five minutes ago hiding in the courtyard. I hate to even think about what could have happened to her if I hadn't been walking through there."

Ethan wanted to point out that the school itself had a responsibility to see every child safely into the hands of her assigned adult during pickup time, but he decided he was in enough trouble. Instead, he did his best to look sufficiently chastised. He really wanted to see Heather, to explain to her, to tell her that this would never happen again, that she was more important to him than work. He would promise to make it up to her.

Heather's tear-stained face and the balled-up tissues in her little, delicate hand broke his heart. He rushed to her side and knelt beside her, but she turned away from him and crossed her arms over her chest. He tried to stroke her hair, but she jerked away from him.

"Heather," he said softly. "I will never, ever leave you again. I promise." He took her gently by the arms and turned her toward him. She was crying again, this time big sobs of pain and hurt and loss and grief, and he embraced her even though her little arms stayed rigidly by her side.

And then he was crying too, and when she pulled away from him and saw his face, she reached out and lovingly patted his cheek.

As they rode home in silence in the cab, Ethan kicked himself for destroying the progress the two of them had made in the past months. He felt ashamed when he thought about how Martha would react when she found out. Surely Heather would tell her when she called tonight. And of course, Autumn would find out. She would have another perfectly understandable reason to despise him.

Autumn had been right after all, and maybe he should have listened to her. He thought about the conversation they had in September. She had asked him if he was doing what was right for Heather. Maybe he wasn't. Maybe he couldn't. Imagining Autumn's disappointment in him made him feel even more miserable.

On the way home Inga texted him that she was having an emergency root canal and wouldn't be home to meet them. He knew she also knew about his catastrophe. Surely the school would have attempted to reach her first. He had no choice but to take Heather with him to the office while he tied up a few things and grabbed the files he would need to work at home this evening.

"Oh, I'm so glad you're still here," he said to Myra when they walked down the hall, Heather keeping her distance from him. She hadn't said a single word.

"Hi, Heather," she called out. "Want to play *Dora* on my computer while Ethan does grown-up stuff?"

Heather nodded and climbed into Myra's lap. Myra studied Ethan with a troubled look he hadn't seen from her before, and then she jerked her head to motion down the hall to the senior partners' offices.

"Mr. Morgan asked to see you as soon as you returned," she said softly.

As he walked into the plush office of the firm's founder, Ethan tried to come up with a plausible excuse for rushing out of the deposition. Picking up Heather would be plausible enough for most people, but Mr. Morgan did not get where he was by being "most people." Ethan hoped Ms. Blenco had not gotten crucified. He hoped even more that he didn't get crucified.

"We are sympathetic with your situation and have tried to accommodate you as much as possible," Mr. Morgan began, gesturing for Ethan to sit in the chair opposite his desk. His boss was powerfully dressed in a blue pinstripe suit and crisp white shirt with the scales of justice embossed on platinum cufflinks. Ethan was painfully aware of his rumpled appearance. He knew he wasn't putting his best foot forward at the moment.

"And I appreciate that, sir. I really do," he answered, bracing himself.

"But we have to consider the other staff in the office and the precedent it sets when we excuse you for leaving at will to take care of your personal business and relying on the firm's resources to accommodate your special circumstances."

"I agree, sir, one hundred percent. It's not right, but I'm on it. I'm going to find a live-in nanny, and this will never happen again."

His mind was whirring with how he would handle things from now on. To begin with, he should have had Inga talk to Myra so she knew that he had to leave at three. So first rule: everything, absolutely everything, related to his and Heather's schedules would be routed through Myra.

"When we made you a partner two years ago," Mr. Morgan was

saying, "you were on top of your game, riding the crest of the wave, but you've lost the momentum that made you such a valuable asset to this firm."

"I'm not exactly sure what you mean," Ethan said. The use of the past tense disturbed him deeply, and he knew he didn't want to hear what was coming next.

"Ethan, it's time for you to resign. It's not unusual for a new parent, especially a single one, to take a less demanding job with a smaller firm. No one would blame you, and certainly we would not judge you. And you can count on a most excellent reference. I will give you a nice severance package to help you keep your feet under you until you find another position. And we will pay your health insurance premiums for a year. It's a generous offer, Ethan. More than I've ever given anyone else. Make it easy on all of us and just resign quietly.

"With all due respect, sir, I won't do that. I am not a quitter."

Mr. Morgan sighed. "I was afraid you would say that, son. And that's one of the reasons we hired you in the first place, right out of law school."

"So what next?" Ethan asked, though he knew. As he was no longer an officer in this firm he was no longer privy to the details of the work done here.

"Myra will pack your personal belongings and have them messengered over to you."

So that was it. After twelve years, he wasn't even allowed to go back into his office one last time. Which was better? To quit or to be fired?

He shook Mr. Morgan's hand even though he would have rather slugged him. He couldn't help but wonder what he would have done if the roles were reversed. He'd call his own lawyer, Hal Jennings, in the morning. He'd get that severance package one way or another, not for himself, but for Heather.

As he walked slowly back toward what used to be his office, he was surprised that he wasn't more upset by the turn of events. He was almost at peace. He supposed from the moment he decided to raise Heather he had known he would have to make some big sacrifices. He just didn't realize how big. He was glad to hear Heather laughing with Myra as he turned the corner.

Myra looked at him knowingly, and he put his fingers to his lips and pointed at Heather. When she saw him she scrambled off of Myra's lap and went over to stand next to him.

"What happened?" she asked.

"What happened," he said, trying to cheerful, "is that we're going to get to spend a lot more time together, for a while at least. How would you like it if I picked you up from school for a while? Won't that be fun?"

Heather took his hand in hers.

"You got fired," she declared in her serious little girl voice. "And it's my fault."

Ethan's eyes smarted with tears as he thought of the load of guilt and anguish this little girl had been carrying since her parents died.

"No, sweetheart, it's my fault for getting fired, because I should have quit the moment you came to live with me. I just didn't know it until now." He squeezed her hand. "Friends?"

She smiled up at him. "Friends," she agreed, and then she threw herself against his legs, and he heard her mumble, "I love you, Ethan."

He bent down so he could look her in the eye. "And I love you, kiddo."

CHAPTER 24

Myra rode with them down the elevator, and Ethan took the opportunity to apologize to her.

"Myra, I'm sorry for all the times I yelled at you these past few months. It was unprofessional and uncalled for."

She put her hand on his arm and squeezed.

"It has been an honor working with you, Ethan. Please don't lose touch. What are you going to do now?"

"Right now, at this very moment, we are going out for pizza and ice cream, and then we're going to stay up late watching *Scooby-Doo* movies."

"It's a school night, Ethan," Heather said, shaking her head.

"Oh, right. Okay, just one *Scooby-Doo* movie."

As Heather munched happily away at Mario's Pizza Parlor down the block from the penthouse, Ethan assessed the day's damage. He had traumatized his child *and* lost his job, all on the same day. So now Autumn would know that not only did he sleep with her sister, not only did he forget to pick Heather up at school, now he had been fired. Wow, he was on a roll. And it had only been six months. Some parent he turned out to be. He remembered his confident "I got this" declaration to Autumn in September. What he "got," he mused, was one big mess on his hands and a little girl counting on him for things, it seemed, he was incapable of giving her.

And part of it was Autumn Hamilton's fault, he thought in a momentary flash of anger. If she hadn't completely cut him out of her life at Christmas, if she hadn't captured his heart in the first place. He shook his head. Of course he couldn't blame Autumn. He was being ridiculous. He thought back to the day they had met, how she had left him speechless, how she had teased him. He had wanted to laugh at her corny jokes, but he had been wound so tight by his circumstances that he hadn't allowed himself to. And he remembered wondering that day if he was happy he met her, or scared, or a bit of both. Now he would never know for certain.

CHAPTER 25

*M*ARTHA'S NEW HABIT of getting up and dressed before dawn when the forecast even hinted at snow had so far not born any results. She had decided to take Peggy's advice and interpret Jack's free mulch and gravel deliveries and snow removal as overtures representing the first steps necessary for courtship. And the next time he came she would be ready for him. Every morning she made enough coffee for two. If the snow ever went away and spring finally arrived, she would keep iced tea on hand in case he came in the afternoon. If he came. She felt her resolve waiver. And winter was coming to a close.

I'm a silly old woman, she thought to herself one morning as she sat alone at her kitchen table. *I've been doing this for a month, and I might as well be waiting for the Easter Bunny for all the good it's doing.*

When she heard the sound of a vehicle in her driveway she almost spilled her coffee as she jumped up and ran to the kitchen door. She slipped into her boots and coat, which had waited by the door, like faithful companions, for weeks. It was just five thirty and dark as pitch. She switched on the outside lights.

What will I say to him? She wondered, pulse racing. *Think Martha,* she commanded herself. *You can do this! All you say is, "Would you like to come in for a cup of coffee?"*

She watched the plow on the front of Jack's truck move the snow into mounds on either side of the driveway, and waved. Much to her relief, he smiled and waved back.

I know he'll get out of the truck to sweep the walk, like he did last time, she reasoned. *That's when I'll invite him in for a cup of coffee.*

The driveway clear, Jack cut the truck engine and hopped out, grabbing a shovel and broom from the truck's bed.

"You're up awfully early, Martha," he said, standing in front of her.

You have no idea, she thought, but instead said, "I like to get an early start on the day."

He nodded.

"It's very considerate of you to do this, Jack. Thank you," she said with feeling.

He wasn't looking at her, but she could tell he was smiling.

"Happy to do it. It's dangerous, you know, if you don't get it up right away. You know, it melts a little in the day and then refreezes at night. That's when people fall."

Martha was about as cold as she wanted to be, and out of necessity, as she desperately wanted to get back inside, she just blurted out, "Would you like to come in for a cup of coffee, Jack?" It was just as she planned, and she couldn't help but be just a little pleased with herself.

He nodded, "Think I will, Martha. That'd be real nice. Just let me shovel off the walkways and then I'll come round to the kitchen." He turned and began to shovel.

Those were the most words she had ever heard Jack Staub say to her at one time. Martha's face burned with a rush of adrenaline, and her heart sang as if she were a schoolgirl. She bustled inside and after removing her outerwear, rushed to the small half-bath and fussed with her hair and applied fresh lipstick.

It was only a few minutes until she heard Jack stomping the snow off of his boots at the back door. She had placed another mug and the sugar and creamer dishes on the table and was just taking a plate of muffins out of the microwave when he opened the door and stepped in, standing awkwardly just inside the kitchen.

"Please come in and warm up," she said brightly, and he took off his coat and hung it on the peg next to hers. The image of the two coats side by side gave her a pang of familiarity.

They sat across from each other, blowing on the hot coffee. Jack had not taken a muffin yet so she lifted the plate in his direction.

"These are homemade," she said. "I hope you like banana. I make a big batch and freeze them so I always have them on hand." *For you*, she thought to herself.

He accepted one and took a hesitant bite and then smiled.

"These are real good, Martha. I'd say just as good as the ones at Miss Elsie's."

"Thank you, Jack," she returned with a smile. "I'd be happy to give you the recipe. And you must give me the recipe for your sweet potato casserole. I am particularly fond of it, you know."

AUTUMN

***

As promised, Ethan's belongings were messengered to his penthouse a few days after his encounter with Mr. Morgan. The boxes arrived while Heather was at school. Unpacking the first one, he pulled out the photo of him and Troy, taken with a group of village children in Afghanistan ten years ago.

I'm so sorry, buddy, he thought, allowing the tears to roll down his cheek, glad Heather was not there to see him. *I let you and Denise down. I just can't get it right. If you knew how badly I've messed everything up, you would change your minds and give Heather to Martha. That's where she belongs. I'm exhausted, unemployed, and it's not right to inflict that on Heather.*

The thought of losing Heather created such an intense hurt inside him that he had to sit down and take deep, calming breaths. He looked around the living room, at the little pink recliner and the baskets of toys and books. Still holding Troy's picture, he went to Heather's room and sat on the frilly pink bed and gazed at her tiny desk where she drew her pictures. He looked at the dollhouse he had given her for Christmas and remembered how she had flung her little arms around his neck to thank him. Later, he had observed her playing with the dolls that came with the house. She had named them Mommy, Daddy, Ethan, and Heather. A little family. That's what she needed. A family, not an unemployed, reckless, unreliable jerk.

He got up from the bed, retrieved two suitcases from the hall closet, and began to pack Heather's clothes and little girl things—things that at first had exasperated him. He retrieved her Barbies from the bathroom and her *Dora* video game from the living room television. When the suitcases were full he called a moving company and arranged for movers to come to pick up the furniture.

After school, he picked Heather up in the car, her suitcases packed and tucked away in the trunk where she couldn't see them. She climbed into the backseat holding a new painting and her violin case and with the enthusiasm he had come to love.

"Look, Ethan," she exclaimed. "This picture is of Dog. He's new."

"Wow, you did a great job, honey. What's his name?"

"I told you already—it's Dog."

When they deviated from their usual route home she scrunched up her face and said, "Where are we going?"

"To your favorite place, to see Nanna."

"Okay," she replied, and she looked down to admire her picture and went on to tell him all about Dog, his wife, Cat, and his puppies, Mike and Debbie.

They reached Finch's Crossing just after seven, and he felt a nervous apprehension rise in his throat as they turned off the highway and entered the town on Broadway Street. By the time they had turned onto Loucks Avenue, he was positively anxious. They passed Autumn's house first, where he saw her yellow Jeep parked in the driveway. The house was dark, and he wondered where she was. He hadn't told Martha they were coming. As they pulled up to the house, she came running out, a black cardigan wrapped around her.

"Is everything all right?" she cried. "Is Heather okay?"

Right then Heather emerged from the backseat and ran to her grandmother. "Nanna! Nanna!" she yelled. "Ethan said we gonna be a s'rprise."

Martha hugged Heather tightly and eyed Ethan suspiciously. He looked disheveled and devastated. She had never seen him like this.

And though she had only known him a few months, more importantly, she had never *expected* to see him like this.

"Hello, Ethan," she said as he came around to greet her and they walked inside. "Don't you have any luggage?" she asked, puzzled.

Ethan pointed to Heather, who had run to the kitchen looking for cookies.

"Not now, Martha," he whispered and put a finger to his lips. "Let's talk after Heather's gone to bed."

They ate together in Martha's cozy kitchen, a familiar happy meal of meatloaf, mashed potatoes, and green beans. *This is the kind of home cooking Heather should be eating,* he reasoned with himself. *Not takeout five nights a week.*

Heather kept some clothes, a nightgown, and a toothbrush at Martha's, so he was able to put her to bed without getting out the suitcases. When he was satisfied that she was asleep, he and Martha sat on the couches around the fire. Martha broke the silence.

"What's this all about, Ethan? I can tell something's terribly wrong. What is it?"

He looked at her, his eyes shining with tears, then buried his head in his hands.

"I've made a huge mess of everything. I forgot Heather at school and lost my job, all on the same day. Can you just imagine how abandoned she felt? It was inexcusable."

"Slow down, Ethan. Take a deep breath." Martha remembered when her own children had come to her so broken and sad with a problem or worry. Her heart ached for Ethan.

"Just start from the beginning," she urged gently, "and tell me what's going on."

Ethan recounted his story. All of it. Not just the school incident and losing his job, but the way he had let Ellen belittle Heather and his inability to make her a nutritious meal, even though he had promised Martha he would. And when he was done, he just stared at Martha, dazed and hopeless. He never thought he would accept defeat like this, but the disaster he had created superseded his promise to Troy.

"I can't do this to her," he said quietly and wiped his eyes with the back of his hands. "I'm not good for her. I've totally messed everything up, so I've brought her back to live with you."

He stood up and headed toward the door, silently crying. "I've got a few of her things, and a moving van will bring the rest and all her furniture."

When he thought of the little pink Hello Kitty recliner in his living room, he broke into sobs.

"Ethan, wait!" Martha called out, clamoring after him as he went to his car and opened the trunk. "You can't do this. This will devastate Heather. She adores you. She needs you. You made some mistakes, that's all. Parenting is hard for anybody. Everybody!"

He brushed past her with the two suitcases and put them in the hallway.

"Tell Heather I'll call her tomorrow, okay?" He suppressed another sob. "And tell her I love her, and I'm sorry I did such a terrible job of taking care of her." He turned and returned to his car, and then he was gone.

Martha watched with disbelief as he drove away and the car disappeared down the avenue.

She sat for a long while in front of the fire, almost paralyzed with uncertainty. All she knew for sure was that when Heather woke up the next morning and realized that Ethan had left her without saying good-bye, she would be devastated. Unsure of what to do, she called Autumn.

"Oh, Autumn," she said when her friend picked up. "Something terrible has happened. Can you come over?"

"Wait, Martha, what's..." Autumn responded, but the call had ended. She flew out of her back door and walked through the bushes that separated their properties. She found a sobbing Martha in the living room.

Autumn kneeled next to her. "What's the matter? Is Heather okay?"

Martha nodded and managed to squeak out, "She's okay for now."

Autumn stroked Martha's back and waited for her to calm herself enough to speak.

"Ethan has brought Heather back to live with me. Just now, tonight. He even left without saying good-bye to her."

Autumn was stunned. "Tell me you're joking."

Martha shook her head.

"But why?" she asked, dumbfounded. "It doesn't make any sense."

"Not to us it doesn't, but it does to him," Martha said, sniffing. And she recounted to Autumn all that Ethan had told her.

When she was finished, Autumn sunk back into the cushions and let out her breath.

"This is terrible," she said. "Heather is going to be devastated. She adores Ethan. How could he possibly think this is the right thing to do?"

"He told me he feels as if he failed Denise and Troy, and if they knew what was happening, they would want him to do this, for Heather's sake."

"That's crazy," Autumn said, more angry than empathetic toward Ethan.

"In any event, it's happened, and I don't know what to do next. I don't know what to tell Heather."

Autumn looked around the living room at the two big suitcases. She got up and took them into the small den that Martha's husband used at one time, and Martha followed her.

"Take out enough clothes and toys for a few days," she instructed.

After Martha had made her selection, Autumn closed the suitcases and put them in the large closet in the room.

"You don't tell Heather any of this, okay?" Martha nodded, and Autumn continued. "Tell her Ethan had a job interview at the last minute and had to leave to catch a train or plane or something. That will explain why he left without saying good-bye."

"You mean, lie?" Martha asked, incredulous.

"That's exactly what I mean," Autumn answered. "Whatever you do, don't let her know the truth. There is no reason to put her through all of this unnecessarily."

"Unnecessarily?" Martha asked. "But…"

Autumn cut her off. "I'm going to New York. Right now. There's a ten o'clock flight from Pittsburgh, and I can make it if I leave now. First thing in the morning I'll talk some sense into him. This is not going to happen, okay?"

Martha sniffed and grasped Autumn's hand. "Okay," she said. And she managed a weak smile.

* * *

AUTUMN

"Autumn," Ethan said, taken completely by surprise when he opened his door, expecting to see movers. "What are you doing here?"

Autumn had booked herself into the Sheraton close to his apartment and after a restless night, appeared on his doorstep at eight in the morning. She immediately noticed how dejected he looked. How lost and confused. It was the way Martha had looked when she had seen her just a few hours earlier.

"May I come in?"

"Suit yourself," he said distantly, and he then walked back down the hallway. She followed him into the living room, where half-packed boxes were scattered around among big rolls of bubble wrap. He went back to packing books and didn't say a word. He wasn't in the mood for a lecture, not even from the woman he loved.

"What are you doing?" She hadn't expected the moving boxes. "Where are you going?"

"I don't know," he said, his back still turned toward her. "All I know is I can't stay here. Too many memories, you know. It would just break my heart every time I walked past her room."

Autumn took off her coat and perched on the side of the couch.

"Martha told me what happened," she said softly. "Why didn't you tell me?"

He shrugged but didn't look at her. "Nothing to tell. I got fired. Happens all the time. People lose their jobs, they move on." And then he did look at her. "You were right, you know. About Heather."

"What do you mean?"

"Last fall, at Martha's, you asked if I was doing what was right for Heather, and I didn't listen to you. I should have. Should have listened to both you and Martha. I've made a mess out of everything.

Heather is better off with Martha. I know that now. I'm a despicable human being." He reached for the packing tape and sealed up the box and then reached for another.

"You're wrong," said Autumn. "Oh, you've messed things up all right, but not the way you think. You will devastate Heather if you abandon her. She loves you, Ethan. And she needs you."

He turned to face her. "Martha hasn't told her yet?"

"I told her not to. She thinks you're at a last-minute job interview and that's why you had to leave without saying good-bye."

Ethan scoffed.

"See, I don't even have a job to provide for her."

"Ethan, what's really going on here? I don't believe for a minute that you've given her up because you lost your job. You'll get another job soon, and I'm sure you have savings and investments to tide you over."

Ethan sank wearily into the love seat and put his head in his hands.

"The job isn't the worst of it. It's unforgivable what happened. I forgot to pick her up after school last week. The nanny had an emergency, and it was my responsibility to get her. And I was so busy in a deposition that I completely forgot. She waited for me for two hours, hiding in the school courtyard. Can you just imagine how frightened she was, Autumn? I scared that little girl half out of her mind because I was selfish and irresponsible."

"You made a mistake," Autumn tried to soothe him.

"A mistake? You've got to be kidding. A mistake is when you drift over the speed limit or let the registration run out on your car. And that mistake I made with your sister," he said quietly, busying himself again with the boxes on the floor in front of him. "I'm despicable.

What kind of person does that kind of thing? I'm a selfish jerk. And you know it."

Autumn was quiet for a moment, trying to decide what to say. She had not expected him to bring up *that* subject.

"Were you in a relationship at the time?"

His head jerked up, and his eyes flashed at her. "Whatever I might be, whatever mistakes I have made, infidelity is not one of them. You probably don't believe me, but I guess that's a moot point. You despise me. I disgust you. You can't deny it."

"No," she responded slowly, "you are none of those things. You are a human being, fallible and tempted and, well, *human*, just like all of us. Do you think you're the only person in the world who has done something like this? At least you regret it, which is more than I can say for my sister."

"Can you forgive me?" he asked, finally looking her straight in the eye.

"There's nothing for me to forgive, Ethan. You didn't do anything to me. I mean, do I wish it never happened? Of course. But I think what you really need to do is figure out how to forgive yourself."

"I don't think I can," he said, with all the sadness that he had been carrying around inside since he took Heather back to Martha's.

"Ethan, why do you think I'm here?"

He thought for a minute and then realized he really didn't have a clue.

"I'm here to tell you that if you go through with this you will break Heather's heart. I mean, it hasn't been that long since her parents died. They were her lifeline, but now you are. And as much as she loves Martha, it's you she adores. You were the one who got her to talk again. She needs you, and more importantly, she wants you, despite the mistakes you have made, and will continue to make."

"I'm not used to making mistakes, and I don't like how it feels."

"Welcome to the human race," Autumn laughed.

"And what mistakes have you made, Autumn Hamilton? Because from where I sit, you haven't made even one since I've known you."

"That's preposterous. I make plenty of mistakes. Everyone does."

"Name one mistake you've made since I met you. Just one, and then you can go."

"Is that really what you want, Ethan, for me to leave? Because I don't believe you do."

He nodded, and she gathered her coat and purse and let herself out. Ethan threw the roll of packing tape against the wall, leaving a small dent. Why did everything have to be so complicated? He loved Autumn. When he saw the hurt in her eyes when she realized his transgression with her sister, and any chance of being with her began to slip away, he loved her even more. He hadn't been able to look her in the eye for the rest of that Christmas afternoon. Every glance from her had scalded and shamed him.

He heard the front door open. The movers were early, and he wasn't ready.

"You can start with the dining room, and then work your way back," he called out distractedly, retrieving the roll of tape from the other side of the room.

"You asked me to name one mistake I've made since I met you." Autumn's voice was steady and warm, and coming from the spot where he had expected to see two big burly and sweaty moving men.

He froze in place.

"I'll tell you one mistake I made," she said softly. "Walking out that door, just now, that was a mistake. And maybe you don't want to know this, but I'm going to risk telling you, because I want you to know what a good man you are so you will go back to Finch's Crossing, bring Heather home, and figure things out from there." She took a deep breath and continued. She was crying. "I love you, Ethan. You are an honorable man. If you weren't, I couldn't love you. I want you to know that I love and respect you and am so proud of what you've done for Heather."

He took one hesitant but hopeful step toward her, then another, until he was as close to her as he had wanted to be for weeks. He took her face in his hands and gently stroked her cheeks with his thumbs, tracing the tear streaks.

"I think I've loved you since you called me a big dirty pumpkin." She gave a little laugh. "I just couldn't admit it to myself."

"I didn't call you a big dirty pumpkin," he said softly against her lips, and she sighed and eased against him, wrapping her arms around his waist and drawing him close to her.

When he pulled back to see her face, he kept his arms around her neck. "I love you, too, Autumn. I have for a long time now, but I knew you would never have me after what happened with your sister." He felt her stiffen in his embrace. "You don't know how sorry I am about that."

"Shhh," she put a finger to his lips. "I don't want to talk about her right now," and she squeezed her arms tighter around his waist, as if to make sure he wasn't going anywhere. "First, kiss me. And then we'll go home to get Heather."

CHAPTER 26

AUTUMN WATCHED AS Meg stirred five tablespoons of sugar into her coffee, cradling her cell phone under her chin. They were sitting in Autumn's kitchen, catching each other up on what had happened in the previous few days since she had returned from New York.

"Am not," Meg declared heatedly into the phone. She paused and then repeated herself. "Am not." Another pause then, "Oh, all right. I'll be there."

Meg ended the call with a slight smile on her lips as she slipped the phone into her back jeans pocket.

"Was that Kyle?" Autumn asked, knowing full well that it was and acknowledging to herself that Meg did not perform her playful "am not, do not" banter with just anyone. It was a clear indication that Kyle's persistence was paying off.

"Yeah, he needs help spiffing up the new office space. You know he took over the atelier building recently vacated by the village twit and is going to live in the upstairs apartment. Peggy and the merchants are going to give him enough of a retainer to cover the rent and utilities. I bet I'll end up feeding him until he starts making some real money. And who knows what he's using for furniture."

Natalie had received probation and the last Autumn had heard was living with her parents.

"Well, I'm sure with your cheery disposition to help him along he will be just fine," Autumn teased. "Surely there must be much more he can do besides the web and social media to supplement his income. There are only so many business websites he can make for a small town."

"He'll overlap into business consulting across the area. He's already got plans to expand Ten Oaks. Hits to my website have tripled, he tells me, since he launched it. He's already picked out the empty back field for the expansion and is writing a business plan. I'm going to have to hire more staff by the time he's done," she groused.

"Is that so?" Autumn responded. "Soon he'll have you on Facebook and Twitter too!"

"Will not."

"Will so."

"Will not. Anyway, he's a convicted felon, you know. Spent two nights in jail for vagrancy until his college president came in and made it all go away."

"Then," Autumn corrected, "he is not a convicted felon. In fact, he doesn't even have a record. At least, that's the word around the lunch counter. Things don't stay secret for too long in this town."

She remembered her own secret, and Meg's, and knew she would never hold onto something like that again. Instead of keeping her secrets to herself she would cling to those who loved her, Ethan and Meg, Martha, and Heather.

"You have to give it to the guy," Meg was saying. "He lived homeless for months, just so he could finish his degree."

"Is that a compliment?" Autumn asked, smiling.

"Maybe. Now let's change the subject. Has Ethan proposed, or do you have some kind of secret engagement you're not telling me about?"

"No," Autumn said, getting up from the island and taking their empty coffee cups to the sink.

"Talked about marriage, then?" Meg pursued.

"He just got here, Meg. He's looking for a job in Pittsburgh and a house to rent. He'll commute to Pittsburgh, and Martha will be overjoyed to provide day care after school."

"Where is he now? Do you have him hiding in your basement until I leave?"

"No, Miss Smarty Pants, they're staying with Martha for the time being. All of his stuff is in storage, and he'll rent a small house for a while until..." her voice trailed off, and Meg completed the thought for her.

"Until you get married?" she offered. She then turned pouty for a moment and continued, "Don't forget your friends when you're an old married lady. I know that happens a lot. That and you'll gain fifty pounds in the first year."

"Nice," Autumn said, smiling. "If you tell Ethan that, I'll smack you. But seriously, I need you in my life, Meg. Remember that day last fall when I started on your portrait in my studio? That was the first time in a year that I had done anything with my art, and you sort of jump-started me, without even knowing it. That was a precious gift you gave me, dear friend. You know I love you."

"Ditto, baby," Meg responded, looking out the window.

Autumn knew that was the closest Meg would get to expressing her feelings. *She'd better not be so hesitant with Kyle,* she thought.

"I should finish that portrait for Kyle. He can hang it in his new office." She laughed.

Meg groaned and rolled her eyes, but to Autumn's surprise and delight, did not object.

"I'm going to give Heather art lessons," Autumn continued, returning to the island to sit across from her friend. "And in fact, I'm thinking about opening the studio for classes and then plein air painting when the weather turns nice."

Meg was nodding her approval. "Yeah, now that you're a celebrity you'll pack em' in."

"You want to try one?"

"No, thank you. I'll stick with the dogs. But you *can* do a portrait of Spike."

"Spike?"

"Yeah, I sort of adopted one of the puppies, a litter runt. Felt bad for him. You probably saw him at the Halloween parade, if you can remember that far back."

"Uh huh, you felt bad for him so you sort of adopted him? I think you needed some company living in that little barn apartment. Admit it!"

"How do you know about that?" Meg asked angrily.

Autumn hesitated. "Kyle told me. Now before you get all huffy about it, he was worried about you and your safety. He didn't know how safe it was for you to be out there all by yourself."

CHAPTER 26

"I told him not to tell anyone. That butthead. But I guess I can forgive him," she reasoned and added, "that was actually kind of nice of him. And you're right about the puppy. I love that dog."

"And that gives me an idea! I could paint pet portraits, too. I never want to find myself in the position I was in this year, with no income stream. I was so mired in what was NOT happening that I couldn't even see the possibilities that were out there. Sort of like it was with you and Kyle."

"Was not."

"Was too"

"Was not."

"Oh, good grief," Autumn said, exasperated. "Why don't I go with you to Kyle's?" She was curious to see how the two were interacting now that Meg had begrudgingly decided she might want to spend time with him.

"Suits me. You can be my buffer."

"You don't need a buffer anymore, remember."

"Do too."

"Do not."

"Do too." But Meg was grinning ear to ear like a schoolgirl, and they walked out into a beautiful day full of hope and promise.

* * *

Balanced on a stepladder, Kyle put the finishing touches on the wall, pleased with the light grey hue he had selected for his new office. Anything was better than the dark burgundy Natalie had selected. Coming down the ladder, he surveyed his new store and office. Jack Staub had helped him build partitions, so he had one area for office work, one for computer repair, and a large front area to meet with clients. He found a rug, a desk, three chairs, and a tall lamp at the thrift shop in Mt. Pleasant. The place looked pretty spartan, but as time passed and his income rose he would spruce it up.

He still couldn't believe his good fortune.

He told himself sternly that he would never be ashamed of his past again. He thought about Meg, squirreled away in the kennel, hiding her fear and loneliness. He still didn't know what she had been so afraid of, but he did know that he wanted to be there when she was ready to talk about it. And he also believed that one day, she would. After all, she had praised his rolls at Christmas, as if he had baked them himself instead of just defrosting them and putting them in an oven. And he was still alive after telling Autumn that Meg was living in the barn. And just the other day, when he sat next to her at Hoffman's lunch counter, she hadn't pretended that she had a meeting to get to. *Love comes slowly*, he thought to himself, *but it comes.*

He heard the bell above the door chime and watched as Meg and Autumn came in. He greeted Autumn but only had eyes for Meg, who looked gorgeous in her work clothes, which, he noticed, were actually clean, and maybe even ironed.

"Not bad for a convicted felon," Meg chirped, walking around the space.

"Meg!" Autumn practically screamed. "There are some things you just don't say, especially to someone who has been so good to you." She looked over at Kyle, who was grinning so wide that she thought he might burst.

"Aw, he knows I'm just playing with him," she replied calmly, seating herself on the office chair and twirling around in it.

"I am not a convicted felon," he said with mock indignance.

"Are too."

"Am not."

"Are too."

* * *

That evening Ethan took Autumn for an after-dinner stroll, even though the chill had returned and they had to bundle up. He promised her a nearby surprise.

"We're only going a quarter of a mile," he promised, hugging her shoulder and drawing her closer to him as they walked. They headed down Loucks Avenue, turned on Grove Street, and stopped on Arthur Avenue, just before the high school, in front of a neat brick bungalow.

"This is it," Ethan said proudly, as if he had just discovered the eighth wonder of the world.

"This is what?" Autumn asked, not understanding what the small, modest house had to do with them.

Ethan pulled a set of keys from his pocket and, taking her hand, led her up the sidewalk and up the three short steps to the front door.

"I rented this today," he said, letting them inside. "It's small, but it's so close to Martha. And you," he added, grinning.

"But, it's so…not you," Autumn blurted out, glancing around the tiny living room. "You have all that beautiful modern furniture in storage."

She couldn't quite see the sleek couch and chairs and the stainless steel and glass coffee and end tables in this living room with the 1950s-style gas fireplace and outdated carpet.

"I'm not worried about it," he said. "Ellen picked out all that stuff.

I didn't spend much time at home, so it didn't really matter as long as I had a bed to sleep in, someplace to eat, and my television and easy chair. That feels like a long time ago," he said absently.

"I suppose it does, though it's only been a little more than six months."

"It's hard to believe how much has changed since you and Heather came into my life," he said, taking her hand as he led her into the dining room. A card table and two chairs had been placed under a modest chandelier fixture, and Ethan lit a candle in the center. A bottle of champagne and two glasses sat on the table.

As they sat down he continued, "If someone had told me six months ago that I would be doing this in a tiny house in a tiny town at a tiny card table, I would never have believed it."

"Doing what?" Autumn asked, looking around the room as if the "what" would suddenly appear.

When she turned back to face Ethan, he was getting up from his chair, and as he knelt down on one knee he said, "I always thought when I proposed it would be somewhere incredible, like the revolving restaurant at the top of the Marriot Marquis or during a horse and carriage ride through Central Park." He paused to catch his breath. He had not realized until that moment how nervous he was. But he plunged on. "But now, here with you, I realize that none of that matters. I would do this in a swamp if I had to, and proudly."

He reached into his pocket and took out a small black velvet box. "Autumn Hamilton," he said seriously, as he opened it and presented it to her. "I'm completely in love with you and want to make a life with you, here in Finch's Crossing. Will you marry me...and Heather?"

By the time he had finally spoken the words, Autumn was trying to dry her tears with the sleeve of her jacket.

"Oh, Ethan, I love you, too. But are you sure you want to live here of all places?"

"I'm sure," he said. "It's the best place for Heather, and I suspect," he added with a grin, "it's also the best place for you. And besides, Pittsburgh is only an hour away, and I have a few leads on a new job."

Autumn just stared at him. "You know I misjudged you when I first met you."

He smiled. "I know. And I may have categorized you as a nosy busybody at first."

She punched him playfully on his arm.

"So, what, you're just going to sit there? Let's see the rock!"

Ethan returned to his chair as Autumn examined the ring, speechless.

"It's a red diamond," he explained, taking the ring out of the box and slipping it onto her finger. "The deep, dark red coloring made me think of your name, and the time of year we met, with the fall leaves all around us. And because you're an artist, I wanted some-thing different, something creative."

"Oh, Ethan," she cried. "This is simply gorgeous. I love it." She held her hand out in front of her to admire it. Set in platinum, two large white diamonds flanked the red stone.

A knock at the door interrupted them as she admired her new ring, and then she heard the front door open and little girl feet as they padded across the floor until Heather practically leapt into Ethan's arms, with Martha on her heels.

While Martha admired the ring, Heather stood on her toes to whisper something in Ethan's ear, which made him laugh, and he pulled her on his lap.

"Heather wants to know if you said yes," he said.

He tapped Heather's nose with the tip of his finger and said, "Well you know, come to think of it, she hasn't answered the question one way or another."

Heather strained to whisper something else in his ear, and he nodded his head in response.

Heather turned to Autumn and said quite solemnly, "Will you please marry us, pretty please, with chocolate syrup on top?"

Autumn gave up trying to contain her tears and jumped up to embrace them.

"Yes, Heather," she said, tears streaming down her face. "Yes, I will marry you and Ethan."

She held out her hand to Martha, who squeezed it tightly, tears gathering in her eyes too.

"I don't even know why I'm crying," Martha said, laughing.

"I do," Autumn offered. "Because you have a family again. And now I have one, too."

As Ethan opened the champagne and produced a third glass and carton of juice from the refrigerator, Autumn felt as if the last piece of the puzzle of her life had found its rightful place the moment Ethan slipped the red diamond ring on her finger. She gazed out the large picture window overlooking Arthur Avenue and saw her beloved Finch's Crossing in an entirely different way. No longer was it just the place where she had grown up and made her mark on the world. It was now the place where she had fallen in love and found the most precious of gifts—a family of her own.

She thought of Meg and Kyle, and of Martha and Jack, and how love had found its way to all of them, in the most circuitous of routes.

CHAPTER 26

For Martha, love came in the form of snow removal and truckloads of mulch and gravel and finally settled at the kitchen table with a cup of coffee. Love persevered for Meg and Kyle despite her fears and stubbornness, and their secrets. And Ethan's love brought passion and vitality back into her life along with a precious little girl to love. She lifted her champagne glass toward the window, toasting all that lay ahead for them in the place where she knew they all belonged.

The End

ABOUT *A*MY *R*UTH *A*LLEN

I'm an American girl who grew up overseas, riding elephants in Thailand, dancing around the Maypole in Sweden, drinking tea in the United Kingdom, and touring castles across Europe. In these foreign (to me) and exotic locales, books were both my anchor and my escape. They connected me to my native land (and English-speakers in general), while introducing me to worlds even more awesome than the ones I lived in.

Fast forward to present day in Minneapolis, Minnesota, where I am the author of the young adult novel, *Stealing Away*, the sweet romance series *Finch's Crossing*, and seven non-fiction books for young adults. In addition to writing fiction, non-fiction, and my blog, I support fellow indie authors by exclusively reviewing indie books.

PLEASE CONNECT WITH ME!

- www.amyruthallen.com
- amyruthallen@yahoo.com
- facebook.com/amyruthallenauthor
- @AmyAllenWrites
- pinterest.com/amyruthallen

Did you enjoy *Autumn*? Please support indie authors and write a review on Amazon.com, Goodreads, and elsewhere so others may enjoy it, too. Thank you.

THE *Finch's* *Crossing* *Series*

❦ WWW.AMYRUTHALLEN.COM ❧

NOW AVAILABLE AS A FREE E-BOOK
A Finch's Crossing Holiday Sampler and Planner

Your favorite characters in Finch's Crossing are gearing up for the winter holidays. Miss Elsie is baking up a storm, Autumn is going overboard with her decorating, and Meg is telling everyone she knows how to keep their pets safe around all those holiday plants and decorations. And Kyle, of course, is using his social media savvy to find Christmas sales and deals. Spend a little time with all of them in the free *Finch's Crossing Holiday Sampler and Planner*. In it you'll find a collection of tips, tricks, ideas, and recipes, plus some holiday planning templates.

Finch's Crossing Book Two: Spring

At thirty-five, Spring Hamilton has reached a crossroads in her modeling career. No longer young, but still beautiful, she has severed ties with her controlling and unimaginative manager, and for the first time must figure out her future, alone. The only thing she knows for certain is that if she doesn't figure out how to transition her career she will end up as a grandmotherly model in mail-order catalogs. As she relocates from Los Angeles to New York she detours to Finch's Crossing for a quick visit with her sister. But a chance encounter with Gabriel, her high school sweetheart, rekindles their love, launching Spring into unbelievable circumstances she never could have predicted. She never thought of herself as the kind of person who would fall in love with another woman's husband. But when life throws you curves, you...

Finch's Crossing Book Three: Summer

Free-spirited, thirty-year-old Summer Hamilton has worked as a chauffeur, waitress, obituary writer, and house painter. But when she is fired from her job as a nanny because she rebuked her employer's advances, she points her pink VW bug east and travels from Seattle to Finch's Crossing. After a ten-year vagabond life, she yearns to decide what she wants to do when she grows up. Upon arriving at Finch's Crossing, she meets carefree Trevor Banks, whose job building adventure parks takes him away for weeks at a time. She is torn between the kind of life she has just abandoned and the one she yearns to make for herself. Having just tamed her wanderlust, Summer must decide whether or not to hit the road again with Trevor in order to be with the man she loves. But as their relationship blooms, a nagging voice in her head keeps asking, "Just exactly how 'carefree' is Trevor?"

Finch's Crossing Book Four: Winter

Winter "Win" Hamilton's high school nickname, "The Ice Queen," has followed her all her life and she is, in fact, just that—cold, selfish, and emotionally detached. But her steely demeanor helped her achieve a full partnership, at age thirty-seven, in a prestigious international architectural firm. True, she doesn't have many friends, but she lives in a beautiful penthouse, has a fat 401K, drives a brand new Porsche Cayenne SUV, and dresses flawlessly in designer clothes. When she breaks her leg in a skiing accident she reluctantly returns to her childhood home to recover. As the broken bones heal, with the help of the handsome local doctor W. Armistead "Trip" Harrison, she rediscovers the traditional values she grew up with, and wonders how on earth her life got so out of balance. As her strength returns and she embarks on a self-improvement campaign, Win realizes that the unflappable and aloof doctor is the one man in town who isn't rendered tongue-tied in her presence. Accustomed to getting her way, she bristles at his lack of interest in her. Realizing she's met the male version of herself, she knows she has her work cut out for her.

12567322R00171

Made in the USA
Lexington, KY
22 October 2018